The Merchant's House

Kate Ellis

PIATKUS

Copyright © 1998 by Kate Ellis

First published in Great Britain in 1998 by
Piatkus Books
5 Windmill Street, London W1T 2JA
email: info@piatkus.co.uk

This edition published 2006

The moral right of the author has been asserted.

A catalogue record for this book is available from the British Library.

ISBN 0 7499 3699 1

Typeset by Phoenix Photosetting, Chatham, Kent
Printed and bound in Great Britain by
Clays Ltd, Bungay, Suffolk

Acknowledgements

With thanks to Roger, Tom and Olly for their patience;
Ruth and Pat for their advice; and my parents,
David and Mona, for their encouragement.

The child flung his tricycle aside and toddled, laughing, towards the basking cat. The creature, sensing the impending assault on her dignity, stalked off with her tail disdainfully erect. She squeezed herself through the bars of the garden gate and headed towards some warm and inaccessible hiding place.

The child began to follow gleefully, but the wooden gate was shut fast, secured against his escape into the lane. He pressed his face against the bars of the gate and watched the cat stop to paw a butterfly, then disappear elegantly into the thick hedgerow opposite.

Then a great purring thing, a shiny black bulk, blocked his view of the lane as it stopped by the gate. The car door opened slowly and the driver climbed out, all the time watching the child, who stood and stared, mesmerised by the sight of the stranger. The driver opened the gate and, after looking round, stooped down to the child's level, offering a hand that held something brightly coloured and desirable.

Elaine Berrisford pressed the mop into the bucket and began the final unwashed section of the stone floor. She would get it done while Jonathon was quiet, happy with the freedom of the cottage garden and his new tricycle.

She looked at the newly cleaned floor with satisfaction. At home this was her cleaner's domain: Elaine had no time for housework – only in the holidays, only when she was at the cottage. In a week she would return to work and Jonathon would be back at nursery. The daily car journeys through ever-thickening traffic would begin again, relentless till the half-term break. The peace of Hedgerow Cottage would be exchanged for the large detached house on the busy main road into Manchester.

She looked at her watch. She would have an hour reading on the sunlounger while Jonathon played. Then maybe they'd drive down to the beach. Jonathon would like that. She remembered the delight on his face as he searched for shells in the gritty sand.

Elaine opened the bottom half of the back door, a stable type. It was kept closed in case that cat got in. She couldn't stand cats, but Jonathon, obsessed with the creature, followed it round everywhere. She picked up her untouched paperback and went outside.

'Jonathon.'

He must be hiding, playing a game.

'Jonathon. Where are you?'

Perhaps he had crept back into the cottage.

'Jonathon.'

The gate – it was shut and fastened, just as it should be; just as she had left it.

She searched with increasing agitation – first the garden, then the house. As her panic grew, so did the sounds. The birdsong, the hum of the insects and the distant throb of the combine harvester became almost deafening as they conspired to mask the only sound she wanted to hear – the sound of Jonathon's voice.

12 September

Neil Watson scraped away at the earth surrounding the white object. Archaeologists know bone when they see it. On a dig in an Anglo-Saxon cemetery they can become quite blasé about the stuff. But in the cellar of an Elizabethan merchant's house . . .

Neil scraped away some more earth. The thing was taking shape. It looked ominously like a skull. He called his colleagues over and offered a silent prayer that it would turn out to be an animal bone, discarded from the kitchens. They were working to a deadline. They couldn't afford the official delays that would follow the unexpected discovery of a body, however ancient.

Jane and Matt began work. The three said nothing, but they knew each other's thoughts. The area of white bone increased: a ribcage; the skull; the limbs.

The tiny thing lay there exposed, clean and bleached. It was obviously human, but so small, Neil thought . . . a baby.

The three exchanged looks. It had to be reported. Neil went to the office to call the police.

19 September

As the young couple passed her, Dorothy Truscot glanced critically at the girl's flimsy sandals.

'Good morning,' she said briskly. It was her custom to greet fellow walkers. The young couple – blond, bronzed and clad in denim shorts – looked slightly startled, grunted a greeting then walked on quickly in the other direction.

Dorothy strode onwards. Her own shoes were of the sturdy, sensible variety; shoes for country walking.

'Rags . . . here, boy.'

The spaniel bounded towards her, eyes glowing with adoration, tail wagging like a windscreen wiper. Dorothy picked up a stick and threw it.

'Fetch.'

She breathed deeply as the dog dashed away, sucking the fresh sea air into her lungs, and looked out towards the vast expanse of glistening sea. It was high here: a hundred yards away the green countryside tumbled down cliffs to unite with the sea. Calm today, the sea held a score of miniature boats; child's playthings. It was only the oil tanker crawling across the horizon which brought a reminder of the outside world of dirt and commerce to this lovely patch of South Devon.

Rags returned with the stick, his exuberance tempered by the demands of nature. As he squatted to add his own personal bit of pollution, Dorothy looked round furtively and drew the plastic poop scoop out of her capacious handbag along with a small plastic bag to contain the offending article. Perhaps true inhabitants of the countryside were accustomed to a bit of muck on their boots and a few

3

dubious smells, but Dorothy was a believer in leaving things as you would wish to find them.

Rags ran on up the path and Dorothy followed. The sun was warm for mid-September, and she regretted wearing her thick Aran jumper. But she climbed the path knowing that the seat – her and Sidney's seat – would be waiting at the top of the slope. When she reached it, panting, she sat down heavily to get her breath back and turned, as she always did, to read the small brass plaque screwed to the back of the seat.

In loving memory of Sidney Truscot
who loved this place.

And he had. She smiled as she remembered how they had bought Dark Lane Cottage on their retirement: sold up and moved down to their holiday paradise. But then came the heart attack; the funeral; adaptation to a solitary country life so different to the Birmingham suburbs. She looked at the grassy ground. His ashes had been scattered here at his request. She felt near to him here.

'Rags. What are you up to, you silly animal? What have you got there?'

Rags bounded up to his mistress and placed the trophy carefully at her feet – a woman's shoe.

'Rags, come here.' He ran away gleefully. This time Dorothy followed. 'Rags . . . Rags. What are you doing, boy? Come here.'

She spotted the wagging tail behind a clump of bushes at the side of the path.

'Rags, come here now, this instant . . . Rags.' He appeared bearing another gift, a shoe to match the first.

'Where did you get that, you silly dog?'

She walked round the bush. Her heart began to beat faster with indignation. Perhaps somebody had left some litter there; fouled her lovely spot with a bin-bag full of old clothes.

Then she saw it. It looked unreal, like a grotesque life-size rag doll – a rag doll without a face. It lay half in the bush. Dorothy's eyes were drawn to where the face had been, now a crusty brown mass heaving with buzzing flies.

Her hand went to her mouth as if preparing to stop a scream or a stream of vomit.

The human body can do extraordinary things in extraordinary situations. If anybody had told Dorothy Truscot that at the age of sixty-five she could run the half-mile to Hutchins Farm without stopping to rest, she would not have believed them. But she managed it in what seemed like a remarkably short time, Rags following at her heels, enjoying the game.

Chapter 1

The Periwinkle is now restored to a goodly condition but Master Cornworthy, the shipwright, doth tell me that the Starfish is in need of a new mizzen mast. She must be ready to sail for the Newfoundland by March.

Elizabeth is sick of a morning and thinks herself with child. I rejoice if this be so. We have awaited the Lord's blessing full ten years this Michaelmas.

Elizabeth hath taken in a new maidservant to help in her time of sickness. The girl's name is Jennet and she is most comely.

Extract from the journal of John Banized,
Merchant of Tradmouth, 15 February 1623

The streets that led from Wesley Peterson's newly acquired house, perched above the town, down to the crazy huddle of buildings that clung to the riverbank were hill-steep, narrow and winding; not built for cars. Wesley felt it would be easier to walk to his new place of work. He told himself that this was a good thing: he would become fit. In London he had never walked; had never really had the time. Downhill was easy; the return journey up those cobbled streets would be the real test of endurance.

It wasn't long before he reached the heart of the town; an ancient heart of timber-framed and whitewashed plaster, interspersed with examples of later architecture; over-confident Victorian and self-effacing modern. The town centre was crowded with people on their way to work and cars pushing ambitiously through the narrow streets. Wesley's pace slowed to a stroll.

To his left, between two shops of Victorian vintage, was a gap, like a missing tooth, filled by a wire fence. In London he would have passed by without a second look, but here in Tradmouth things were different. He stopped and stared at the exposed site: the small mounds of brickwork; the intriguing holes dotted here and there; the skeletal layout of a building revealing itself on the brown earth. A dig was in progress, unmistakable. Wesley was on familiar territory.

Three dusty figures behind the wire screen bent over the ground with trowels, brushes and concentration. One of them he recognised.

'Neil!'

A young man in torn muddy jeans and with a mess of brown hair looked up. When he saw Wesley he grinned.

'Wes! Good God, man, what are you doing here? You look a bit smart. What are you selling?' He abandoned the tools of his trade and hurried to admit Wesley to the site via a wire gate set in the fence.

Wesley looked around. 'What's this, then?'

'You tell me,' Neil said, throwing out a good-natured challenge.

Wesley noted the features of the site and thought for a moment. 'House? Sixteenth ... seventeenth-century? Courtyard? Bit like that one we worked on in Neston, remember? Outhouses, by the look of it. Situated in the centre of an old seaport. Merchant's house?'

'Spot on. Demolished at the turn of the century ... shops built on it. Now they've knocked down the shops to build flats, so here we are. Got six weeks before the concrete's poured in. Usual story. How's life in the police force, then? I thought you were pounding the beat in London.'

Wesley smiled. 'I gave up the beat years ago ... joined CID. Now I've got a transfer to Tradmouth. We've always liked the place and it's near Pam's mum.'

'Great. How's Pam?' asked Neil quietly. 'Any kids yet?'

Wesley shook his head and looked at his watch. 'Look, Neil, I'm late. I'll have to go ...'

'If you're doing nothing tonight come down the Tradmouth Arms about eight thirty. We're always in there. It'd be nice to see Pam again.'

'Yeah, that'd be good.'

'And I'll tell you all about this place. We had a bit of excitement about a week back. Should interest you in your line of work . . .'

Wesley, intrigued, would have questioned Neil further, but time's winged chariot, in the shape of a passing patrol car, reminded him that he had to make a quick exit if he was to make a favourable impression. The first day in a new job is invariably the worst.

Sergeant Bob Naseby looked longingly at the steaming mug of tea behind the counter, hidden discreetly from public view. When he had dealt with Miss Beesby's lost budgerigar he promised himself five minutes' peace before he started on his paperwork.

Satisfied with the sergeant's assurances that the entire force would be on constant lookout for little Joey, Miss Beesby left. But no sooner had the station door swung shut than it opened again and a tall, smartly dressed young man entered and walked confidently up to the counter. Bob Naseby hadn't seen him before; he would have remembered. The dark brown face was pleasant and the eyes intelligent. If Bob had to hazard a guess he'd put the newcomer down as a new doctor at the local hospital.

'Morning, sir. Can I help you?'

'Detective Sergeant Peterson. I've been told to report to Detective Inspector Heffernan.'

'Oh, yes. We've been expecting you. Transfer from London, isn't it?'

'Word gets round.'

'It does in a place like this. You'll find it a bit different from what you're used to.'

'I hope so.'

'What is it they call us up there? Turnip heads?'

Wesley Peterson smiled but said nothing.

Bob picked up the phone and dialled. The new man had to be an improvement on his predecessor, who had recently shaken the dust of Tradmouth off his boots and headed for the Met's bright lights. And the Chief Constable would be delighted. He was forever sending memos about attracting more ethnic minorities into the force. The acquisition of DS Peterson would do his statistics no end of good.

'Hello, Rachel? I've a DS Peterson here to see DI Heffernan. Can you come and fetch him? Thanks, my luvver.'

Wesley smiled to himself at the use of this Devon endearment which could have caused considerable misunderstanding in London.

Bob put the phone down. 'Someone'll be along in a minute . . . show you round.' He put out the large hand that had delivered so many wicket-taking balls for the police cricket team. 'Bob Naseby, by the way.'

'Wesley Peterson.'

'Know this area at all, do you?'

'Yes. I used to be at uni . . . used to live in Exeter.'

The door at the side of the counter opened and a young woman stepped out. She had straight blond hair, wore a crisp linen suit and sensibly flat shoes; pretty in a practical sort of way.

'DS Peterson? I'm Rachel Tracey . . . Detective Constable.' She looked him up and down appraisingly. 'A call's just come through. Suspicious death. Little Tradmouth Head.'

Bob's face clouded. 'Not the kid?'

'I don't know yet. The inspector's not here. I've just rung him and he said to pick him up.' She turned to Wesley. 'You'd better come along with me.'

She set off with bustling determination. Wesley followed. DC Rachel Tracey was a woman who knew exactly where she was going.

'You can't park by his house,' she added as they got into the police car. 'I'll get as close as I can, then we'll have to walk.'

She parked on double yellow lines in a narrow street leading to the harbour. Then Wesley followed her at a frantic pace through a dark, restaurant-lined cobbled street which opened out onto a picturesque quayside with castle walls at

9

the far end and a startling view over the river to a hill-hung town on the opposite bank. Seagulls yelled their hearts out overhead, drowning the gentle chug-chug of the nearby car ferry, and the air was heavy with the scent of seaweed.

'He lives here.' She pointed to a row of waterfront houses of indeterminate age, probably very old; the kind of dwellings favoured by retired sea captains in the last century. The end house was smaller than the rest, almost a cottage. She opened the rusting white front gate, marched up to the door and knocked loudly.

An upstairs window was flung open and a tousled head appeared. 'That you, Rach? I'll be down in a sec.' The accent was more reminiscent of the Mersey than the West Country. The head disappeared before Wesley had a chance to get a proper look at his new boss.

Then he emerged out of the front door, a big untidy bear of a man with curly hair and a well-worn anorak: more like an off-duty local fisherman than a detective inspector, Wesley thought. He shook Wesley's hand firmly and listened to Rachel's report on the situation as they walked to the car.

'So we don't know if it's Jonathon Berrisford or not.'

'They didn't say . . . just a body. SOCOs are up there now, and Dr Bowman.'

'Has the super been told?'

'He's over at Morbay . . . at a meeting. They've been trying to get in touch with him.'

'And Stan Jenkins?'

'He's in Bristol. Someone reckons Jonathon Berrisford's living next door.'

'Let's hope he is, then.'

Heffernan turned to Wesley. 'It's all happening, Sergeant . . . body on your first day.'

'I hope it's not Jonathon, sir.' Rachel's mask of efficiency slipped for a split second.

'So do I, Rach. So do I.'

Rachel Tracey was a good driver. Her father, a farmer, had taught her to drive a Land Rover at the age of twelve, and she had passed her test on her seventeenth birthday. Wesley closed his eyes as she swept confidently down the narrow lanes which were walled with hedgerows that made the fields beyond invisible. The bends were blind and the roads single-track, but when they met a vehicle it would invariably back up to let them pass. Such is the influence of the law.

They parked in the small carpark thoughtfully provided by the National Trust for visitors to Little Tradmouth Head. In high summer they would have had difficulty getting a space, but in mid-September the only vehicles parked there were those belonging to the SOCOs and Dr Bowman's brand-new Range Rover which stood, gleaming, in their midst.

It was a long, steep walk, and Wesley regretted that his shoes were more suited to driving round London than walking through the countryside. He made a mental note to buy himself something more substantial. He spotted the fluttering blue-and-white tapes, like the bunting of some grim village fête, ahead of them on the path. White-overalled figures went about their work with professional preoccupation while flashing cameras recorded the scene.

A tall, thin, balding man approached them, grinning like a genial host at a party.

'Gerry Heffernan. Haven't seen you in ages. Margaret's been asking after you, you know. How are you? How's the diet?'

'Non-existent, Colin. You know me – too fond of my grub. This is my new sergeant, Wesley Peterson. Replacement for you know who.'

'Nice to meet you, Sergeant. You won't mind if I don't shake hands. Rubber gloves – occupational hazard.'

The inspector surveyed the scene. 'So what have we got, Colin? Is it the kid?'

'No, thank God. It's a woman. Early twenties. About five foot seven. Fully clothed. No sign of sexual assault that I can see but you never know. Fair hair . . . face bashed in. Your lot have found bloodstains and disturbed ground near the path, and they reckon she was moved into the bushes after death to conceal the body. I'd go along with that.'

'Time of death?'

'Couple of days ago, I'd say.'

11

'How soon can you do the PM?'

'First thing tomorrow. Report by tomorrow evening?'

'Fair enough.'

Heffernan turned his attention to a spotty young uniformed PC who was hovering nervously outside the taped-off area, studying Wesley with undisguised curiosity.

'Morning, Johnson. Any sign of a weapon?'

'Not yet, sir. Nothing obvious.'

'Who found her?'

'Lady by the name of Mrs Truscot, sir. Walking her dog. Gave her a bit of a turn.'

'I'm not surprised. Where is she now?'

'Up at Hutchins Farm. That's where she rang from.'

Heffernan grinned at his new sergeant.

'I'm going to be generous seeing as you're new. Go and interview this Mrs Truscot, will you? Hutchins Farm's over there; you can just see the chimneys. If Cissy Hutchins is there, which she will be if anything interesting's going on, you'll get a cup of tea, and she bakes the best scones in Devon. Off you go. You can take PC Johnson here as your native guide. I imagine he's partial to a home-made scone or two. And organise a house-to-house, will you?' He looked round. 'Or should it be cottage-to-cottage? It shouldn't take long. And see if anyone's been working in the fields in the last couple of days – they might have noticed something. And try to find out who walks here regularly.'

'Right you are, guv.'

Johnson smiled to himself. He'd never heard the inspector being addressed as 'guv' before. But rumour had it the new bloke was from London. You had to make allowances.

'Hedgerow Cottage is just down the lane.' Rachel Tracey looked concerned. 'We don't want to go barging in, do we? If Mrs Berrisford saw two policemen at the door she might think . . .'

'Good thinking, Rach. You do Hedgerow Cottage . . . and go easy, eh?'

As the photographers packed up, Wesley followed Johnson up the steep path towards the culinary pleasures of Hutchins Farm, wondering what it was about Hedgerow Cottage that made his new colleagues so nervous.

12

Chapter 2

We did meet in the church today to talk of the work
to be done. Methinks the Mayor's memorial to his
wife be too large and showy. It doth take up a goodly
part of the wall on the south aisle. Master Rankin
doth agree. Mayor Rawlins was ever a man to seek
his own glory and that of his kin.

The mizzen mast of the Starfish be mended at
much expense to myself and the master is ordered
to assemble a goodly and sober crew . . . a hard task
in these ungodly times.

Elizabeth suffers still from the sickness and her
monthly courses have ceased still. I rejoice to think
she may be with child. She hath much praise for
Jennet who proves willing about the house.

Extract from the journal of John Banized,
21 February 1623

Pamela Peterson sat down on an upturned tea chest and
looked at the phone. She was torn between wanting it to
ring, wanting to hear the voice at the other end offering her
work – cover for somebody sick or on a course – and wanting
to be left in peace to try to create at least a semblance of
order in her new home. She knew from past experience
of supply teaching that once you got one job, once you had
established yourself, the phone never stopped ringing. But
that was in London. Things might be different here.

But whatever the world of education had in store for her,

it was no use sitting around. When she was unoccupied she had time to think of the other phone call she was expecting.

She began to unpack the dinner service from its newspaper cocoons. It emerged, butterfly bright, only to be stacked away in the dresser. At least she was making progress with the house, getting things done. Perhaps Wesley would give her a hand when he got in. He was late – but then that wasn't unusual.

When she heard the key in the door she stood up and tidied her hair with hands filthy from handling the newsprint.

'How did it go?' She watched her husband, trying to gauge his mood. He stood back and smiled.

'Fine. Any luck with work?'

'Not yet but it's early days. Give them a chance to catch flu or have a nervous breakdown. So how was it?'

'The DI's a funny character . . . can't make him out.'

'He must be an improvement on your last one.'

'He seems popular from what I can see. Did you ring your mum?'

'Thought I'd wait till tomorrow.'

'And the clinic . . . did they get in touch?'

She turned away, her shoulders tense. 'Not yet. I might give them a ring.'

'I'm not sure about this clinic.' Wesley put his hand on her shoulder. 'I don't know why you won't talk to my parents about it: they'll recommend someone, someone good. Or you could speak to Maritia . . .'

'I don't want your family knowing all my private business,' she snapped, determined.

'But they're doctors . . . they've got all the right contacts. They're the best people to discuss it with.'

Wesley's parents had had their misgivings when he had married Pam: misgivings about a racially mixed marriage; misgivings about Wesley's choice of Pam rather than his former girlfriend, a black solicitor who attended their church. But the Petersons had come to accept their daughter-in-law, even grown to like her. It was embarrassment, or the fear of being branded a failure, that made Pam keep her silence and seek the help of strangers.

14

She bent down and continued unpacking the dishes. 'It said on the radio that a body's been found.'

'Yes. That's where I was most of today. Up on the headland. Lovely spot.'

'And?'

'And what?'

'Was it a murder? It said on the radio that the police were treating it as suspicious.'

'Looks like murder – some poor woman with her face bashed in.'

Pamela shuddered. It wasn't safe anywhere these days. Every paradise had its serpent.

Wesley changed the subject. 'I met Neil Watson on my way to work this morning. He's working for the County Archaeological Unit, on a dig in Tradmouth town centre, fairly near the police station. I said we might go for a drink with him tonight. That okay?'

She turned away. 'You can go. I've got too much to do.'

'But we've not seen Neil for . . .'

'I don't feel like it. Okay?'

Wesley knew when he had to tread carefully, when things were getting to her. Matters might improve when she had her work to distract her.

'Shall I get some supper on?'

Pam turned round, looked at him and regretted her sharpness.

'Yeah,' she said quietly, apologetically. 'Have a look in the freezer.'

They ate the meal in silence, relieved only by the babble of the television in the corner. Wesley packed the dishwasher then went upstairs and changed into jeans and denim shirt.

As he went out of the front door on his way to the Tradmouth Arms, he hoped that Pam wouldn't spend the evening reading and rereading those medical books and crying.

Neil introduced his colleagues. There was Jane, young, blonde and classy, who wore her torn jeans and ragged sweatshirt with style. There was Matt, a little older, who wore a ponytail, a sweatshirt pronouncing the virtues of a

Shropshire public house and a worried expression. They greeted Wesley casually. Neil made no mention of his friend's profession, but merely said that they had been at university together.

Wesley was glad to be back amongst the archaeological fraternity, the camaraderie of the post-dig drinks session. He felt the tingle of recaptured youth and independence as he downed his second pint. He was glad he'd come.

'Where are you staying, Neil?' he asked, curious.

'Bed and breakfast just outside the town. Cheap and cheerful. Jane and Matt are luckier. They're on board Jane's uncle's yacht on the river.'

Wesley looked impressed. 'Very nice.'

Jane looked him up and down. 'You don't know Jamaica at all, do you, Wesley?' She spoke with a slow, well-bred voice.

He shook his head. 'Sorry. I've been to Trinidad – that's where my parents are from – but never Jamaica.'

'I've got a chance to go to Jamaica next year. Marine archaeology . . . wrecks. I dive. It's one of my hobbies.'

'Great. Go for it.'

'We could do with a few donations of Spanish treasure,' chipped in Matt bitterly. 'God knows we're underfunded. Just think of us freezing in the mud when you're sunning yourself in the Caribbean, won't you, Jane.'

Jane picked up her drink and looked away. This was obviously a thorny subject. Neil winked knowingly at Wesley, then took his pint and drank thirstily. He still seemed to have the drinking capacity of his student days: Wesley's had decreased with age and responsibility.

'Pity Pam couldn't make it,' said Neil as he put his glass down.

'Another time. What was this exciting find you mentioned this morning?'

'We turned up a skeleton . . . in what would have been the cellar of the merchant's house. We've been assured by all the experts it's contemporary with the house.'

'What sort of skeleton? Man . . . woman?'

'A baby, newborn or very young. Probably some servant girl had it in secret and it died or she did away with it. Went on all the time in those days. Still, it's interesting. I'd like to find out something about the house – who lived there and all that. There's bound to be records.'

'Well, you can do all the detective work,' said Wesley. 'I've got enough on my plate with this murder up at Little Tradmouth.'

'I heard about it on the radio. Mad rapist, was it?'

'No sign of anything like that. And I never talk shop out of working hours.'

'So our Jane can sleep easy in her bed. Not that she does much sleeping when Matt's about.'

Wesley raised his eyebrows and looked across at the seemingly incongruous couple. Now he knew why the subject of Jane's Jamaica trip had aroused such acrimony.

'Another pint?' he asked. He looked at his watch. With any luck Pam would be asleep when he got back.

Rachel Tracey lay restless in the bed that had been hers from childhood. In the dark she could make out the shapes of the cups and rosettes that still stood on the mantelpiece of the cast-iron fireplace in the corner of the room, a reminder of past gymkhana triumphs. Being the only girl, she had never had to share a room; it was hers alone, a refuge from the uncertainties of the world.

She curled up, pulled the duvet further around her and listened to the sounds of the country night: the screech of the owls; the bark of a fox in the nearby woodland. Sleep wouldn't come. As she closed her eyes she could see only the face of Elaine Berrisford.

When she had gone to Hedgerow Cottage she had hardly liked to ask the routine questions: had Mrs Berrisford seen anyone, anything suspicious on or around the seventeenth? She had asked apologetically and hardly listened to the monosyllabic answers. To be there at all had seemed like an obscene intrusion on grief. Having done her duty, she had made a rapid exit.

Rachel turned over, switched on the bedside light and picked up the book she'd been reading. But she couldn't concentrate on the printed words. She saw only the image

of Elaine's desperate, empty eyes. If only they could find
the child alive . . . if only they could find Jonathon
Berrisford.

Chapter 3

The ships are nearly prepared for sail. I have set Oliver in charge of the loading and he has so far proved trustworthy. One of the coopers fell ill with a sweating fever yesterday which did cause some delay, yet we should have the work done by Friday if the Lord be willing.

Elizabeth is no better and keeps to her bed and Jennet doth wait upon her.

The girl doth have a modest manner and fine eyes.

Extract from the journal of John Banized,
1 March 1623

Wesley arrived at work bright and early the next morning. To his surprise DI Heffernan had beaten him to it.

'Don't get too comfy, we're going out in a minute,' the inspector called as he disappeared into his office.

'Right, guv.' Wesley sat down at his new desk and opened the drawers. They were empty apart from the bottom one which contained a pile of magazines. He pulled them out. He wasn't easily shocked but he found the sight of the bored-looking women in various states of degradation distinctly distasteful. He pushed them back into the drawer.

'Found his little comics, have you? I didn't know they were still there. I'd have organised a bonfire. No doubt he left them there hoping I'd find them.'

Wesley felt embarrassed. He hadn't realised Rachel was behind him.

'I don't, er, really know how to get rid of them. I don't want to put them in the bin.'

'The sooner they're gone the better. He used to sit there reading one whenever he thought I was looking. Sexist pig.'

'Who did?'

'Your predecessor. Harry Marchbank . . . DS.'

'I thought you meant the inspector.'

She laughed. 'You've got to be joking. He's a love.' She perched herself on the edge of the desk. 'Heffernan and Marchbank never got on. There was always a bit of an atmosphere. If Harry hadn't got out when he did, I reckon Heffernan would have got him transferred. Mind you, I didn't think he'd stay round here long anyway.'

'How do you mean?'

'He couldn't stand Tradmouth. Never fitted in. It was his wife who wanted to move down here, and when they split up he was straight back to London. Best place for him.' She blushed. 'Oh, no offence. . . . I didn't mean . . .'

Wesley smiled. 'Don't worry, no offence taken.'

Their eyes met and Rachel returned his smile. He was an attractive man, she thought, with a gentle, thoughtful manner. It was going to be a refreshing change working with Sergeant Peterson. She stifled a sudden yawn.

'Tired?'

'Mmm. I didn't sleep too well last night. I went to see that poor woman at Hedgerow Cottage and I couldn't get it out of my mind. It must be awful to lose a child like that . . . not to know what's happened to him. She looked so desperate, poor thing.'

Heffernan emerged from his office like a bear waking from hibernation. 'Come on, Sergeant, get your skates on. We've got to be there in half an hour. Don't want to miss curtain-up, do we?'

'Don't we?'

'You're not squeamish, are you, Sergeant?' asked the inspector with relish.

'Er, no . . .'

'We'd best get going, then.'

'Anything from the house-to-house?' Heffernan asked as they went out of the station door.

'Nothing. No one's seen anything out of the ordinary. Mind you, there are quite a few properties empty up there . . . holiday cottages.'

'You get a lot round here.'

'What about Hedgerow Cottage?'

'What about it?'

'Rachel mentioned it.'

'Thought you might have seen it on the news. It was about a month back. Little boy of two went missing – Jonathon Berrisford. He just vanished into thin air. It's an isolated spot and nobody saw or heard anything. The only person there was his mother in the house. And there was a farm worker, Bill Boscople, in a field nearby harvesting. Not a sign of the kid.'

'So what do you reckon, guv?'

'Probably wandered off somewhere. They might find the poor little blighter in a ditch or something when the vegetation dies back. We had the helicopter out every day for a week. No sign.'

'What about his mother? Most murders are family affairs.'

'Well, it's not my case. Stan Jenkins is in charge . . . you've not met him yet. He reckons there's no chance it's her and I trust Stan's judgement.'

'She might be very convincing.'

'She might be but my money's on the ditch.'

'And the father?'

'He wasn't there. They live up north somewhere. She's a teacher or lecturer of some kind and she spends the holidays in their cottage down here. He's a wine merchant, I think . . . just comes down when he can. She's still at the cottage now. Wanted to stop down here just in case. I don't know if I'm a big softy or what but I hate anything to do with kids.' He sighed. 'Come on. We'd better shift ourselves. We don't want to be late.'

They reached the station carpark but Heffernan kept on walking.

'Aren't we going in the car, guv?'

'No. It's only down the road. You young ones nowadays . . . you'll lose the use of your legs if you're not careful.'

21

Heffernan moved quickly for a big man, and they arrived at the post-mortem room early. The two policemen stood some way away from the action, and Wesley spent half the time studying the floor or the ceiling. For someone who came from a medical family he felt decidedly squeamish. During his archaeological training the bodies had been piles of dry bones: he would never get used to post-mortems.

Colin Bowman went about his work with an air of detached nonchalance which he had cultivated over many years of proximity to death. He addressed the occasional remark to the inspector, who leaned against the wall, arms folded, looking on with interest.

'So what do you reckon, then, Colin?'

'I'd say that the cause of death was severe head injuries caused by ... I don't really know. Something heavy, uneven; not something like a baseball bat but around the same size. I'd say a thick heavy branch, something like that. I've found traces of bark in the wounds. I'd say she was struck from behind and that's what killed her, then some maniac went to work on her face. Not very nice.'

'Anything else? Murderer right-handed or left-handed? Man or woman?'

'Now you're asking. If I had to guess, just off the top of my head before I do further tests, I'd say right-handed. As for sex ... either, I suppose, if the weapon was thick and heavy enough, but I'm just guessing. The victim was in her early twenties. Natural blonde. Healthy. Average muscle tone – not an athlete or one of your aerobics freaks. Five foot seven. Pretty average all round, really. All her own teeth, what's left of them. We can try and reconstruct them, see if they match dental records. Any idea who she is yet?'

'No missing person round here matches her description. She might have been doing seasonal work in Morbay and they assume she's gone home and not bothered to turn up. It happens. We'll need publicity if nobody comes forward. Any chance of an artist's impression ... something like that?'

Colin Bowman shook his head. 'Reconstruction's pretty specialised work. Can be done, of course, but it takes time.'

Wesley looked up. 'I know of someone in Exeter who

22

might be able to do it. Professor Jensen from the university. I saw him reconstruct the face of a pharaoh's daughter.'

Heffernan raised his eyebrows. 'I've no objection to calling in a bit of outside help if nothing turns up in the next few days.' He patted Wesley heartily on the back. 'Good thinking. You can tell me all about this pharaoh's daughter over a steak and kidney pie at lunch-time.'

Bowman shook his head. 'You're the only man I know who can eat steak and kidney pie after a post-mortem. Your sergeant looks like a salad'd scare the daylights out of him.'

Wesley made for the door. He longed to get the smell out of his nostrils, out of his clothes. He longed to get home for a bath.

'There's just one more thing, Gerry.'

Heffernan turned. 'What's that, then, Colin?'

'She's had a baby fairly recently . . . say in the past couple of years.'

The inspector made straight for the Fisherman's Arms, trailing Wesley in his wake.

'Got the victim's clothes back from forensic, sir.'

'Right, then, Rach. Let the dog see the rabbit.' Heffernan, comfortably full after an unsurpassable steak and kidney pie, sorted through the neatly labelled plastic bags.

'Any report come with these?'

'That's to follow, sir.'

'As usual. What have we here? Let's have a shufti.'

'Where's Sergeant Peterson, sir?'

'I took him out for one of Maisie's specials at the Fisherman's Arms. Just the thing after a post-mortem – kill or cure.'

'And which did it do, sir? Kill him or cure him?'

'He's up at Little Tradmouth organising another search for the murder weapon. Fresh air'll do him good. And I've asked him to see Mrs Truscot again. I thought the name was familiar. I know her – she sings in the choir.'

Rachel had difficulty imagining her boss singing his heart out in a church choir, but she had heard from various sources that he had a good voice. 'So you had a good lunch?'

'He's a bright one, that new sergeant of ours . . . degree in archaeology.'

She raised her eyebrows. 'He never said.'

'And his parents are both doctors. So's his sister. His dad's a consultant – heart surgeon – from Trinidad. That's in the West Indies.'

'I did do geography at school, sir.'

'I'll tell you what, he's a breath of fresh air after the last one.' Heffernan chuckled wickedly. 'And I like the idea of his replacement being black. Marchbank was the most bloody racist sod I've ever met.'

Rachel smiled to herself. Gerry Heffernan rarely swore – only when discussing Detective Sergeant Marchbank.

'I know, sir. I . . .' She hesitated.

'What is it, Rach?'

'It's, er, well, I've heard Steve Carstairs making a few comments. Not to Sergeant Peterson's face, of course. When he thinks he can't hear. You know the sort of thing.'

'He'll have picked up nasty habits from Marchbank. He thought the sun shone out of his backside. What a role model, eh? You did right to tell me, Rach. I'll keep an eye on things.'

'Sergeant Peterson found Marchbank's little comics, sir.'

'Did he now?'

'Didn't know how to get rid of them. Wasn't going to put them in the bin and shock the cleaners.'

The inspector chuckled again. 'I'm sure we'll think of something.'

'And a call came through half an hour ago. There's been another theft – building materials. Looks like the same gang.'

'Send Steve Carstairs over, will you? And tell him I want a full report. In joined-up writing with full stops and capital letters.'

'Will do.'

He turned his attention back to the pile of plastic bags. 'Now then, what have we here?'

'There's nothing to identify her, sir. No handbag.'

'Do you ever go out without a handbag, Rach?'

'No . . . no, I don't. You've got to have somewhere to keep your purse and your keys and all that.'

24

'So we can assume her handbag's been taken. Either by the murderer or someone who found it lying about.'

'Her murderer could have driven her there and she left it in the car.'

'Mmm, could be. Anything found in the pockets?'

'Only this.' Rachel produced a smaller plastic bag containing what looked like a business card. 'Hairdresser's, sir. The card was in her jacket pocket. It's fairly new and Gwen from forensic said they found bits of hair all over her sweater. Like when you have your hair cut and you keep finding bits of hair on your clothes for the rest of the day. I reckon she'd just been to the hairdresser's.'

'Let's have a look at that card.' He studied it closely. 'Anything from missing persons?'

'Nobody fitting the description on this patch, but I've been in touch with some other local forces. There's one here ... Newquay. A surfer and his girlfriend staying in one of those backpackers' hostels. She walked out and he reported her missing. Blonde, medium height ... I've written down the details.'

'Do these look like backpacker's clothes to you?'

'Not a chance.' She picked through the plastic bags, studying the labels on the clothes. 'She was wearing a skirt. Far too conventional. And this jacket – this stuff's not cheap.'

'Worth following up, though. She might have come into money and fancied a change of image. Anything else?'

'Girl from Dorset ... sort of fits the description. She had a row with her mother's boyfriend and walked out.'

'Check on that as well. And this hairdresser's ... do you know it?'

'Snippers and Curls. I know of it.'

'Ever been there?'

Rachel looked disdainful. 'No. There's someone comes to the farm to do our hair.'

'Well, get over to this Snippers and Curls place. See if they can come up with a name.'

'I'll find out who did her hair. They might have chatted.'

On her way out Rachel looked in the mirror, then in her purse to see if she could afford Snippers and Curls' prices.

An hour later Rachel found herself opening the art deco front door of Snippers and Curls. She wished she'd had a chance to wash her hair that morning. She was certain she looked a mess.

A young woman in her late teens, sitting behind the reception desk, greeted her with an insincere smile.

'Have you got an appointment?' Her voice had an automatic quality.

Rachel showed her identification and the smile disappeared.

'Do you want to speak to Mr Carl?'

Rachel wasn't going to let her get away that easily. 'Did you work on reception last Saturday . . . the seventeenth?'

The girl looked worried. 'Er, yeah.'

'Can you remember a customer, a young woman in her early twenties: slim, five foot seven, blonde hair?'

The girl hesitated, looking uneasy.

'Why don't you have a look in the appointments book? Might jog your memory.'

The book was examined. The girl shook her fashionable curls. 'They're all regulars.'

'Anybody who might fit the description I gave?'

'Well, Mrs Bolton's blonde . . . but she's eight months pregnant.' She looked at Rachel enquiringly.

'Anyone else?'

'No. But she might have come in without an appointment.'

'Everything all right, Michelle?' The girl jumped to attention as a tall, waistcoated man in his thirties with a ponytail glided towards them.

'Oh, er, this lady . . .'

'Are you the manager, sir?' Rachel thought she'd better relieve Michelle of the awesome responsibility of explanations.

'This is Mr Carl, Artistic Director,' Michelle chipped in helpfully as Rachel showed her identification again.

'I was enquiring whether a blonde lady in her early twenties had her hair done here on the seventeenth . . . last Saturday.'

'Have you looked in the appointments book, Michelle?'

'Yes. There's nobody like that, but I wondered if she came in on the off-chance. I can't remember anyone, but it happens, doesn't it, Mr Carl?' She looked at her boss anxiously for support.

He spent a moment in obvious thought. 'I can't remember anyone that day. I'll have a word with my staff. I've got another salon in Neston so I'm in and out. May I ask what it's about?'

'We're trying to identify a body found at Little Tradmouth yesterday. Her hair was newly cut and she had one of your cards in her pocket.'

Rachel thought she detected relief on the man's face. 'I leave those cards round in a lot of places ... cafés; that beauty place up on Fossway Hill. She probably just picked it up. It doesn't mean she had her hair done here.'

'If you could just ask your staff, sir.'

Rachel waited while he went round the chairs, whispering to the snipping staff. Each of them shook their beautifully designed heads.

'No. Sorry. Looks like she went somewhere else.' Mr Carl studied Rachel, looking her up and down with a practised eye. 'Have you ever considered a perm? Nothing strong, just a gentle one ... give you a softer look.'

Rachel shook her head and left, making a mental note to ask her hairdresser, Gladys – a motherly creature a world away from Mr Carl and his staff – about perms.

Mr Carl watched her go. The police were asking questions: that meant trouble. He went into the back office and picked up the phone.

Chapter 4

The ships sailed today for the Newfoundland. I pray God that the voyage be safe and prosperous and I beg His blessing upon my ships.

Robert, the apprentice, hath been taken with the toothache and did ask Master Webb, the apothecary, for physic when he did visit my wife. Elizabeth fares a little better with Master Webb's mixture and the child doth seem to grow well. I keep from her bed as Master Webb doth advise.

Last night I did see Jennet in her shift through the open door to her chamber. She is slender with full breasts and I did feel much roused with desire. She spied me and did shut the door. Lead us not into temptation, oh Lord.

Extract from the journal of John Banized,
14 March 1623

'So what have we got?' Heffernan sat down in the swivel chair which rocked precariously under his weight.

'I've seen Mrs Truscot, guv. She gave me a better description of the young couple she saw on the coastal path. And she reckons the girl was carrying a handbag – a small one which didn't really go with the rest of her get-up, if you see what I mean.'

'Put out a description of this pair. Someone might have seen them. Or better still, know where they are.'

'They could be miles away by now.'

'You know what you are, Wesley. A born pessimist.'

'Just being realistic, guv.'

'Well, be realistic in your own time. And don't keep calling me guv. Sounds like something out of *The Sweeney* . . . and I've never driven a Ford Capri in my life.'

Wesley suppressed a grin. 'Sorry, sir.'

'Never mind. Anything else?'

'No sign of the murder weapon. But if it was chucked over the cliff, the tide would have carried it away.'

'Could have been caught in all that vegetation on the way down. Ever do any climbing at that university of yours?'

'Can't stand heights, sir.'

'There's a DC over at Neston who climbs. Can't remember his name but Rachel might know. See if you can sort something out. Any luck with that reconstruction expert at the university?'

'He's away on a lecture tour in the States. I could contact some other places if you want.'

'No. Leave it for now. We'll see if anything turns up first.'

The door opened.

'Come in, Rach.' Heffernan looked her up and down. 'It doesn't look any different.'

'What doesn't?'

'Your hair. I thought you were getting it done.'

'Not at those prices I wasn't. Looks as though our murder victim didn't get hers done there either. They said she hadn't been there. I even saw the Artistic Director, as they call him – Mr Carl.'

Heffernan snorted. 'Mr Carl? You mean Charlie Grubbing? We did him for drink-driving about eighteen months back. Did you try anywhere else?'

'Every hairdresser in Tradmouth, sir. Nothing. I could try Neston next.'

'Good idea.'

'There was one thing, sir. That Mr Carl . . . Charlie Grubbing; he seemed nervous about something.'

'Did he, now? Let's hope he hasn't been driving that BMW of his while he's still banned. If only the good ladies of Tradmouth knew that their hair was in such reckless hands. Anything from forensic, Rach?'

29

'I'll get on to them again.'

'Ta. And have a look through her clothes; see if they give you any ideas. Where she shopped, that sort of thing. Apply a bit of feminine intuition.'

'Now, sir, we agreed. No sexist remarks.'

'That wasn't sexist, Rach, that was a compliment.' He turned to Wesley. 'Talking of sexism, have you got shut of those magazines yet?'

'I'd forgotten all about them.'

'Well, don't let Steve Carstairs get a sniff of them or it'll give him ideas, and we wouldn't want that; he's got enough as it is. Chuck 'em out, Wes, before your wife decides to visit you at work and thinks you've taken up a new hobby. How's she settling in, by the way?'

'Fine. She's looking for a job supply teaching – help her get to know the area before she applies for something permanent.'

Heffernan looked up. 'My Kathy used to work for one of those nursing agencies. Similar thing – got sent to different hospitals.' He smiled at this memory of the past, then his face clouded, almost imperceptibly.

As Wesley followed Rachel out of the office, he looked back. The inspector had got something out of his drawer and was staring at it blankly. Wesley thought it was a photograph.

The small town of Neston, eight miles downriver from Tradmouth, attracted followers of alternative philosophies as a flower attracts bees. New Age bookshops, healing centres and occult emporia stood alongside the butcher's, baker's and gift shops of the steeply sloping high street. Jangling metal hung from the pierced ears and noses of the young incomers, while the old ladies of the town looked on with tolerant amusement.

But the sprawling site just outside the ancient town walls, where the travellers parked their ancient buses and fifth-hand caravans, was not so well tolerated by the locals.

In one of the caravans, a rusting box of 1960s vintage, Julie Day wriggled into her denim jeans while her companion watched appreciatively from the grey-sheeted bed. He patted the vacant pillow.

'Come back to bed, Jules.' He reached out and touched her naked midriff. She moved away.

'Sludge said the flea market's worth a visit. We've got to get there before it shuts.'

Dave lay down again, defeated. He could hear Sludge's gentle snoring from the other end of the caravan.

The tattered curtain that separated their bedroom from the living area parted and a kohl-eyed face, bejewelled with a jangling nose-ring, appeared.

'Jules, are you coming or what?'

'Yeah, right, Donna. I'll be out in a minute.'

Donna withdrew with her habitual expression of boredom. Julie had seen nothing like Donna, with her black-beaded hair and clothes to match, in her native Wongatoa. But then that was why she was travelling: to see the world; to broaden the mind. Everything at the travellers' camp was new to her: the beautiful unkempt children running wild; the scruffy mongrels on leads made of string. She was glad they had met up with Sludge and Donna. It was one more experience for their album.

'Sludge is still asleep,' pronounced Donna flatly. 'It's time we went.'

Dave reached across lazily and hit the button of a battered radio. It was the news.

'Switch that off, Dave.'

But Dave was listening. He held his hand up. 'Shhh.'

Julie sat down on the end of the bed. Donna, bored, retreated behind the curtain.

'You heard what it said, Jules. Police want to interview a young couple seen . . .'

'So?'

'So! That's us. We were there. That old woman with the dog saw us. They're looking for us.'

They studied each other. 'You had it last, Jules. Where did you put that bag?'

There was no privacy in the caravan. Sludge had been awakened by their conversation and had drifted through from his bedroom, bleary-eyed.

Julie scrabbled under the bed and pulled out a small black

leather bag; quilted; expensive. 'I'll get rid of it. Chuck it away.'

'We can't do that. It might be important evidence.' Dave, the good citizen.

'So?' Sludge opened the can of cider he was holding and took a swig.

'What are the police going to think if we come forward now, Dave? And what about the money? Sludge is right.' Julie looked at Donna for support, but Donna lit the strangely thick cigarette she had just rolled and said nothing. 'How can we walk into a police station? Just think, Dave. We could land up in trouble, and that's the last thing we need.'

Dave stared at the bag. Julie had a point. They had planned to move on in a couple of days, and he had no more wish to get involved than Julie had. The radio news had said they could be important witnesses. The bag could be important, could help to trap a killer. He put his head in his hands and tried to come up with an answer.

'Just forget about it.' Donna's voice was slurred in a haze of smoke.

Dave looked up. 'We'll put it back.'

Julie rolled her eyes. 'Get real, Dave. I'm not going back there.'

Sludge looked up from studying the label on his can of cider. 'So what's with this bag anyway? What's in it?'

It was Julie who answered. 'Purse with thirty quid in it, make-up, key, few photos down the lining. We used the money . . . ran a bit short.'

'You've got to get rid of it. Think of the hassle.' Sludge shook the can. It was empty; he chucked it aside with contempt.

'It said on the radio that the police haven't identified this body yet. We've got to take it back.'

Julie looked at Dave. She'd always known he had a stubborn streak. 'Okay, Dave. You win. We'll take it back there and hide it under some bush. They'll think they've missed it.'

Sludge smirked unpleasantly. 'Yeah, put it under some bush and if they find it some pig'll get a right bollocking for not seeing it earlier. I like it.'

'Okay,' said Dave, relieved. 'We'll go this afternoon. It's the best thing, believe me. Then we can get out ... move on.'

Sludge and Julie grunted reluctant approval. Donna, eyes closed in oblivion, had no opinion whatsoever.

The kettle was boiling. Pamela Peterson watched the steam rise and frost half of the kitchen window. She was starting work the next day, covering for someone's maternity leave. This would be her last chance for a while to drink tea at leisure in the afternoon. But she needed to get back to work ... to take her mind off things.

They had promised to phone today. She looked at the telephone on the wall and picked up the receiver, just to make sure it was still working: it always was.

Pam carried the tray through to the living room and put it down on the coffee table. She looked at her guest; her new neighbour who had called to introduce herself. A baby, tucked discreetly inside its mother's sweatshirt, made little snuffling noises as it sucked.

The neighbour, a young woman about Pam's age, looked up and saw that Pam was staring.

'I'm sorry. Er, you don't mind? He was hungry and I didn't want him to bawl the place down,' she said, hoping she hadn't caused offence.

'No, no. Of course not.'

'Only some people are a bit ... you know.'

The baby disengaged itself and gave a satisfied sigh.

'I was really pleased when you moved in next door.' The neighbour had the rare knack of talking intelligibly while munching a chocolate digestive. 'It's about time we had someone young on the road. It's been full of geriatrics for years. Good for baby-sitters, though – all those frustrated grannies.'

Pam smiled weakly.

The neighbour glanced at her slyly, cradling the relaxed and sated baby in her arms. 'I saw your husband going out this morning.' She raised her eyebrows, a comment or a question left unsaid. 'What does he do?'

'He's a policeman ... CID.'

'Oh,' mouthed the neighbour, obviously surprised. 'You've no kids, then?'

Pam shook her head and looked away.

'I suppose you'll wait till you've settled in. It must be a big upheaval moving from London.' She looked at the baby, now asleep. 'Look, I'm sorry. I must get back. My sister's calling round in half an hour. Thanks for the tea. It was really nice to meet you.' She stood up. 'Can you hold him a minute while I get my things together? I've left his bag in the hall.'

She passed the sleeping bundle to Pam, who took it gingerly. Left alone, she gazed down at the tiny bald creature in her arms and ran her finger fleetingly across the soft, flawless cheek. She could smell him: that vanilla smell that babies possess to enslave their mothers and other members of their court. She felt him move softly against her breast, and the tears started to roll down her face.

Then the phone shattered the silence. Pam tore a tissue from the box on the windowsill and wiped her eyes.

Julie, Donna, Dave and Sludge sat at the back of the single-decker bus, filled with pensioners making full use of their cheap bus passes and a smattering of harassed mothers with noisy, dripping-nosed children. The other passengers carefully avoided staring at the chains dripping from Donna's nose, apart from one dirty-faced toddler who studied them earnestly throughout the journey. The English public transport user prefers to ignore the existence of anything out of the ordinary.

When the bus stopped at the harbour, they were the last to get off. The driver watched the four disappear into the distance, shook his head and mumbled something to himself about National Service.

They strolled along the harbour embankment, too preoccupied to enjoy the watery September sun. The busy craft plied like scuttling insects up and down the shimmering river. There was more activity on the water than on the out-of-season riverfront. The cobbled embankment was quiet.

'Is it far?' Sludge spoke for the first time since they had set out from Neston.

'Fair walk . . . past the castle and along the cliff path,' replied Dave, matter-of-fact.

Sludge pulled a face. 'We'll stay here in the town, eh, Donn?'

Donna nodded in agreement. She hadn't realised that the expedition might involve a long walk; somehow she had imagined the spot to be on a bus route, the idea of walking for pleasure being incomprehensible to her. The two couples parted, agreeing to meet later at the bus stop.

Dave and Julie strode through Tradmouth's narrow streets, having decided to forgo the wave-tossed excitement of the little castle ferry owing to lack of funds. The day was pleasant, and Dave began to enjoy himself as they passed the castle walls and headed for open country. Then the sight of the carrier bag Julie was carrying reminded him of why they were there. It would all be over soon; out of their hands; not their responsibility. They had wiped the bag carefully; removed all possible fingerprints. There would be nothing to connect them with it. They would dump it near where they had found it and get away from the place as fast as they could. They wouldn't want to hang about anyway – not after what had happened there.

The police tapes were still hanging there, marking the spot. Dave looked at Julie, who responded with a nervous smile. There was nobody about.

The six pints PC Johnson had had in the Red Bull with his mates the night before were still having an unfortunate effect on his bladder, as was the flask of tea thoughtfully brought to him by Mrs Hutchins from the farm that lunchtime. He was glad of the abundance of bushes.

He was bored. He had counted the boats on the sea, tried to become an avid birdwatcher, even told himself that he was lucky to be enjoying a beautiful bit of Britain's coastline and getting paid for it. But the inspector knew best, he supposed: if he wanted the site watching, it had to be watched.

Johnson stationed himself behind a tall bush and sighed with relief as his bladder lost its heavy burden. He was glad it wasn't the height of the tourist season: discreet urination

35

would be difficult with lines of walkers trudging by, however high the bushes.

But there *was* someone. He could hear the crack of undergrowth and the murmur of voices. He decided to stay where he was. The sight of a policeman emerging from the bushes might alarm some innocent walker; besides, he could see everything from his hidden vantage point.

He watched as the young couple stopped and opened the carrier bag. They turned it over, careful not to touch its contents. Something fell to the ground at the foot of a high hawthorn hedge and they kicked it under the foliage so whatever it was was well hidden. PC Johnson switched on his radio and called the station.

It was ten o'clock that night when Donna and Sludge returned to their caravan. They had waited for Julie and Dave but there had been no sign of them. Sludge showed no curiosity about their whereabouts. They just hadn't bothered turning up; had found something more exciting to do. People move on.

But Donna, unconvinced by Sludge's explanation, felt uneasy. Something had happened to Dave and Julie. She opened a can of cider and tried not to think about it.

Chapter 5

Elizabeth's sickness doth not abate. In the church on Sunday she felt much discomfort and kept to her bed for the remainder of the day.

In church I prayed the Lord to forgive my weakness. There is a small hole in the wall in the empty chamber at the top of the house next to where Jennet sleeps. I am drawn there to watch her in secret. When she doth undress she fires my lust and I cannot help myself. I go to the spying hole like one that hath no will of his own. To see her naked is my only desire and to know that she doth not suspect inflames the lust within me.

Oh Lord, forgive me. It must cease forthwith.

Extract from the journal of John Banized,
20 March 1623

On Wednesday morning Wesley set off for work early: a murder investigation generates work as a nuclear explosion generates heat.

He was surprised to see Neil at his post so early, although there was no sign of Jane and Matt. He crossed over the road and called his greetings through the wire fence.

'Come in, man. Don't stand there like a spectator at a zoo.'

Wesley pushed the wire gate open and entered the site.

'Coming for a drink tonight? Same time, same place.

I've been doing a bit of research . . . thought you might be interested.'

Wesley was, but a glance at his watch told him Neil's information would have to wait for another time.

'The place was built in 1585, three years before ships sailed from here to fight the Armada.' Neil's eyes shone. History, the sense of great events experienced by a location, had always set his imagination alight. That was why he was a good archaeologist. Wesley looked at his watch again. Once Neil got going there was no stopping him. 'Built by a Thomas Banized. In the family for two centuries – merchants involved in the Newfoundland trade.'

'Rich?' Wesley began to be infected by Neil's enthusiasm. Just for that moment the Banized family loomed more real than the dead woman at Little Tradmouth.

'Very comfortably off, I'd say.' Neil looked about him. 'Nice place this in its day. There are some Victorian photographs I've seen, and Matt's drawing up a proper plan. You'll have to have a look when it's done. We might even get as far as a computer simulation of the place, if we're lucky. I'm having a look in the church registers tomorrow, see what I can find out about the Banizeds. Look, Wes, I can see you're in a rush . . . see you tonight, maybe? And see if you can get Pam to come.'

'I'll try.'

They parted with a wave. It might do Pam good to get out, to see Neil again. She seemed a bit better since the phone call telling her about the appointment at the clinic, but still jumpy, nervous. He'd play things by ear.

'Just tell him what you told me.'

'But it's embarrassing.' Wesley shook his head, beginning to regret confiding in Rachel . . . anyone. It was a personal matter. He also felt a twinge of conscience. Was he being disloyal discussing his wife's problems with an attractive young woman?

'You'll have to tell him something. You'll need the time off for the appointments.'

Wesley looked through the glass partition at Heffernan

in his office. He saw the inspector put the phone down. He was smiling; in a good mood. Now would be the time.

Heffernan emerged from his office, the grin still illuminating his chubby face.

'They've found it – the handbag. And two suspects to go with it. They were brought in after you'd gone home yesterday. They fit Dorothy Truscot's description perfectly, and they were caught trying to dump the handbag back on the murder scene.'

'Could I have a quick word, sir?'

'Go on, then, I'm listening.'

'I need to take Friday afternoon off, sir. I know it's a bad time, but . . .'

'What for?'

'An appointment . . .'

'What kind of appointment? With your hairdresser? Dentist? What's the latest these days? Personal fitness coach?'

'A medical appointment, sir.'

'What's the big secret? Not got the clap, have you? Nothing to be shy about. I saw a lot of it in the navy.'

Wesley didn't know whether or not to take Heffernan seriously. He swallowed hard. He might as well get it over with.

'It's my wife who's got the appointment and I've got to go with her. We've been trying to start a family for a while and . . .'

Wesley braced himself for another joke at his expense, but he saw Heffernan's expression soften.

'Look, I know it's an awkward time and we're . . .'

'No problem. I'm sure the criminals of Tradmouth and district won't go on overtime just 'cause you've got a few hours off.'

Wesley thanked him and turned to go.

'Wesley.'

'Yes, sir?'

'Best of luck.'

The phone rang and Heffernan answered it.

'Right, Wes. They're down in the interview room. Come on. This could be interesting.'

Julie sat on the plastic chair, biting her nails. She had seen police interview rooms in countless television programmes, but she found the reality of the spartan surroundings – the beige-painted brick walls decorated only by an institutional clock – unnerving. This was it, reality; this was trouble.

Why were they keeping her so long? She could hear the blood pumping in her ears. Where was Dave?

She crumpled the empty plastic cup in front of her and the noise reverberated around the room. The policewoman by the door looked at her disapprovingly.

The young black man who entered the room greeted the policewoman with a nod and sat down opposite Julie. He gave her a quick sympathetic smile. A solicitor. He could be the duty solicitor they'd mentioned. She closed her eyes in silent thanks.

'Have you made a statement?' His voice was soft and well educated.

'Yeah . . . she's got it.' The policewoman produced the handwritten forms and gave them to the newcomer, who put them on the table in front of him. Julie sat in silence while he read them through. When he had finished he looked up at her and smiled again. She felt almost relaxed.

'I'm Detective Sergeant Peterson and I'd just like to go over your statement with you, if I may.'

Julie gave the plastic cup another crunch. No rescuer, no one to extricate her from the situation – just another policeman.

Wesley let Julie go through her story without interruption, only prompting her where necessary to clarify the odd point. By and large his instinct told him that she was telling the truth. But she was hiding something, and he suspected that he knew what it was.

Rachel found Dave only too anxious to talk. She had to ask him to slow down at times so that she could get the sequence of events clear in her mind. He was keen to get it all off his chest. Of course, it hadn't been his idea to take the bag. He had wanted to leave it where it was. And he had insisted that they return it as soon as he heard about the murder.

Yes, they had taken the money. He was sorry: it wasn't his idea.

'What money?' asked Rachel pointedly.

'How are our two guests?' Heffernan sat back in his swivel chair which tilted dangerously under his weight.

'Talkative, sir. I couldn't shut him up.' Rachel grinned. She had rather enjoyed her encounter with the suntanned young Australian.

'On the whole I think she's telling the truth,' Wesley added. 'But I get the feeling she might be leaving something out.'

The inspector read the two statements in silence.

'They're the same but for one thing.'

'The money, sir?' Rachel had read the statements through already and had noticed the anomaly.

'Right. They nicked it when they found the bag, heard about the murder then panicked.'

'So why didn't they just get rid of it, chuck it away anywhere? Get out of the area?' asked Wesley.

Heffernan grinned. 'First of all we had their description and they thought they could be identified, but I also detect a small-town Sunday school upbringing here. They're out of their depth. It's one thing to give in to temptation and walk off with a bag that's just lying there unclaimed, but it's another to bugger up a murder inquiry by destroying vital evidence. One of them's got a conscience. Like they say in their statements – they realised it was important but didn't want to get involved.'

'So who's the one with the conscience?'

'Him, I reckon. You go and have a word, Wesley. See what else you can find out. And get us a coffee from the machine, will you, Rach. I'm spitting feathers here.'

Rachel's lips tightened. She hadn't joined the CID to run around getting coffee for men; but as the junior officer present, she supposed she didn't have much choice. She left the office slowly and resentfully.

'What have I said, Wes?' Heffernan asked as he watched her go.

'No idea.' If his boss didn't know, he wasn't going to enlighten him.

'She's a good copper but she doesn't half get some moods on her.' He looked at the handbag in front of them on the desk encased in a plastic bag. 'We'll wait till she comes back to go through it, eh?' He began to stare at the bag as if he were willing it to give up its secrets.

Wesley interrupted his thoughts. 'Heard anything new about Jonathon Berrisford . . . that missing kid, sir?'

Heffernan sighed and looked up. 'I was talking to the super earlier. Some woman reckons she's seen him with a bloke in Morbay. She's convinced it's him . . . keeps ringing in.'

'Have there been many sightings?'

'The usual . . . from John O'Groats to Land's End; usual crop abroad and all. Lord Lucan eat your heart out.'

'So why's this woman so convinced?'

'Stan Jenkins is interviewing her later, but I wouldn't get your hopes up. I've been around too long to believe in fairytale endings, if you know what I mean.'

Rachel entered bearing a plastic cup filled with a non-descript steaming liquid which she deposited rather too firmly on the inspector's desk, so that some of it spilt onto the papers beneath. Heffernan mopped up the spilled coffee with a grey crumpled handkerchief. The phone rang and he picked up the receiver with his free hand.

'Another one for Steve Carstairs,' he said as he rang off. 'Building materials nicked again, from those new houses they're building up by the marina at Saltway this time; they're getting around. Tell Steve to get over there right away, will you, Rach, and tell him to take a couple of uni-formed bods with him. He'll need to do the rounds of the builders' yards . . . see if any of this stuff is turning up in the system yet. Okay?'

Rachel bit her lip and left in silence.

The bag sat there on the table; fat; bloated with potential information. When Rachel returned, Heffernan stood up and looked at it with the air of a Lord Mayor about to cut a ribbon and declare something open.

He drew the contents out carefully: a make-up bag stuffed

42

was seventy. Smoked sixty a day, drank navy rum like it was lemonade and lived on fish and chips. Died when he was eighty-three.'

'Perhaps they have stronger constitutions up in Liverpool, Gerry.'

'Don't know about that, but they've got stronger tea. Just look at that – it's like a urine sample. I'd take it back if I were you.'

Stan looked across at the two amazons behind the counter and rejected the idea of complaint. He sat down and tried to muster some enthusiasm for the green creation on his plate.

'Any news of Jonathon Berrisford?' Heffernan spoke with his mouth full.

Stan shook his head. He was used to being asked about this particular case: everyone in the station concerned themselves with a child's disappearance. 'Drew a blank with that woman up in Morbay. I did a check on her. She's staying in a hostel down here, getting a bit of sea air – care in the community job. She's known to the West Midlands force; apparently she makes a habit of this sort of thing. Every crime or disappearance, she's always the star witness.'

'Suppose it makes the poor cow feel important.'

'Don't feel sorry for her, Gerry. She's wasting police time. Lucky I didn't charge her. You must be getting soft in your old age.'

'How's Jonathon's mother? She still down here?'

'We finally persuaded her to go back home. It wasn't doing her any good sitting in that cottage staring at the wallpaper. And she couldn't be left on her own; we had to have a WPC stay with her and that didn't do the budget much good.' He sighed. 'She's better off up there. She'll have her husband and relatives, and I dare say the doctors up there can dish out the tranquillisers as easily as the doctors down here. She rings me every day, though. Sometimes I can hardly bring myself to pick the phone up.'

Heffernan bowed his head and said nothing.

Stan changed the subject. 'How's your new sergeant settling in – the black chap?'

'Fine. I've actually caught him in possession of a quantity of brain cells, unlike others I could mention.'

Stan eyed Heffernan's plate enviously. 'How are your sausages?'

'Want one?'

'I can't take your last one.' His eyes gleamed as he pushed the remains of his salad to one side.

'Go on, Stan, nobody's watching ... and your need is greater than mine. Must be going.' His metal chair clattered as he stood up. 'See you, Stan. Don't eat anything I wouldn't eat.'

Stan Jenkins raised a hand in farewell, his mouth being full of forbidden cholesterol.

As soon as Heffernan had padded into his office, Rachel descended on him, her mouth set in determination.

'Why did you let them go, sir? Shouldn't we be charging them?'

He sank down wearily into his chair. 'Who?'

'Those Australians. Surely there's been an offence committed.'

'What offence? Being Australian's not an offence ... at least it wasn't last time I looked.'

The inspector maddened her when he got into these moods. She tried to keep calm. 'The money, sir. They stole the money.'

'Borrowed it, Rach. They've promised to repay it and I don't think for one moment they've got anything to do with the murder. Still, it's worth checking, I suppose. We can have a word with those hippies they've been stopping with, establish their movements at the time of the murder. Fancy going on the hippie trail to Neston, Rach? Could transform your life.'

He looked up at Rachel, trying not to grin. The look of disapproval on her face reminded him of his Great-aunt Beatrice who did charitable work for distressed sailors and reputedly possessed the largest knickers in Liverpool. Eventually he took pity on her.

'Don't worry. Our antipodean friends are quite safe at the youth hostel and they've sworn a solemn oath not to leave Tradmouth till we've finished with them. I reckon we've scared the excrement out of them – him especially. They won't budge. Look, Rach, get down to Neston to that travellers' site and see if you can track down this pair they were staying with. You've got the details.'

'Yes, sir.' Sullenly.

'Take DC Carstairs. I wouldn't recommend taking anyone in uniform. And go home and slip into something more comfortable – jeans or something – or they'll think you're from the DSS or Social Services. Off you go. And don't look like that. They're mostly harmless . . . even the dogs.'

'Yes, sir.' Coming from local farming stock, she was unconvinced by her boss's last statement, but nevertheless went in search of Steve Carstairs to break the news. The outer office appeared to be empty, but as she closed the door a head rose slowly from behind a desk.

'What are you doing down there, Wesley? Lost something?'

Wesley looked sheepish. 'I thought I might try and get rid of . . . you know. I've brought a bin-bag from home and I can tape up the top and . . .'

'Had a good look, then?'

Wesley looked up at her, irritated by the accusation. 'We're not all like my predecessor, you know. Some of us have better taste.'

She looked distinctly sceptical. 'Come on, Wesley, I know what men are like. I've got three brothers, the original sexist pigs.'

'No boyfriend?' He couldn't resist the question.

'Not at the moment.'

Their eyes met and there was a moment of awkward silence. Then Wesley, self-conscious, turned his attention back to the bin-bag.

One of the magazines he was coaxing into the bag fell to the floor and opened itself at a particularly provocative page, the pose owing more to an anatomy textbook than the annals of erotic art. His eyes were first drawn to the obvious places, but then he saw the face, blank and dehumanised. The girl was blonde and under other circumstances Wesley would have described her as attractive. It was a face he knew well; a face he had last seen, destroyed and battered, on the pathologist's table. He bore the magazine triumphantly into his boss's office.

'So that's what Madam got up to in her spare time.' Heffernan studied the picture from every angle while Rachel looked on with distaste. 'Very observant of you, Wes, noticing her face. That's what years of expensive education do for you.'

'The publishers are an outfit in Manchester,' said Wesley, turning to the front page. 'I'll get someone to run a check on it now.'

'Looks like we're headed up north tomorrow, then. Ever been to Manchester, Wes?'

'No, sir. Can't say I have.'

'It'll be a whole new experience for you. You know what they used to say? If you've never been to Manchester, you've never lived.'

Wesley looked sceptical.

It had just gone six thirty when Mr Carl switched the burglar alarm on and the salon lights off, then emerged into the grey drizzle that had brought the Indian summer to an abrupt end. Coat collar up, he made his way down the cobbled hill past shutting shops and figures with newly resurrected umbrellas, past the fenced gap in the shopfronts where they were digging up the foundations of some old house or other. There was nothing much to see for their efforts, only some old brickwork and some holes ... and that skeleton he'd read about in the local paper.

He could see the welcoming beacon of the Angel's mullioned windows. The pub was late-fourteenth-century with a smart twentieth-century clientèle He found it comfortably full of post-work drinkers. The Artistic Director of Tradmouth's foremost hairdressing establishment sat on a blackened pew and waited, soothed by the music of Vivaldi. One pint ... two pints; he was late, three-quarters of an hour late. Carl stood up to leave; he would phone from home, see what had happened. Then the door swung open. The newcomer spotted Carl and weaved his way through the standing drinkers. He stood there, without speech. Carl could see there was something wrong from the panic in his eyes.

Chapter 7

The Lord has punished me. Elizabeth has lost the child. She keeps to her bed in her grief and will not see me.

This morning I went into the chamber by Jennet's and I did block up the gap in the wall lest I be tempted more to sin.

Extract from the journal of John Banized,
5 April 1623

Manchester lived up to its reputation. It was raining . . . and they were lost.

Wesley stopped the engine. 'Got the *A to Z*, sir?'

'Don't worry. Navigation was always my strong point. Just give me a chart and I'll get us there. Don't look like that. You're in the capable hands of an officer of the merchant navy.'

'I thought it was the police force, sir.'

'That and all. Turn right and straight on. Should be the university then some hospitals on our left.'

The traffic was light. Wesley was glad he didn't have to do this in the rush hour. Heffernan navigated them successfully through litter-strewn streets lined with ancient and modern shops selling Indian food and saris; past student accommodation built in the sixties brutalist style; past Victorian redbrick shops, many selling takeaway food, catering to the burgeoning student population. They turned a corner and drove down a road of large Victorian terraces and villas, lined with mature trees. The rows of plastic bellpushes by the flaking front doors indicated that the once-prosperous houses were now divided into flats. Fallowfield had seen better days.

'My daughter, Rosemary, lives off this road,' Heffernan said quietly. 'She's at the Royal Northern College of Music.' He paused for a few seconds. 'I worry about her, you know.'

'I'm sure she can take care of herself, sir.'

'You're probably right . . . but I still worry.' He looked down in silence at the *A to Z*. 'Take the next turning on your left and then it's second on the right. Cul de sac. Kempthorn Close.'

Kempthorn Close was flanked by the now-familiar Victorian terraced flats, modern metal fire escapes jutting from their façades like angular warts. At the end of the cul de sac a large villa stood in littered overgrown gardens; a recently Tarmacked drive, like a fresh scar on a wrinkled face, led to the entrance. The battered, once-imposing front door bore a number of mismatched name-plates; some tarnished brass, some dark plastic with bold white lettering. Venusian Publications was one of the latter and bore the qualification 'First Floor'. They stepped into a dingy hallway, floored with shabby linoleum, and climbed the impressive staircase. The sound of muffled typing seeped through glass-panelled doors.

They reached their destination. Wesley was about to knock, but Heffernan had pushed the door open before his knuckles could reach the glass. A startled secretary looked up. She was hardly what Wesley would have expected an employee of a pornographic publishing company to look like: a bespectacled, demurely dressed lady of mature years, she would have looked at home behind the counter of a suburban public library. Her mouth twitched into a nervous smile. She scented trouble, and when the visitors showed their identification her suspicions were confirmed. Heffernan explained the purpose of their visit, and Wesley watched the woman's face as she was shown the picture of the dead girl. She shook her head.

'It might have been before my time. I've only been here three months.'

'Is there anyone else I can speak to?'

'There's Mr Keffer, but he's out this afternoon.'

'Out where?'

'On a shoot.'

The inspector had an idea what he'd be shooting, and it wouldn't be pheasants. 'Where can I find him?'

'I really can't say. They tend to move around . . . different locations.' She made it sound almost glamorous. 'He'll be in first thing tomorrow,' she added helpfully.

'Have you got his home address?'

'Er . . .'

'This is a murder inquiry, madam.'

She drew a card from an index on her desk and wrote down an address.

'We might need to speak to you again, Mrs, er . . .'

'Webster. I've only been here three months . . .'

With her pleas of ignorance ringing in their ears, Heffernan and Wesley clattered their way down the uncarpeted staircase.

Pamela Peterson had had misgivings when her then boyfriend had shown an interest in joining the police force. The nightly portrayal on television of hardened cops with broken marriages and a drink problem had sounded warning bells. She had grown used to the anxiety and erratic hours over the years, but she still felt a stab of anger as she put the phone down.

She debated whether or not to ring her mother, but decided against it. Then she considered calling Maritia, her sister-in-law. The prospect of talking her problems over with a qualified doctor was tempting. But Maritia might be on duty, or too tired to be sympathetic. Besides, Pamela wasn't really in the mood to talk to anyone. She had a bath and went to bed.

How could Wesley let himself get stuck in Manchester tonight of all nights, when tomorrow was so important? Everything depended on tomorrow.

The bar at the St Dominic Hotel – a name that had attracted Heffernan with its solid monastic associations – added a

51

whole new dimension to the concept of blandness. The walls were laminated, the bar was laminated, the lager tasted as though it had been created in a sterile environment using laminated barley. The greenery, growing up the trellis at the side of the bar, looked decidedly artificial.

Keffer had proved to be elusive. Twice they had returned to bang on the door of his flat in the up-market modern block with its decorative wrought-iron balconies – probably inspired by the architect's annual holiday to the Continent. There had been no sign of Keffer or any other human habitation in the carpeted communal corridors. All was silence. So much for Northern neighbourliness.

Heffernan looked down at his lager, urine-sample gold. He didn't feel like drinking any more. He had hoped for a paternal drink with Rosemary, but when he had rung to tell her he was up in Manchester she had claimed a prior engagement, a date with some young man – very likely unsuitable. He took another unsatisfying gulp from his glass. Wesley was upstairs on the phone, probably trying to appease an irate wife. Heffernan had been there. Now, as he drained his glass and looked round the lonely bar, he realised how much he missed Kathy. He wished he were up there talking on that phone; he wished he had somebody to appease. He took his glass back to the bar and climbed the stairs to his room.

They set out early next morning. Producers of pornographic magazines didn't strike Heffernan as potential early risers, but you could never tell.

Keffer's block of flats seemed just as deserted at half past seven in the morning as it had done the evening before, the only difference being that there were more BMWs parked in the residents' parking spaces.

This time they were lucky. After five minutes of earnest doorbell-ringing their endeavours were rewarded by the appearance of a bleary-eyed man in his forties. A short towelling robe, insecurely fastened, fell open to reveal a pair of garish red boxer shorts decorated with a yellow slogan which, Wesley guessed, was probably rude, but he wasn't prepared to study it long enough to read it. They produced

52

their warrant cards and the bleary eyes widened into suspicious wakefulness.

They were led into a darkened living room. It looked as though someone at least had had more fun the previous evening than Heffernan and Wesley had experienced at the St Dominic Hotel. An empty wine bottle stood on the tiled coffee table amongst tumbled lager cans, overspilling ashtrays and dirty glasses. The fuggy air reeked of cigarette smoke and perfume. Keffer made himself decent and drew the curtains back. The place looked more squalid in the grey daylight.

Heffernan addressed the wary Keffer with impeccable formality. 'Ever been to Devon, sir?'

'What's this? Tourist board making house calls now?' Keffer smirked at his own wit.

'Just answer the question please, sir.'

Keffer shook his head. 'Florida's more my scene.'

'We're investigating the death of a young woman. She was found near Tradmouth. Know where that is, sir?'

'No idea.' He looked as if he might be telling the truth.

'I wonder if you'd have a look at this photograph, sir.' Heffernan nodded to Wesley, who handed the photo over. They watched Keffer's reaction.

'Karen . . . it's Karen.'

Heffernan's eyes shone with the excitement of the chase. 'Karen who?'

'She's not, er . . . is she?'

'What can you tell me about her?'

Wesley got his notebook out and prepared for some serious writing.

'Look, I didn't know her well and it was three years ago . . . more. She only modelled for me a couple of times – tasteful stuff, you know.' Wesley raised his eyebrows. 'She was a nice kid, just a bit short of cash; you know how it is.'

'No, I don't. You tell me.' Heffernan leaned forward, challenging.

'Well, there are girls who've been in the business years but sometimes the punters like a new face – someone different.' He paused, waiting for a reaction. He got none. 'Karen was a friend of a friend. She needed the money.'

'Drug habit?' Even though no traces had been found in the body, it was worth asking.

'No way. She wanted to go on a modelling course. I was offering her some experience.'

I bet you were, thought Wesley.

'Look, I was helping the girl out, giving her some modelling experience, and she was getting paid for it. What's wrong with that?'

Heffernan assumed the question was rhetorical. 'What can you tell us about her?'

'I've told you. I hardly knew her.'

'Anything you can tell us . . . anything at all.'

Keffer sat in silence for a few seconds, gathering his thoughts and his dressing gown round him. 'I didn't know her well, mind, only professionally. I just arrange the models and take the pictures.'

'So who introduced you?'

'One of my usual girls.'

'Name?'

'Sandra.'

'Sandra what?'

'Don't know . . . forgotten. Something ordinary. Smith or something.'

'Where can I find her?'

'Dunno. Haven't seen her in eighteen months. They come and go.'

'This Karen. Where did she live?'

'With her mum.' The policemen exchanged glances. Now they were getting somewhere.

'Got an address?'

'No.'

'Surname?'

'Something foreign. She said her dad was American, killed in a car crash. Dunno if it was true. Sometimes they make things up to make themselves more . . . you know . . . glamorous.'

'Who do?' The man's attitude was beginning to needle Wesley.

'The girls. They all see themselves on the front cover of

Vogue, poor cows.' He paused for a second, lighting a cigarette. 'Gordino, that was her name. Something like Gordino.'

'Would you have such a thing as a phone book, sir?' Heffernan enquired with measured politeness.

The phone book produced no Gordinos but one Giordino. Wesley wrote down the address.

'What do you think of our photographer friend?'

Wesley looked disdainful. 'The word sleazy springs to mind.' He decided on a direct approach as hints seemed to have no visible effect. 'Look, sir, I'm going to have to make a phone call. I've got that appointment this afternoon and . . .'

'Don't worry, Wes, I've not forgotten. We'll call on this Mrs Giordino then we'll be straight off. If she's the girl's mum we'll be taking her back with us anyway. We'll be back in time. Trust me.' He grinned and slapped the sergeant on the back in an avuncular manner.

After consulting the *A to Z*, they found themselves on a small council estate. The redbrick semis, of 1920s vintage with front gardens, had once achieved the pinnacle of municipal respectability; the lawns cut, paths swept and net curtains snowy white. But now, although most looked well kept, some were letting the side down, and a few overgrown gardens displayed broken toys and rusting cars mounted on bricks.

Wesley opened the wooden gate to a neat garden path. The house beyond, although the curtains were beige rather than white, gave the impression of being well cared for. Their knock at the recently painted front door was answered by a woman in her fifties who stared at them suspiciously from behind a door chain. The beige cardigan and cheap brown skirt she wore gave an impression of unrelieved dowdiness.

Wesley was struck by the gentle way in which his boss spoke to the woman, the sympathy with which he broke the news. As she sat on the beige Dralon sofa, surrounded by cheap-framed photographs of her dead daughter as a schoolgirl, sipping tea from a chipped flowered mug – the first one Wesley had been able to lay his hands on –

Heffernan continued speaking softly to her, asking questions with a delicate tact, gauging the woman's feelings. Wesley, not hearing clearly most of what was said, looked at his notebook in despair.

Mrs Giordino silently packed a small suitcase then went next door to leave her key with a neighbour.

'I didn't get most of that, sir. What's going on?' Wesley looked down at the notebook's virgin pages.

'Plenty of time for getting things on paper when we're back on home ground. Time and a place for everything.'

Heffernan sat in the back of the car with Mrs Giordino and Wesley drove – an arrangement that filled him with relief. Like most of his generation who had never encountered death and grief in their personal lives, he felt awkward with the bereaved: it wasn't that he didn't sympathise, he just didn't know what to say. He ran through a mental calculation: the journey would take four and a half hours, five at the outside – he wasn't a reckless driver. It was ten to ten. They would be in Tradmouth by three. The appointment was at four thirty. It wouldn't be a problem.

The carpets at the Morbay Clinic were thicker than those Pam had been able to afford for her new home. She sank her toes into the pile, feeling its depth, as she sipped freshly percolated coffee and scanned an interior design magazine.

Her palms felt clammy and she needed the toilet again. Nerves. They always affected her like this: interviews, exams, her wedding day. Where was Wesley? He should be here. He should be going through this with her.

The receptionist was still giggling furtively into the phone. She was dressed in what appeared to be a nurse's uniform, although her heavy make-up and blond curls hinted that she was employed more for her appearance than her professional qualifications.

Pam's opinion of private medicine had been the same as Wesley's, but when she had discovered the NHS waiting time for even an initial investigation, she had decided that political principles could be overridden and savings broken into.

It was two years now since she had come off the Pill: two

years of waiting to see what each month would bring; two years of disappointment. It had hardly mattered at first, but then, month by month, as every street seemed to throng with pregnant women and babies and every advert, every magazine, every TV programme showed babies in abundance, it had started to matter a great deal. The mothers of the children she taught seemed to leave rabbits in the shade when it came to breeding as they routinely provided new fodder for the education system. For a year now Pam had felt empty; a freak of nature.

The receptionist spoke with a soft Devon accent. 'Mrs Peterson, Dr Downey will see you now. Did you say your husband was coming too? Dr Downey does like to see couples together,' she added disapprovingly.

Where was Wesley? Pamela, flustered, dying for the toilet, opened her mouth to speak, but no words came out.

Chapter 8

Elizabeth's sister Anne doth stay with us and she hath taken on the running of the household. Elizabeth prevails upon me to find Anne a husband from amongst our acquaintances but she is not young and well favoured so the task may not be easy.

The raising of the church roof hath commenced and the builders are about their task. The carpenters have used fine carved timber for the new gallery, from the Spanish galleon captured by the Roebuck some forty years past. It doth look exceeding well and hath saved the cost of new timber and carving.

The Reverend Wilkins did ask last night for more money from the town for the new windows. Mayor Rawlins hath promised two new windows. He is ever trying to buy a good reputation with his wife's wealth.

I have seen little of Jennet now that Anne hath the household well in hand.

Extract from the journal of John Banized,
10 April 1623

When lorries overturn on motorways the effects are usually spectacular. The M5, being heavily burdened with traffic that Friday lunch-time, ground to a complete stop. Wesley Peterson, his hands tensed on the steering wheel, experienced the worst seven-hour car journey of his life.

But Gerry Heffernan reckoned he'd learned more about

Karen Giordino in the back of their stationary car than he ever would have learned in an interview room. Mrs Giordino's grief poured out as a non-stop monologue about her daughter. At the end of the journey he felt he knew everything about the girl and her mother, beginning with their abandonment by the council clerk father for a siren of the corporation typing pool when Karen was four years old. There was no American connection; the surname came from a long-forgotten Italian great-grandfather. Karen had opted for a more glamorous version of her history.

Of Karen's recent past, her mother knew very little. In the last few years there had been long silences, the longest lasting over a year. Heffernan ascertained, by tactful questioning, that Mrs Giordino knew nothing of her daughter's brush with the seamier end of the modelling industry – she had been told office work. This had been followed by Karen's decampment to Blackpool 'to do some seasonal work', the nature of which was vague. Mrs Giordino seemed to have displayed a remarkable lack of curiosity about her daughter's career.

'She met this boyfriend of hers there. He was up on business – you know how they have these conference things.'

Heffernan leaned forward, willing her to continue.

'Sorry, sir. I'm going to have to make a phone call.' Wesley picked up the car phone.

'Okay, okay,' Heffernan snapped impatiently. The sergeant had broken the atmosphere of quiet confidence. Mrs Giordino stiffened. The moment was lost.

They sat in silence in the stationary traffic while Wesley tried to get through to his home number. There was no reply. He spent the next ten minutes ringing directory enquiries for the clinic number, then another ten trying to leave a coherent message with a dizzy receptionist. He had done all he could.

Heffernan decided to try again, gently. 'This boyfriend? Did you ever meet him?'

'Oh, no.' She spoke as if this were obvious.

'And as far as you know they're still together?'

'Far as I know. Living together down south somewhere.'

'Do you have their address?'

'She said she'd send it once she'd settled but. . . .' Heffernan nodded sympathetically. 'I never had a card last Christmas. She's got her life to lead, I suppose.' She looked at her clenched fingers. 'Had her life.'

'She'll have told you his name?'

'John . . . it was John.'

'Surname?'

'She never said. I mean, you don't, do you.'

'Did she say where he was from?'

'Down in the south-west somewhere. Cornwall?'

Heffernan looked up sharply. 'Could it have been Devon?'

'Could have been.'

'What about the baby? Did she let you know when it was born?'

Mrs Giordino's eyes widened. 'What baby? I never heard she had a baby.' The woman looked at him, her face full of the pain of neglected motherhood. 'No. She never had a baby. She would have told me. She would.'

Heffernan nodded and continued. 'Is there anything else? Please think hard, Mrs Giordino. Anything she might have told you about her boyfriend . . . anything at all?'

'I think he was married when she met him. Left his wife.'

'Did she tell you that?'

'Don't know. Must have done.'

'Did you have a phone number where you could contact her?'

She shook her head as if nothing really mattered now: Karen was dead, gone.

Wesley picked up the phone and dialled again.

Armed with an authentic picture of the murdered woman, Rachel had drawn a complete blank at the travellers' site at Neston. She had seen Sludge and Donna, who backed up Dave and Julie's story, but they made it clear by their monosyllabic answers that they didn't know anything else about the matter and didn't particularly care.

She had then resumed her crusade among the hairdressers of Tradmouth with more gusto than before. Snippers and

Curls was her last port of call. It was always best to double-check and she had a feeling . . . just a feeling.

Mr Carl was putting the finishing touches to a scrunch-dry when he spotted Rachel walking with determination down St Margaret's Street. He signalled to Damien, the junior, to take over the hairdryer and, with a word and a charming smile to his client, hurried into the back. When he heard the front door of the salon open he let himself out into the alleyway at the back of the shop and disappeared in the direction of the Butterwalk.

It was no use going to the clinic. Pam would already have left. Wesley sat in front of the television screen which might just as well have been blank for all the notice he was taking of it. She should have been home by now. She must have driven to Plymouth, to her mother's: the traditional refuge for disgruntled wives.

He picked up the phone and began to dial his mother-in-law's number. He got on well with Della, a recently widowed and formidable sociology lecturer. He hoped she would help her daughter to see things in perspective.

Wesley was halfway through dialling when he changed his mind. He'd let Pam cool off.

The sound of the key in the front door brought him to his feet, his heart racing. He grabbed the remote control and angrily silenced the television, then he stood still, waiting. He heard her put her keys away, take her coat off. This was how a suspect must feel before being questioned. She walked in. He rushed to her and tried to take her in his arms, but she turned away.

'We got stuck on the M5. A lorry overturned. How did you get on? What did they say?'

She pulled away from him. 'I don't want to talk about it. I've just spent the last few hours with my private parts on full display. I felt like a lump of meat on a bloody butcher's block, and you weren't even there. I don't think you care at all.'

She slammed the door behind her to make the point.

Wesley wondered if Neil would be in the Tradmouth Arms that evening. He needed a drink.

'You look pissed off, Wes.' Neil had never been one to sidle tactfully round the obvious.

'How are you getting on with that research?' Wesley had no desire to discuss his troubles, even though tonight Neil was alone, Matt and Jane having gone off to see a film in Morbay.

'I've been looking up the old parish records. The first Banized at that address was a Thomas – died in 1601; his wife Margaret died a year later. I reckon he must have been the one who built the place. If you're free one lunch-time I'll take you to see their tomb. Pretty fancy, they weren't short of a sovereign or two. The tomb's damaged at the corner. Legend has it it was done when the church was being renovated in the early seventeenth century. A workman dropped something on it. Nothing's new.'

Wesley went to the bar to get more drinks. He was beginning to relax; to enjoy himself. When he returned Neil resumed his narrative.

'This Thomas had a son, John, who took over the business. It must have done well 'cause his tomb's quite an elaborate affair and all. He married the only daughter of a prosperous merchant from Neston, Elizabeth Pilner, and they had a son, Thomas, who became mayor in 1663. The vicar's a bit of a local historian – he's been a lot of help. He says there are documents about the Banized family in the local museum. I'll have a look when I've got some free time.'

'No clue about the skeleton?'

'Not a thing. Probably some servant girl's bastard.'

'Where was it found?'

'About three feet below what would have been the cellar floor.'

'Did servant girls get that much privacy in those days to go digging up cellar floors?'

'How should I know? You're the detective. We're starting to dig the other part of the cellar tomorrow. Come along if you're interested.'

'Wish I could, Neil, but we're in the middle of this murder inquiry.'

He looked at his watch. It was nearly closing time. As it

was Friday a few members of the weekend yachting fraternity had occupied a corner of the bar and were regaling each other loudly with tales of their nautical deeds. In another corner sat a huddle of elderly locals who threw occasional curious glances in Wesley's direction.

'Look, Neil, I'll have to go. You in here most nights?'

'Where else? We tried the Angel but it was a bit posh.'

Neil raised a hand in casual farewell and Wesley stepped out into the salty night air. Heffernan's house was virtually round the corner, and from where Wesley stood he could hear the lapping of the water against the quayside. He wondered fleetingly how his boss spent his evenings.

He walked slowly back home up the steep narrow streets that led away from the harbour, preoccupied with two questions. Would Pam be asleep when he got back? And would the cellar of the merchant's house hold any more grisly secrets?

Chapter 9

Today Elizabeth was recovered enough to attend church. When we returned to the house she again took to her bed as the service had tired her greatly. The work on the church proceeds at a goodly pace. I have had words with the workmen who did allow a block of stone to fall and damage my father's tomb. Anne returns to her home next week. How I do fear her departure for Jennet will then be once more in our quarters. God grant me strength.

Extract from the journal of John Banized,
19 April 1623

'The boss said he wanted to see you as soon as you got in.'

Rachel dumped a pile of reports on Wesley's desk. He looked at them despairingly and took his coat off.

'Anything new?'

'I think we've got the murder weapon. That DC from Neston went down the cliff, found a big lump of branch caught in the bushes. No prints, of course, but a few traces of blood and hair that hadn't been washed away by the rain. It's all in the report. You'd best go and see the inspector. He's waiting.'

Heffernan beamed magnanimously as his sergeant entered, and told him to take a seat. At least somebody was in a good mood.

'Mrs Giordino okay?'

Heffernan sighed. 'Aye. She's settled at Betty Pargeter's

B and B. Got one of the WPCs looking after her. I'm nipping round to see her in a minute.' He paused. 'Hope you didn't get into trouble yesterday.'

Wesley looked up, surprised. To have a superior officer concerned about the effect of unexpectedly lengthened working hours on your domestic arrangements was a whole new experience.

Heffernan continued, 'If you need time off again we'll arrange something.'

'Thank you, sir.'

'How's your wife?'

'She wasn't too pleased.'

'Yeah. Emotive subject, having kids. People get very . . .'

'Yes, sir.'

The door opened and Steve Carstairs's tousled head appeared. Why, Heffernan wondered, did DC Carstairs always have to look as if he'd spent the previous evening at an all-night party. Perhaps he had, if station gossip was anything to go by.

'Excuse me, sir, there's been a call from the manager of a bank in Morbay. He's recognised the photo in the paper, says she's got an account there.'

'Right. Get over there, will you.'

'No need, sir. The branch is open Saturday mornings so he's faxing me all the details.' Carstairs stood there like a child expecting the reward of a sweet.

'Go and see him anyway. If he recognises her, he's obviously met her. Find out what he knows.'

Crestfallen, Steve Carstairs left the room.

When the fax arrived half an hour later, Wesley entered the inspector's office and placed the information on the desk. Heffernan studied it and looked up, his eyes glowing with renewed interest.

'Well, we've got an address now. The rest should be plain sailing.'

Rachel looked through the glass and saw the boss at his desk, head in hands. Her instinct was not to disturb him, but police business came first. She knocked briskly and opened the door.

'That address, sir. Wesley's about to go over there with Steve. You okay, sir?'

The inspector looked up. 'I've just had to explain to a woman why it wouldn't be a good idea to see her daughter's body. Apart from that, I'm fine.' He took a deep breath. 'Sorry, Rach, I shouldn't be taking it out on you. Tell Wesley to take that key that was found in the bag, will you – see if it fits the door to her flat.'

'How did Steve get on at the bank?'

'The manager didn't know her. Just seen her the once when she came in to get some passport photo signed. He shouldn't really have done it if he didn't know her, but Steve reckons he fancied her.'

'Steve would reckon that, wouldn't he, sir. What about her bank account?'

'The current account fits in with what we know about her. No regular salary but whatever she was up to didn't pay too badly. Let's just hope it wasn't immoral or illegal. You've run her name through the Police National Computer?'

'Nothing known, sir. Our best bet is to trace this boy-friend. Did the mother say anything this morning?'

'She wasn't really in the mood for a cosy chat. Poor cow, she's not had much of a life, and now this . . .'

'Yes, sir,' said Rachel sympathetically.

The address the bank had given turned out to be a flat in a white-stuccoed villa in the better part of Morbay; 22 Peasgoode Avenue. Not a bad address, thought Steve Carstairs. Could do with something like this myself.

'Nice place,' commented Wesley.

Steve didn't reply.

Wesley rang the doorbell marked 'Flat 2'. There was no answer. He took the key that had been found in the handbag from his pocket and tried it in the lock. It didn't fit.

'Let's see what the neighbours can tell us.' He rang the bottom of the three bells. The door was opened by a well-dressed middle-aged woman, elegantly coiffeured and carrying a minuscule dog, the breed of which Wesley didn't know, not being a dog lover himself. The woman looked them up and down with practised disdain, expecting them to begin a sales pitch for a new concept in double glazing. Wesley thought it prudent to produce his warrant card. The polite, well-spoken graduate touch would be needed here.

'Sorry to disturb you, madam, but we're making enquiries about the tenants of Flat two. I wonder if you could help us.'

The woman, doyenne of the local neighbourhood watch and only too eager to be a good citizen, invited them in and provided tea and biscuits. Unfortunately, there was nothing much she could tell them. The couple had lived there only for six months and, as the cliché goes, kept themselves to themselves. Apart from a nod and a mumbled good morning if they happened to meet in the communal hallway, she had had nothing to do with them. She had noticed no visitors and she hadn't seen them for the last month or so. No, they definitely did not have a baby; the walls were thick but not that thick; children weren't allowed in the flats anyway. What did the man look like? Well, ordinary; mid-thirties – older than the woman; dark; average build; average height . . . just average. Yes, she would be willing to try to build a picture of him – anything to help the police. Wesley wished all his interviewees were so co-operative.

The inhabitants of Flat three weren't. The immaculately dressed young couple who drew up in their red Porsche as Wesley and Steve were leaving made it clear that they had nothing to do with their neighbours, nor did they want to: they hadn't time for that sort of thing, they explained frostily as they unloaded their brown paper bags full of French sticks and sun-dried tomatoes. They made it absolutely clear that they wanted nothing to do with the matter.

The landlord was the next step – a property company in the up-market redeveloped end of Morbay. Not cheap.

As soon as their warrant cards were produced, Wesley and Steve were hustled into the back office of the plushly carpeted premises as though the staff were afraid of contamination. A grey-suited woman with too much make-up introduced herself as Liz, found the relevant file and grudgingly handed it over. The flat was in Karen's name and she had written the rent cheques. The deposit had been paid in cash. There was no sign of any references but then, Liz explained, they weren't always insisted upon. If tenants didn't cause trouble and paid their rent on time, it wasn't the job of a landlord to pry into their private lives, she added self-righteously as an afterthought.

When asked for access to search the flat, Liz looked at Wesley as if he'd made an obscene suggestion. Torn between exercising what she had learned in assertiveness classes and being accused of obstructing the police, the latter won. She produced the key disapprovingly and announced that she had better go with them.

When they asked Liz to wait outside the flat while they made their search, she was about to argue but thought better of it.

It was obvious that nobody had lived in the flat for a while. The fridge had been cleared out and the bread bin was empty. Karen had left the flat not intending to return for some time. It reminded Wesley of a house left by someone going on holiday for a few weeks. There were female clothes in the wardrobe and women's magazines scattered about, but there was little sign of male occupation apart from a sports bag in the hallway containing a selection of casual clothes and underwear, all from well-known chain stores. Perhaps the man of the house had moved out some time before. Was that what this was all about? A lovers' quarrel? Most murders, Wesley reminded himself, were domestic: find the boyfriend and you've found the murderer.

Steve was flicking through a small pile of CDs on a shelf near the fireplace. 'No rap or reggae, I'm afraid, Sarge,' he said with a smirk.

'I prefer classical myself,' replied Wesley casually as he searched through a selection of blockbuster paperbacks, brimming with sex and violence. He looked across at Steve, who was engrossed in one of the glossy magazines.

'Come on, Steve, put that down and get searching that bureau. I'll radio through and get them to send someone over.'

Steve hesitated and shot Wesley a resentful look.

'Is there a problem?' Wesley asked calmly. Perhaps he was imagining things.

Steve stood up slowly, his eyes downcast. 'No, Sarge,' he mumbled.

Wesley went over to the window and looked out. Liz was standing frostily by her car. She would have a long wait.

'How's it going, Rach?' Heffernan burst into the office and flung his anorak onto the coatstand with some aplomb.

'Fine, sir. Just entering this into the computer.'

'Rather you than me. Any tea going?' She looked up at him coolly and he thought better of his request. 'No, love, don't bother. Don't want to be spending all afternoon in the gents'. Anything new?'

'Wesley and Steve are searching the flat now, sir. They called in for some help so a couple of uniforms went down.'

'Anyone in the flat?'

'Don't think so, sir.'

'Rach, can you get down there and have a look through this woman's things – see if they give you any ideas.'

'Will do, sir.'

Rachel picked up her jacket and made a quick getaway before the boss had a chance to change his mind.

Heffernan opened the door to his office and looked at his desk, overflowing with paperwork. Something would have to be done. He sat down and began to sift through the mountain, putting things into piles: forensic reports; post-mortem report – he must look at that in more detail, maybe he would take it home tonight, though it would hardly make suitable bedtime reading.

The new section had been cleared ready for the detailed dig. It was a slow process but Neil by nature was a patient man; he had to be.

The flags of the original cellar floor, photographed and documented, were carefully laid aside and the painstaking trowelling and brushing burrowed away into the foundations in the hope of finding an earlier building on the site; a glimpse into Tradmouth's more distant history.

Seagulls circled overhead, shrieking so loudly that Neil almost missed Jane's voice calling him over.

She stood back from where she'd been digging and Matt,

sensing an important find, strolled over to her. The three of them stared down at the disturbed earth.

'Could be an animal bone,' said Neil optimistically.

Chapter 10

Anne is gone and Jennet hath resumed her duties. I am grieved to find my old feelings do return but with prayer we can but hope to drive out sin.

Elizabeth feels well once more and doth not now keep to her bed. Yet she is still much fatigued and I should not presume upon her to resume the full duties of a wife at this time. But my body hath needs and when I cast my eyes upon Jennet I am reminded of them. I pray for strength.

Extract from the journal of John Banized,
30 April 1623

Gerry Heffernan was partial to church bells. They reminded him of his childhood when they had summoned the faithful out of their pebbledashed Liverpool semis to prayer at the red sandstone church on the corner of the main road. He had been in the choir then, *Beanos* and gobstoppers hidden beneath the angelic white of his surplice, and he was still singing now, minus *Beanos* and sweets and with a considerably deeper voice. The bells increased in volume as he approached the church and he felt his step lighten as they swung in celebration.

His spirits needed raising on this dull Sunday morning. He had just called on Mrs Giordino, who had politely refused his tentative invitation to church. She was a Catholic, she explained, lapsed. Heffernan had left, saddened that he could offer so little comfort.

Taking his place in the oak choir stalls behind the elaborately carved and painted screen, reputedly one of the finest in Devon, he was aware of a grey curly head in the row in front. Dorothy Truscot's grim discovery hadn't affected her warbly singing voice adversely.

After the service and the unmemorable sermon, he emerged from the porch of St Margaret's as so many had done since the days of the fourth King Henry, when the church had been built with money donated by prosperous local dealers in wine, fish and wool whose earthly remains had long ago been consigned to the crypt and forgotten.

When he arrived home he checked the carrier bag that contained the food. He had told Wesley half past twelve – best time for the tide and the working lunch he had planned; a chance to get away from the office and the paperwork; to clear the mind and get the facts in some sort of order.

The invitation had come as a relief to Wesley. He had left Pam preparing for tomorrow's lessons. She had seemed so preoccupied with her work and her own thoughts that she hardly seemed to notice him going out. The atmosphere in the house was still somewhat chilly.

Heffernan greeted his sergeant heartily and invited him in. Wesley looked round the living room, making a quick appraisal.

It was neater than he had expected; no sign of the squalor that had surrounded him in his own single days. The walnut baby grand piano dominated the room; sheet music scattered over its top showed that it wasn't there merely for decoration. The plain white walls were hung with pictures of ships of varying types and sizes, and a brass sextant lay in pride of place on the oak sideboard. If Wesley had had to hazard a guess about the owner of such a room on one of the more popular television quiz shows, he would have suggested it belonged to a musical sailor. No sign of a police connection, but then his own house was hardly adorned with handcuffs and copies of the Police and Criminal Evidence Act. Home was a place of escape.

Heffernan emerged from the kitchen carrying a large carrier bag and led Wesley outside onto the cobbled quayside. He was expecting a pie and a pint in the Tradmouth

Arms but Heffernan was heading across the quay towards the water.

'Here she is,' the inspector announced with obvious pride.

Wesley looked around, expecting to see a woman approaching down the quay – a hidden aspect of his boss's private life. But there was nobody in sight. Heffernan had climbed aboard a small yacht moored a few yards away from his front door. Wesley prayed silently that the seasickness he had experienced on the storm-tossed cross-Channel ferry last year wouldn't return today. He eyed the vessel nervously. The weather was calm, hardly a breath of wind; he stood a chance.

'What do you think of her?' Gerry Heffernan gazed at the boat lovingly.

Wesley had seen some men get like this about their cars, but hadn't known the phenomenon extend to boats. 'Very nice, sir.'

'Got her three years ago and did her up. Completely refitted her and gave her some new keel bolts.'

Wesley nodded, trying to appear knowledgeable.

'She's a sloop, East Anglian class. Twenty-seven foot nine, four-berth,' Heffernan continued proudly. 'She was in a state when I got her, I can tell you.'

Wesley tried to look enthusiastic as he clambered aboard. He didn't know one end of a boat from another, but he was loath to let his ignorance show.

Once aboard, in the surprisingly neat cabin, the carrier bag was opened to reveal the delights of fresh crab, prawns, salads and what appeared to be a home-made fruit pie.

To his astonishment, Wesley found he was hungry. They ate at anchor. The meal, washed down with a chilled bottle of Chardonnay, was as good as it looked. But the trip down-river to the sea which followed left Wesley feeling distinctly queasy. His boss observed happily that even Lord Nelson had been prone to seasickness.

'I hadn't expected this,' Wesley said as Heffernan steered the streamlined craft through the waves.

'Just thought we could do with a change of scene.'

They stood for a while on deck, Wesley watching as the craft was navigated skilfully round the headland, topped with the twin castles that guarded the entrance to the River Trad.

'You seem to know what you're doing. Been sailing long?'

'Seems like all my life. I was in the merchant navy – first mate – before I joined the force.'

They stood for a while in amicable silence, watching the waves and the receding ruggedness of the cliffs.

'What made you join the force, Wesley?'

Wesley thought for a while. He had not been prepared for the question and he wasn't even certain of the answer. He did his best. 'It was always assumed that I'd become a doctor like my parents – and my sister read medicine at Oxford.'

Heffernan looked impressed.

'The family got a bit of a shock when I chose to read archaeology and an even bigger one when I joined the Met. But my grandfather back in Trinidad was a detective, a chief superintendent. When we stayed with him he used to entertain us at bedtime by telling us about his more lurid cases.' He grinned. 'And all those Sherlock Holmes books I used to read when I should have been revising for exams probably had something to do with it too.'

'Bet he's proud of you, your granddad.'

The suggestion of praise almost made Wesley forget his queasiness. 'Would have been. He died five years ago.'

'I'm sorry.' Heffernan stood in silence, remembering his own early days: his uncle, a bridewell sergeant, the choice between the force and the sea, the sea winning until a burst appendix landed him in Tradmouth Hospital after being winched off his ship by helicopter. He smiled to himself. Such a fuss for such a small part of the human anatomy.

'I joined 'cause of my appendix.' Wesley looked at him curiously. 'There was this nice young nurse in the hospital and the sea lost its appeal. We got married and I stopped here. Joined the force. Kathy, my wife ... she died three years back.'

'I'm sorry.'

The inspector said nothing. He stared in front of him at the outstretching sea.

Wesley thought it best to change the subject. 'Any news about Jonathon Berrisford yet?'

Heffernan shook his head. 'The mother rings Stan Jenkins every day. It's really getting to him. Fancy having to tell a mother every day that there's no news. I'm just glad it's not my case.'

'Have you had any thoughts on the Karen Giordino case, sir?'

'You had any?'

'Looks like a domestic so far. Body found in beauty spot: sort of place you'd go walking with your girlfriend or whatever . . .'

'I believe partner's the word these days, Wes.' Heffernan grinned.

'They had a row; a violent quarrel. He bashes her head and face in and runs off. Panics, clears out of the flat. He could be anywhere. We don't even know who he is.'

'We will soon. Someone must know them, and if he's got an ex-wife or in-laws down this way they might be only too happy to turn him in. It shouldn't take long.'

'Straightforward, then?'

'We won't know that till we find him, will we?'

Heffernan turned the boat round skilfully. It was time to go home.

It was clear to Heffernan that Sir Arthur Conan Doyle had never been in the police force. Irritated by the good doctor's low estimate of the number of brain cells collectively possessed by the Metropolitan Police, he flung the book across the room, blaming Wesley for his unfortunate choice of reading matter. It was Wesley's mention that lunch-time of his adolescent literary tastes that had made Heffernan pick the smartly bound volume off the bookshelf. Now he remembered why it had been left untouched all these years. If he had been Lestrade, he would have devised some fiendishly cunning way of ridding himself once and for all of that unbearably smug, violin-playing drug addict.

He turned to his bedside table for more reading fodder. Since Kathy's death he had got into the habit of reading till the early hours.

It wasn't what he normally classed as bedtime reading, but he hadn't yet had a chance to examine it in detail. The post-mortem report lay on top of a pile of tempting novels. Duty overcame hedonism: he picked it up.

Ploughing through the medical jargon wasn't easy, not with a drowsy brain. But when he came to page five something caught his eye and he stopped, went back to the previous paragraph, and began to read more carefully.

Chapter 11

I did go into my chamber when Jennet was changing
the linen. I stood in the doorway and watched her
and she was unaware of my presence. I saw the
whiteness of her neck and her breasts and was quite
overcome with desire for her. She looked at me as
if she comprehended my need. I withdrew from the
room lest I be tempted to kiss her

Extract from the journal of John Banized,
14 May 1623

Neil had spent all Sunday worrying about the dig. They
couldn't afford any more wasted time.

After the fragment of white bone had been uncovered,
he had thought it best to abandon work until Monday. Jane
and Matt had readily agreed. Although nobody voiced their
fears, they were all thinking the same thing.

As he unlocked the gate at 8 am on Monday morning, Neil
felt uneasy. He retrieved his equipment from the wooden hut
at the edge of the site and removed the protective tarpaulin
from the trench they'd begun work on. Jane and Matt arrived
to find him already at work. He stood and turned as they
approached, and stepped aside so that they could see what
he'd begun to uncover.

Jane's hand went up to her mouth.

Neil spoke quietly. 'I'll ring Wesley. At least there's
someone in that police station now who knows what they're
doing and won't trample all over the bloody site.'

* * *

The minicab stopped by the newly painted Victorian gate-posts and the driver, instructed to wait, picked up his copy of the *Daily Mirror* to read while the meter ticked away.

Mr Carl looked back at the throbbing taxi and cursed the police force which had temporarily deprived him of the use of his BMW.

He felt in his pocket for the key – it was there. He strode confidently up the gravel path: if you did anything with enough confidence nobody ever questioned your right to be doing it. He had found that out at an early age.

But today was an exception to that rule. On the steps leading to the front door stood a uniformed policeman, an expression of boredom on his freckled face. He would be only too eager to relieve the tedium with a few questions about Mr Carl's presence.

He turned and walked quickly to the waiting taxi, praying he hadn't been noticed.

Constable Parsons took the notebook out of his top pocket.

Heffernan poked his head out of his office and bellowed. 'Wesley, can I have a word when you've got a minute?'

Rachel, behind a pile of computer print-outs, raised her eyebrows. 'What have you been up to?'

Wesley gave her an innocent shrug and joined his boss in the glass-partitioned office.

'Sit down.' The inspector seemed to be in a good mood. 'Good trip yesterday. Bit of a swell, though – not too good for seasickness. What did you think of *Rosie May*?'

Wesley looked puzzled.

'The boat. What did you think of her?'

'Very nice, sir . . . very nice.'

He saw Wesley's eyes glazing over. It was a shame his new sergeant didn't share his passion for things nautical. Never mind. Back to the matter in hand.

'I was just arranging rosters and all that. Have you got another appointment at that clinic? Want to make sure you get there this time . . .'

'Nine thirty, Thursday. I was just about to tell you.'

'That was quick.'

'It's surprising what they can do when you cross their palms with silver. I don't really agree with private medicine but . . .'

'Will you be there long?'

'Well, they did all Pam's bit last week, so I shouldn't be long. They say there's nothing to it – more embarrassing than anything else.'

'Have they said anything yet? Any ideas?'

'They did some tests and didn't find anything wrong. She might have to have one of those laparoscopy operations. You know, when they stick a camera . . .'

'I know.' Heffernan had heard of the procedure but wasn't well up on the detail. Nor did he want to be. 'What's that for exactly?'

Wesley, amazed at his boss's sudden interest in gynaecology, explained in simple terms, the only kind he knew.

'Only I've been trying to get in touch with Colin Bowman all morning but he's out. Some meeting or other. Have a look at this, will you.' Heffernan chucked the post-mortem report across the table. 'Page five, last paragraph.'

Wesley read aloud. ' "Scarring of both fallopian tubes most likely caused by pelvic infection." '

'Could that infection be caused by childbirth?'

'Yes. And other things: abortion, sexually transmitted disease, all sorts of things. But certainly infection after childbirth.'

'Is that the sort of thing they look for at the clinic? I mean, can that cause infertility?'

Wesley nodded. It was a subject Pam was always reading up on, almost to the point of obsession. 'Is it important?'

'No idea. Probably not.' He stared at the report open on his desk. 'But where's this child Colin Bowman said she had? It must be somewhere. Get Rachel to run a check on all the hospitals and clinics in the areas she's been known to live in, and all the adoption agencies; she obviously didn't have a kid in tow in Morbay.'

Wesley nodded as the inspector sorted through the jumble on his chaotic desk and produced a piece of paper – the face of a man. They looked at the picture jointly created by the regular police artist, a solemn, ponytailed young man, and Karen Giordino's public-spirited neighbour. The face of a dark-haired man in his thirties with no distinguishing features. He looked disconcertingly ordinary – the elusive John.

'Get it put in all the local rags. Someone's bound to recognise him.'

Wesley nodded. It was easy to remain anonymous in the metropolis, but South Devon out of season . . . He said as much to the inspector.

'Don't you believe it. Maybe that was true a few years back but now there's a floating population all round the coast . . . if you'll pardon the pun. Lots of people coming and going. Doesn't make life any easier.'

After a perfunctory knock, Steve Carstairs burst in. 'Phone call for you, Sarge,' he said sulkily. 'A Neil Watson . . . says it's urgent.'

Wesley excused himself and took the call. Neil sounded more annoyed than worried. It was one more delay for the dig, using up valuable time. Wesley promised to be round there as soon as he could. He returned to his boss.

'Another skeleton, sir, at the dig in St Margaret's Street. The archaeologist in charge is a friend of mine. He says it all looks contemporary with the site.'

'We'll still have to go through the motions. Do the necessary, will you. Get Dr Bowman to pronounce life extinct and all that. You'd best get up there but don't be long.'

'I'll make sure everything's done to Home Office regs, sir.'

Wesley left the room, trying hard not to show his enthusiasm for the task ahead. A bit of time spent with Neil on the dig would be a welcome diversion.

Heffernan heard the phone ringing in the outer office and once more Steve was the bearer of tidings, this time good.

'There's been a message from the PC posted at the dead girl's flat, sir. A bloke arrived in a minicab and turned tail as soon as he saw him. He got the minicab's number.'

'Well, you know what to do,' Heffernan snapped. A display of initiative now and then wouldn't have gone amiss with DC Carstairs.

'Shall I interview the driver, sir?'

'What a good idea. Off you go.'

Carstairs bit his lip and closed the door behind him.

Rachel was hovering by the door. 'I had a look through the dead girl's things yesterday, sir, like you asked. She had some good clothes. Fashionable.'

'Like the stuff she was wearing when she died?'

Rachel hesitated. 'Not really, sir. The stuff in her flat was more . . . you know, flashy.'

'So she wanted to look the picture of respectability, eh?'

Rachel shrugged. 'Maybe.'

'You'd better go with Steve and hold his hand, Rach. Someone's got to. Let me know what you turn up. I'm off to see Mrs Giordino.'

'When's she going home?'

'I don't know, and I haven't liked to ask.'

Heffernan lifted his coat off the standard-issue inspectors' coatstand. It was a chilly day.

'Where's he off to, Rachel?' asked Steve outside, as he donned his jacket.

'Visiting the bereaved. Full of good works, our inspector. Come on.'

'Where to?'

'We're off to find that minicab. I'm coming with you.'

Rachel marched out of the office. Steve Carstairs followed behind, studying her legs.

Carl paid the minicab driver and navigated his way down the driveway of the white-stuccoed cottage, avoiding the rusty skip full of building rubble. He hammered with his fist on the glass front door. There was no answer. He hammered again till the glass shook, then watched as the dark shape in the hall grew larger. The door opened.

'I heard you the first time. Have you got the bag?'

'I couldn't. The police were outside.'

'Shit. I need those bloody clothes. Come on in. I was just going to have a shower.'

Carl stepped into the narrow, woodchip-papered hallway, nearly tripping over a child's tricycle that lay in wait behind the front door. He looked at his companion's stained towelling dressing gown and bleary eyes.

'You look awful.'

'Those bloody builders were here first thing this morning banging and crashing. I hadn't slept all night and I'd just managed to get off.'

'Where are they now?' Carl looked around.

'How should I know? They're a bloody law unto themselves. They knocked off at lunch-time. The police didn't see you, did they?'

'Shouldn't think so.'

'Only I don't want them here. I don't want them asking all their questions. It's bad enough . . .'

'Okay, John, okay.' Carl opened a can of lager from the stock on the sideboard and handed it to his companion. 'I understand, believe me, I understand . . .'

Desk Sergeant Bob Naseby recognised the woman who had just shuffled in, swathed in woollen scarves, grey and brown, like a giant moth seeking the light of the reception desk. He sighed and drew himself up to his full height. He wished they wouldn't let them out – they only caused trouble.

'I've seen him again.' She looked Naseby straight in the eyes with the absolute conviction of the deranged. 'Where's that Inspector Jenkins? I want to talk to him.'

'Now then, my luvver. Who did you see and where?'

'I want to see Inspector Jenkins.' She bit her lip petulantly. 'I want the mechanic, not the oily rag.'

'All right, all right. No need to be like that. I'll just ring through for you.'

She stared at him, a stare of intense hatred. Bob picked up the receiver. He was a patient man. There was no answer.

'There's nobody there right now. Take a seat over there. I'll try again in a minute.'

She leaned forward. For a moment he thought she was going to spit at him.

'I'll not go away in a corner and shut up. You're trying to stop me seeing him. You tell him I've seen the boy. You tell him I know where Jonathon Berrisford is.'

Bob Naseby dialled again.

Chapter 12

Last night I did have my pleasure of Elizabeth who
doth give me her assurance she is once more well.
But I sinned in my thoughts for I did in my imagin-
ings have my will of Jennet. I would the mind were
controlled with as much facility as the body. It may
be that I should send Jennet from the house.

> Extract from the journal of John Banized,
> 15 May 1623

'If she asks to see me again, Bob, tell her I've gone on a
round-the-world voyage ... retired ... anything.' Inspector
Jenkins watched the swing door shut on his departing visitor.

'I used to have that problem thirty years back, women
chasing after me.'

Stan Jenkins swung round and saw Gerry Heffernan
grinning.

'It's that woman again, Gerry, the nutcase. The one who
says she's seen the kid. It's getting so she won't leave me
alone.'

'Fancy a pint? She won't find you down the Tradmouth
Arms.'

Jenkins looked sheepish. 'Beer's out, I'm afraid. The diet.'

'Slimline tonic, then. Come on. You look as though you
need it.'

Jenkins hesitated for a moment, then followed Heffernan
out through the swing doors. Bob Naseby smiled to himself
as he watched them go, wondering how long Jenkins would

take to crack, given the proximity of the Tradmouth Arms' best bitter.

One taste of slimline tonic was enough. Jenkins went to the bar and ordered himself a pint. The pub was pleasantly full but not overcrowded. Locals on their lunch hour, relieved that the tourist season was over and they could get a seat, tucked into the landlord's much-acclaimed crab sandwiches. Heffernan and Jenkins did likewise.

They sat in amiable silence, jaws munching. Stan Jenkins spoke first. 'How's your new sergeant? Still shaping up okay?'

'Fine.' Heffernan took a sip of his beer. 'He's a good bloke. Did you know he's got a degree in archaeology?'

Stan shook his head. 'How's he getting on with the others?'

'Very well on the whole. But I've heard through the old station grapevine that our DC Carstairs has been making a few racist remarks to his buddies in the canteen – you know the sort of thing. At least Wesley outranks him so he can't say much to his face. I'll have a strong word if things don't settle down once the novelty wears off.' He sighed. 'I put it down to bad influences.' He sat back and drank deeply. 'So what did your girlfriend have to say?'

'My girlfriend? What do you mean?'

Jenkins looked quite put out. If Heffernan didn't know better he would have said he'd touched on a guilty nerve. 'The woman who keeps following you about.'

'Oh, her,' Jenkins said with some relief. 'She just keeps saying she's seen Jonathon Berrisford, that's all. She believes it and all, poor cow.'

'Maybe she has.'

'What?'

'Maybe she has seen him.'

'Come on, Gerry. She just passes a kid of about the right age in the street and comes straight to us. Ten years ago she would have been locked up. I mean, I feel sorry for her, but it's wasting our time.'

'So is it always the same kid or what?'

'How should I know? By the time we get there the kid, whoever he is, is long gone. I put a couple of uniforms to keep watch on the area but they come up with nothing. There's nothing to come up with. She's a nutter.'

'Same story today?'

'She's branching out. She reckons she saw the kid go into a house with a man. We'll follow it up. No choice. It's a million-to-one shot but it's all we've got. I won't tell the Berrisfords, though. I don't want to get their hopes up.'

'What are they like, the family?'

'Hard to say under the circumstances. Seem like a decent couple. Middle-class, father a wine merchant or something like that. He's the stoical type, doesn't show his feelings much.'

Heffernan downed the last of his pint. 'Any chance they're involved?'

'No way. I'd stake my pension on it. He's their only kid, after years of trying apparently.'

'She wouldn't be the first adoring mother who couldn't cope; something just snaps and . . .'

'No, Gerry, you're on the wrong track there. The poor woman's desperate, rings every day.'

'Can't be easy.'

'It isn't, Gerry. It gets to me, I can tell you.'

Heffernan looked at his watch. 'Come on, Stan. Drink up. Work calls.'

Stan Jenkins drained his glass but showed no signs of moving. He looked up at Heffernan. 'Do you know, Gerry, I've actually started praying that we'll find this kid alive. I'm getting past it, getting too involved.'

Heffernan gave his fellow inspector a comforting slap on the shoulder and made his way through the assembled drinkers towards the door. Stan Jenkins rose to follow him, his face troubled.

Cedric Mutch didn't trust officialdom. Taxmen, VAT men (and women – they were usually worse than the men), snoopers from the Social Security . . . and police: police were the worst of the lot; police meant trouble.

When he got back to the office, his colleagues had greeted him with all the enthusiasm that medieval peasants must have reserved for one who brought the Black Death to their village. The police were waiting for him. And police were about as welcome in the shabbily appointed offices of Cab-u-like as plague rats.

Rachel's eyes stung with the fog of smoke as she invited Cedric Mutch to sit down. Mutch, a weasel-like man with thinning hair and an insignificant moustache, did so, and lit a cigarette with a cheap disposable lighter. Remembering the desirability of buttering up the law (and his manners) he offered the packet to Rachel, who politely refused, and Steve, who resisted temptation.

'Now, Mr Mutch,' Rachel began. 'You took a fare to Peasgoode Avenue earlier today. Could you give me a description of the man and tell us where you took him next?'

Mutch couldn't get the information out fast enough, relieved that he himself wasn't the focus of the investigation.

Rachel could almost hear the sighs of relief as they left the premises and climbed into their car.

The address Mutch had given them was just outside the village of Whitstone, about four miles from Tradmouth. They drove out of the town past the whitewashed council estate, banished to Tradmouth's farthest end. They passed the holiday park, uninviting in the autumnal drizzle, with its insubstantial chalets. Rachel's hand tightened on her seat belt as Steve turned left off the main road and tore down the narrow, hedge-walled lanes. She wished she had insisted on driving herself.

The cottage was easy to find. It had started small but had sprouted a couple of single-storey extensions over the years. It had the unfinished look of a house undergoing major renovation, an impression confirmed by the half-filled skip in the driveway and the piles of building materials in what had once been a well-kept front garden. There was no sign of life.

Rachel noticed that something had caught Steve's attention. He wandered around the garden examining bricks, guttering and bags of cement, consulting his notebook as he picked his way round the obstacle course. Rachel watched with curiosity; she had rarely seen Steve so conscientious.

'Hey, Rach, this stuff. I reckon it could be some of the gear nicked from those building sites. Same makes.'

'You're sure?'

'Well, I can't be sure, but . . .'

'Well spotted.' Rachel thought a bit of encouragement wouldn't go amiss. 'You can look into it when we've dealt with the other business. Come on.'

He knocked at the door; a glass door of 1960s vintage. The flaking paint had encroached on the frosted glass; Rachel hoped that the renovations would include a replacement front door. A dark figure approached down the hallway. The door opened.

'Hello, Charlie.' It was Steve who spoke, macho, swaggering, like he'd seen it done on the telly. 'Mind if we come in?'

Rachel showed her warrant card; at least one of them should be doing things by the book – she'd have a word with Steve later. 'Detective Constable Tracey, Tradmouth CID. I presume you know DC Carstairs?'

'He was at school with my brother,' Steve chipped in helpfully.

Mr Carl stood aside to let them in and led them sullenly into the living room, seemingly the only room untouched by the hands of the absent builders.

'This your house, sir?' Rachel looked around.

'My sister's. She's away in Canada for a few weeks visiting her husband's brother.' Carl shuffled uncomfortably.

'Anyone else in the house, sir?'

A floorboard creaked above their heads. Rachel looked at Steve. Carl swallowed hard and shook his head.

'What were you doing in Peasgoode Avenue at around ten this morning, sir?'

'Er, I was on my way to visit a friend. I realised I'd forgotten something. I asked the taxi to bring me back here.'

'Bit expensive, taking taxis and changing your mind,' Steve said meaningfully. He stood blocking the door, arms folded. Rachel wished he wouldn't try quite so hard to play the macho copper. He'd clearly been watching too much television.

Carl shot him a dirty look. 'If you lot hadn't taken my licence off me I wouldn't have to rely on taxis, would I?'

Rachel tried charm. 'Who were you going to see?'

'A girl.'

'Could I have her name, please, sir? It might help to clear this up.'

'Look, I've not committed any crime, right?'

Rachel smiled politely. 'We can always discuss this down at the station if you prefer, sir.' The old ones were always the best. She saw the fight go out of Carl's eyes.

The door opened, almost knocking Steve sideways.

'It's okay, Carl. Thanks. I'd rather get this over with.'

Standing in the doorway was a man: average height; average build; mid-thirties; dark hair beginning to recede slightly. He wore jeans and a grey T-shirt. The type of man you'd pass in the street without a second glance.

Rachel spoke. 'Hello, John.'

Steve Carstairs watched open-mouthed as their quarry strolled into the room and sat down on the battered green Dralon sofa, a look of resignation on his face.

He spoke quietly. 'Look, I'm sorry for causing so much trouble. I panicked when I heard she was dead. I needed time on my own. I loved that girl. I did . . . I loved that girl.'

The remnants of his composure disappeared. Near to tears, John wiped his arm across his moistened nose and eyes. Rachel watched him carefully. As far as she could tell the grief seemed genuine. But you never could tell.

'I think we should get down to the station, sort things out,' she said gently.

John followed her meekly to the waiting car.

In the recently screened-off section of the site Dr Bowman smiled as he bent over the exposed skeleton.

'Well, I can just about say with certainty that she's dead.'

'She?'

'Oh yes, it's a she. And there's still some fragments of hair and clothing. Look. Quite well preserved. Doesn't look modern, I can tell you that much. Not much else, though, at the moment.' He looked at Neil. 'You're sure this wasn't a burial ground of some kind?'

'You're standing in what was the cellar of a late-sixteenth-century merchant's house. The shop would have been at the front over there with a parlour behind, then the courtyard, then the kitchens and warehouse at the back. Look, you can see the remains of the well in what would have been the courtyard.' The doctor nodded. 'I found this near the hand; it might have been buried with her.' Neil held out a coin, not yet cleaned up. 'We've photographed it *in situ* but I thought I'd have a look at it. Might help with the date.'

'And does it?' Dr Bowman asked, curious.

'It's James I, a sovereign.'

Wesley had been watching the proceedings with interest. 'I think we can take it the police needn't be involved, then?'

'There'll be formalities, of course, but I think this one's out of your jurisdiction, Sergeant,' said the doctor. 'About four hundred years out, so you can relax.'

'Can you tell how she died?'

'That depends. I'll get her back to the mortuary and have a look. Just out of interest, of course.'

Jane was hovering nervously. 'If you could be careful with any fabric that's there, Doctor ... I'd like to examine what there is, if I may. Maybe send it for conservation if it's suitable.'

'Naturally.'

It was over an hour before the skeleton was gently released from its resting place by trowels and brushes. Colin Bowman took the opportunity to go to lunch, but Wesley helped as much as his unsuitable clothes would allow.

When the doctor returned, he bent over the skeleton which lay awaiting its journey in the mortuary van. He turned to the archaeological team, who were standing awkwardly, unsure what to do next.

'You're absolutely certain that this section of the site didn't show signs of recent disturbance?'

'Yeah,' said Neil with conviction. 'There was a layer of concrete on top of this lot which dated back to the turn of the century, then soil and rubble filling in the cellars, then the flags of the old cellar floor. This is about three feet under the flags.'

'Thank God for that,' said Bowman with evident relief.

'Why?' Wesley asked, his curiosity aroused.

'I won't know for certain till I've made a proper examination, maybe not even then. Look at those dark stains on the facial bones. They could have been caused by the rupture of blood vessels. That's often an indication of suffocation or strangulation. And look at this round the neck. Looks like the remains of a strip of leather, a belt or something. Would you agree?' He looked up at Wesley. 'I think you might have a murder victim on your hands, Sergeant.'

Chapter 13

Trade is good and I am needing more help in the shop. This morning I did meet with a captain in the Butterwalk who had news of my ships. He assures me all is well and the weather fair. Elizabeth is desirous of moving the stair from the passage to the back of the shop. It would be better for her to keep watch on the shop were I to be out of the house. Master Mellyn, the carpenter, saith he knows of a ship's mast which can be used in the construction.

I did see Jennet this morning in the garden, gathering herbs. She did not see me.

Extract from the journal of John Banized,
18 May 1623

Heffernan switched on the tape machine, uttered the legally required words, then sat back and looked at the man on the other side of the table. Sometimes this was how killers looked – defeated.

'When did you meet Karen Giordino?'

'Couple of years back. Business trip to Blackpool. She worked at the hotel.'

'What do you do for a living, Mr Fielding?'

'Sales executive – agricultural chemicals.'

'And you were selling these in Blackpool, these agricultural chemicals?'

'No. It was a conference.'

Heffernan sat back. 'Very nice. Conferences in hotels, pretty girls. Unfortunately Sergeant Peterson and I never get the chance, do we, Sergeant?' Wesley shook his head co-operatively. 'We leave that sort of thing to chief superintendents and the like. Are you married, Mr Fielding?'

'Divorced.'

'Was this before or after you met Karen?'

'Er . . . I was separated then.'

'Did you move in with Karen right away?'

'No. That was about two years ago. I was seeing her every weekend and she wasn't having much luck with her modelling work so we decided to rent a cottage together. Other side of Morbay. Then the owners wanted us out so we got the flat.'

'Were you happy?'

John looked up. It seemed a strange question. 'We were okay. Had our ups and downs like everyone.'

'And a couple of weeks ago you had a down, eh?'

'I didn't say that.'

'What made you do a runner? Why didn't you stay in the flat?'

John sat for a while contemplating his fingers. 'I was scared. Karen had disappeared and I heard that a blonde woman had been found murdered. Then when I saw her picture in the papers I panicked. All right?' He looked up defiantly.

Wesley spoke softly. 'Surely it would have been better to have come forward, if you had nothing to hide.'

John shuffled nervously in his seat. Wesley had seen his type before: salesmen flashing down the motorway cocooned in the company car; the loud chuckles over business lunches; wife number two (preferably blonde); the drink problem; the 'mid-life crisis'. But as one who had himself experienced prejudice, he told himself firmly that he mustn't let it cloud his judgement now.

Heffernan took another tack. 'When did you last see Karen?'

'Seventeenth September. I know 'cause I had to travel to Birmingham that day. Stayed overnight.'

'Tell us about it.'

'Oh shit, I might as well tell you. We had a row that night. She wanted to go for some modelling job. I don't mind her doing a bit here and there but this meant her going abroad.'

'Why didn't you want her to go?'

'I just didn't.'

'Nobody to wash your shirts?' the inspector threw in mischievously.

John gave him a look and Heffernan regretted his flippancy. There was a long pause before John broke the silence.

'I was scared she was getting sick of me. I could feel it. She'd started getting more modelling work, and then this travelling abroad . . .'

Wesley nodded. He understood. 'Did she get much modelling work?'

'Yeah, she wasn't doing too badly. Catalogues, mainly – stockings, tights, trousers. She had good legs. So when she said she was meeting this man in Tradmouth and she might be . . .'

Heffernan sat up. 'What man?'

'She was meeting him in Tradmouth. He'd arranged this job.'

'Did she tell you his name?'

'No. I don't know anything about him.'

'So you don't know how he contacted her?'

'Could have been through the agency.'

'What agency?'

'Tradmouth Models. They used to get her work.'

'Tell me about them.' Wesley was interested.

'They're a small outfit, somewhere in Tradmouth, but don't ask me where. She never talked about it much. She didn't have to work, you know, I'd have paid for everything; but she liked the modelling. She liked to look good.'

'The flat's in her name. Why?'

'Everything is. Don't want the ex-wife to get her hands on anything, know what I mean?'

Wesley knew. He wondered how many enemies Karen had made in Devon. There was probably no love lost between her and the woman she replaced. 'So you can't tell me anything else about this agency or who she met at work?'

John shook his head. 'Was she keen on this job, meeting this man?'

'I'll say. Gave herself the works. New hairdo, facial, leg waxing. Trip to Plymouth to buy some new clothes – the lot.'

'Who did her hair?'

'Charlie . . . Carl. He did her hair at the flat. He always did her hair. She doesn't . . . didn't trust anyone else. He's my sister's ex-husband. We stayed mates when him and Claire broke up. He lent me the cottage. I couldn't stay in the flat when I knew she was dead. I had to get out . . . get all my stuff out . . .'

Heffernan watched as John's eyes filled with tears. 'I hope you catch the bastard who did this. I hope. . . .' The tears came faster and John tried vainly to wipe away the mucus that glistened on his nose. Heffernan nodded to Wesley, who turned off the tape machine.

'Detective Sergeant Peterson terminating this interview at seventeen twenty hours.'

Heffernan handed John a crumpled handkerchief.

Rachel hadn't joined the police force to fill in forms any more than she had joined it to make cups of tea. It was with relief that she picked up the phone and heard Bob Naseby's voice on the other end summoning her downstairs to the front desk. A lady wanted to speak to her.

She ran lightly down the uncarpeted stairs, glad to be out of the office. When she reached the front desk Bob pointed out a young woman, sitting on the padded bench, her face bearing the stoic expression of a patient waiting to see the dentist.

'Her name's Denise Wellthorne,' Bob whispered confidentially. 'She asked to see you.'

'Did she say what it was about?'

'You'd best go and see, my luvver.'

The woman looked more nervous as Rachel approached. She was young with blonde curls and a noticeable suntan. Rachel introduced herself and waited expectantly.

'I'm a hairdresser,' the woman blurted out. 'I work at

Chez Danielle down by the market. I've been away – Tenerife.'

'Very nice.' Rachel smiled to put Denise at her ease.

'When I got back to work this morning they said you'd been round asking about a blonde lady who had a cut on the seventeenth.'

Rachel started to take interest.

'Well, I did a lady's hair on the seventeenth. She came in without an appointment, just for a cut and blow. I've been away, you see. I didn't know. And it was lunch-time so I was the only one in . . .' She stopped gabbling and looked at Rachel enquiringly.

'We've identified the dead woman and we've traced the person who did her hair. But thanks for coming in anyway. If I want to talk to you again, I'll get in touch.'

Denise Wellthorne gushed out her name, address and phone number and tottered out on her high heels.

'If only all hairdressers were as public-spirited,' Rachel commented cryptically to Bob before she disappeared upstairs.

'We can't hold him much longer without charging him.'

'Come off it, Wesley, we do know the rules down here, you know.'

'I don't think he did it, sir.'

'Put money on that, would you?'

Wesley shrugged his shoulders. Gut feelings were hard to put into words.

'We'll get an extension. We need more time. I'll tell the super. How did you get on with your skeleton, by the way? More work for us, is it?'

'Dr Bowman says it's murder, sir.'

Heffernan looked up sharply. 'Then why the hell didn't you say? We'll have to get—'

'Don't panic, sir. It happened about four hundred years ago.'

'Thank God for that. As if we didn't have enough to deal with here. You'd best get back to our friend Fielding. We don't want him getting lonely, do we?'

Wesley nodded and returned to the interview room, where John was devouring a sandwich hungrily.

'You all right?'

John nodded. His solicitor, a balding man with the face of a middle-aged goat, scowled and looked at his watch ostentatiously.

'Can I see her?'

Wesley raised his eyebrows. 'See who?'

'Karen.' The reply was almost a whisper. 'I'd like to see her.'

Wesley sat down. 'Well, she's a bit ... it's not very ...'

'Please.'

'I'll see what I can do.'

Wesley nodded to the bored-looking constable in the corner and left the interview room in search of his boss. He found him in his office with a ham sandwich smuggled from the canteen.

'It's being arranged. Another thirty-six hours.'

'Fielding wants to see the body.'

'Not a pretty sight.'

'If he killed her, he'll know that already. What about this man she was supposed to meet?'

'Rachel's been on to the model agency she used. They say the man's a photographer, a Maurice Brun. It was arranged through the agency and he uses their models quite regularly. All seems to be above board. Rachel's trying to trace this Maurice bloke at the address the agency gave her but she's not had much luck. The agency reckon he could still be abroad. Do you think Fielding's ready for another little chat?'

Ready or not, John Fielding had no choice. The tape machine whirred into action and Heffernan resumed the questioning, this time on different lines.

'What happened to the child?'

John looked genuinely perplexed. 'What child?'

'She had a child recently, within the last couple of years. What happened to it?'

'She never had a child. Who told you she had?'

'The post-mortem showed ...'

96

'Well, it's wrong. Karen never had a baby. They must have got it wrong.'

Wesley and Heffernan looked at each other.

Heffernan spoke. 'I believe you've asked to see the body, Mr Fielding?'

Chapter 14

Master Mellyn hath begun the work upon the staircase. A new consignment of wool hath come into my warehouse so I must move the leather to the cellar which, thank the Lord, is good and dry.

Elizabeth is well and is a good wife to me once more. But I still think upon Jennet. I do try not to see her about the house. That is the best way.

Extract from the journal of John Banized,
25 May 1623

The smell of formaldehyde spoke to Wesley of unspeakable things. Standing behind John Fielding, he looked away as the attendant gently removed the sheet from the corpse's battered face. He was quite unprepared when Fielding took a step back, nearly knocking him off balance, and vomited onto the floor.

Taking John firmly by the arm, Wesley steered him from the room to join the uniformed constable waiting outside.

John gasped, eyes disbelieving, like one who had seen a glimpse of hell. 'I never thought . . . oh my God . . . oh my God . . .'

'Take him back to the station, will you.'

The constable nodded and took John's arm to steady him as he staggered away down the corridor.

Dr Bowman was an easy man to find. He greeted Wesley with a cheery smile and an amiable enquiry as to how the sergeant was settling down in Tradmouth. It was a full five minutes before Wesley had a chance to broach the subject of skeletons and murder.

'Almost definitely asphyxiation. I've done the relevant tests. Of course, we can't tell very much after four hundred-odd years, and we can't get the culprit banged to rights, can we.' He laughed at his witticism. 'She was female, early twenties. She'd given birth to a child at some stage; the pubic tubercle was present. It's a spur of bone that grows to support the uterus during pregnancy.'

'And the baby?'

'Oh yes, I'd forgotten about that. Buried in a different part of the cellar. Strange. If they'd been together I would have said it was the master of the house covering up his indiscretions.'

Wesley sighed. 'Don't expect we'll ever know for sure.'

'Did your suspect identify the body, then?' Bowman's question brought Wesley sharply back to the present.

'No. He just threw up all over your nice clean floor.'

Colin Bowman shook his head. 'I told Gerry Heffernan it wasn't a good idea.'

'That friend of yours has been on the phone again,' Rachel remarked casually as Wesley returned to his desk.

'Neil?'

'That's the one.'

'Did he say what he wanted?'

'I never asked. I'm not your personal secretary,' she said with a half-smile, a challenge in her eyes.

'Sorry.' Wesley looked away, embarrassed. 'Is the inspector back?'

'Not yet. How did it go? Did Fielding identify the body? Did he confess all?'

'No. He just threw up. Which begs the question, if he killed her and knew she was in that state, why ask to see her?'

'We concentrate on the man she was meeting, then? This Maurice?'

'Might be an idea.'

'Forensic haven't come up with anything on Fielding's

clothes and shoes.' Rachel sat back in her chair. 'Did Fielding identify the clothes she was wearing?'

Wesley thought for a moment. 'No. No, he didn't.'

'Maybe he never noticed what she wore. Do you notice what your wife wears?'

'Not usually. Only when she dresses up to go out.'

'She's lucky. Most men don't even notice that.'

Wesley laughed, but noted that Rachel spoke with conviction and a trace of bitterness.

'Did Neil leave a number?'

'On there.'

He dialled but there was no answer. They were probably outside on the site. He'd drop by at lunch-time; it was only down the road.

He found Neil digging alone. Jane and Matt had gone for a sandwich.

Neil looked up, his face serious. 'We had bloody treasure hunters in here last night. They broke the lock on the gate and tried to break into the hut and all but they must have been disturbed. Probably the publicity about these skeletons. Thought they'd try their luck with their bloody metal detectors. Look at this.' He indicated a few roughly dug holes near where the woman's skeleton had been found.

'Let's hope they didn't get too much,' said Wesley. 'I'll get the police patrol to keep a special eye on the place and tell the local antique shops to keep a lookout. Did you say they dug near the body?'

'Very near – bit underneath we haven't dug yet. Bastards.'

'Found out any more about this place?'

'I've rung the local museum and asked if they had anything on the house or the Banized family. It seems they've got some household and business records, that sort of thing. I'll go up there when I've got the chance. And I'm doing well with the parish records and all. Nice bloke, the vicar – interested in local history. He's looked up all the entries for Banized in the church registers and made a list of the inscriptions on their tombs, been a great help. I've not had a chance to look at his stuff properly yet but I'll get you a photocopy. Give you some bedtime reading. You coming out to play tonight?'

'It depends what time I finish work; I'll see.'

A few minutes later, furnished with a photocopy of the relevant parish records, Wesley returned to the station, blissfully unaware that it was going to be a very long day indeed.

Heffernan was in a bad mood. He trudged through the office, face set, and slammed his door. Wesley looked at Rachel, who shrugged her shoulders and returned to her computer screen, then he tapped tentatively on the inspector's door.

'Come in, Wesley. I thought I might go for a trip down the river this afternoon. I'd ask you along only you've got too much to do.'

Wesley smiled to himself. 'Yes, sir.'

'If the super asks where I am, say I'm out pursuing enquiries, okay?'

Wesley nodded.

'Did Fielding manage to identify her this morning?'

'That's what I wanted to see you about. He took one look at the body and threw up.'

'Understandable. We've not all got stomachs like Colin Bowman's.'

'If he did it, sir, he wouldn't have asked to see her. He would have known what state she was in.'

'That's your opinion, is it, Sergeant?'

'Yes. I suppose it is.'

'Another twelve hours and we'll have to let him go or charge him. What's it to be?'

'I'd let him go.'

Heffernan shrugged. 'Maybe.'

'Sir, Mrs Giordino didn't actually identify the body, did she?'

'She identified the photograph. What are you getting at?'

'But nobody's identified the body as Karen's?'

'Fielding's given us her dentist's address. His records'll clear up any doubt.' Heffernan began to sound irritated. 'Why?'

'Nothing, sir. Just a thought. Do you remember that key that was found in the bag. It didn't fit her flat and . . .'

'If you stopped trying to be clever, Sergeant, and found

us that Maurice bloke that Karen Giordino was supposed to be gallivanting off with at the time she died, we'd all be a bloody sight better off.'

'Rachel's been to the model agency. We've tried to contact him. He lives on his own in Morbay and there's nobody at his address. The agency say he's in France somewhere. So does his neighbour who's looking after his cat. And according to the agency he's supposed to be with Karen. I've contacted the airlines. No luck. He's probably gone by ferry or the tunnel.'

'Well, we all know where Karen is. The man's either a suspect or a vital witness. Contact the French police. We've got to find him.'

'But if the body's not Karen's . . .'

The inspector didn't give him a chance to finish. He left the office, slamming the door. Wesley watched him go, open-mouthed.

'Where's he gone?' Rachel seemed unconcerned about the boss's display of temper.

'Sailing.'

'That figures. It's really got to him.'

'What has?'

'He went to see Mrs Giordino this morning. She's going back home tomorrow. Sailing's his way of dealing with it.'

'Thought it was something I said.'

'No. You were just the nearest available officer of lower rank.' She smiled and their eyes met. Rachel looked away, and shuffled some papers self-consciously.

Five minutes later the phone rang and Rachel answered it. She covered the mouthpiece and spoke to Wesley. 'It's Bob Naseby on the desk. He says we should both get down there quick.'

'Why? What is it?'

'How should I know?'

They clattered down the uncarpeted stairs and arrived at the front desk. Bob gave them a meaningful look and pointed to a figure standing in the corner of the reception area reading the notices. When the figure turned, Wesley's heart began to beat faster. He opened his mouth to speak.

But what do you say to someone who has returned from the dead?

The woman approached the desk and Bob Naseby broke the silence.

'This lady wants to speak to you, Sergeant Peterson. She says her name's Karen Giordino.'

Chapter 15

Methinks Elizabeth may be with child. Her courses
have ceased and she doth feel most sickly of a
morning. I rejoice if this be so. The staircase is
finished and is well but Master Mellyn did charge
more for the work than he first did say. I had thought
that as he did use an old ships mast instead of new
timber it would prove less dear. Robert, the apprentice, hath the toothache once more. Elizabeth is tired
and I do keep from demanding she perform the full
duties of a wife.

I am drawn to thinking once more of Jennet
who I do see often. Today I came upon her in our
bedchamber putting down fresh rushes and I did feel
the stirrings of desire as I did watch her shapely
arms all bare and the whiteness of her bosom. I must
be strong and avoid her company.

Extract from the journal of John Banized,
1 June 1623

Years back Darren Watts would have joined his father on
the fishing boats as soon as what passed for his formal
education was over. But the fishing industry in the West
Country and beyond was experiencing lean years and
Darren, like so many of the friends he met down at the
amusement arcades of Morbay, had signed on.

It was his elder brother who had introduced him to the
delights of metal detecting, first demonstrating its potential

in the garden of their whitewashed council house in the middle of the estate that squatted beside the main road out of Tradmouth, then venturing down into the town onto the river-edge mud when the tide was out.

It was the anticipation Darren loved; the prospect of the big find. He had never, in fact, found anything very remarkable . . . until last night.

He had read the report in the local paper and his brain had slowly turned over the possibilities while he sat with his family passively watching an American film on satellite television. He had rung his friend Gary, who was always ready for a bit of excitement. Tradmouth was a bloody boring place.

Breaking through the fence last night had been easy. They should have put a stronger padlock on the gate – it was asking to be busted.

They had ducked down, hearts racing, when the police patrol car passed by. Then they had begun. Darren had been quite unprepared for the effect of nerves upon his bowels. He wanted the toilet. He wanted to go home. But Gary had told him to fucking pull himself together and get working.

They had come up with a coin, then some buckle thing that looked like it was off a belt. It all looked like a load of crap to Darren, but it might be worth something. Then he'd found the ring – all filthy, needed a good wash. Darren said he'd show it to his brother who knew about things like that.

Satisfied with the night's finds, they had gone home, and Darren had let himself into the house furtively, wanting no questions asked. Then that morning he had shown the mud-caked ring to his brother who told him to take it to an antique shop when he'd cleaned it up. It might be worth something.

Now that his mum had gone off to her work at the chicken factory, Darren filled the bathroom sink and gently lowered the ring into the lukewarm water. As he moved it around and the mud gradually floated off it, he could see the glint of gold and the green and blue of the stones in their settings. He lifted it from the water and studied it carefully. It was old, beautiful – a real prize. There was writing on the inside.

Darren squinted and held it close but he could only make out one word: 'Jennet'.

Wesley and Rachel reckoned the first thing somebody'd need when they'd come back from the dead would be a cup of coffee. They sat across the table from the young woman, trying not to stare.

Rachel thought she looked older than her photograph, harder. She was taller than Rachel had expected, and a pair of enviably long legs protruded from beneath the black leather miniskirt. Her face was carefully made up and her fair hair fell in an immaculate bob. Mr Carl evidently knew his stuff. But for all the changes it was still clear that this was the woman in the photograph: this was Karen Giordino. They'd recognise her anywhere.

'You've given us a bit of a shock, Miss Giordino,' Wesley began. 'We thought you'd been killed. Have you heard about the body that was found up at Little Tradmouth?'

'I've been out of the country.' Her accent betrayed her Manchester origins. 'On a modelling assignment. I went back to my flat this morning and one of the neighbours said the police had been round looking for John. She said they thought I was dead.'

Her hand started shaking as she lit a cigarette.

'I'm glad to see you're still with us, Miss Giordino. But there are one or two things I'd like to clear up.'

'Where's John?'

'He's here at the station. You can see him in a few minutes, but first I'd like to ask you a few . . .'

'I had nothing to do with all this. I've been out of the country. It's nothing to do with me. What makes you think it's anything to do with me?' She inhaled the cigarette smoke deeply.

'Your mother's down here,' said Wesley, playing for time. 'If you'd like to see her . . .'

Karen flicked ash onto the floor with her long scarlet nails. 'What would I want to see that old cow for?'

'She thought you were dead,' said Rachel, affronted.

Karen blew out a contemptuous cloud of smoke. 'Haven't seen her in years. Don't want to neither.'

Wesley looked over at Rachel, hoping the police launch had managed to track down their boss's boat.

'Why did you think I was dead, then? You've not told me that. Anyone could have told you I was in France. Why didn't you ask John or Phil from the agency?'

'The reason, Miss Giordino, that we thought you were the victim is that passport photographs of you were found in the victim's bag.'

'Then surely even the bloody police force could tell it wasn't me. God help us all if you lot are that useless.'

'The victim's face had been disfigured. She was unrecognisable. But she fitted your general description: same colour hair, eyes, build. There was no other identification on her. It was natural to think the photographs belonged to her. We then traced you through, er, connections in Manchester and found your mother.'

'What connections?'

Wesley tried not to catch Rachel's eye. 'A Mr Keffer. You worked for him, I believe.'

'Bloody hell. That was years ago. Look, John doesn't have to know about that, does he? I mean, it was just to get some cash together for this modelling course and . . .'

'Don't worry, Miss Giordino, your secret's safe with us.'

'I don't do anything like that now, you know. It's all respectable stuff,' she added indignantly.

Wesley thought that here was a woman with a past she'd rather forget. He continued. 'I'm sure it is, Miss Giordino. I'm afraid I'll have to ask you a few more questions. Can you prove that you went on this trip to France on the seventeenth? Any witnesses? This Maurice, for instance?'

'Look, are you accusing me of something? I was with Maurice. We travelled over on the seventeenth. I met him in Tradmouth and we got the ferry over from Plymouth. We drove to Paris.'

'We haven't been able to trace this Maurice.'

'He stayed on. He's got friends who live near Paris. He went to visit them for a few days. I wanted to get back.'

'How did you get back?'

'Ever heard of Le Shuttle? Got it to London then got the train back to Morbay. Don't you believe me?'

'Will anyone else confirm your story?'

'The hotel we stayed at in Paris . . . in the Pigalle. They didn't speak much English but they'd know us again. Maurice punched one of the waiters 'cause he thought he was trying it on with me. And Maurice was always ordering champagne to be brought up to our room. Didn't seem to care how much he spent.' She smirked, enjoying the memory. Suddenly Wesley felt extremely sorry for John Fielding.

Rachel produced the black handbag from its plastic shroud like a conjurer producing a rabbit. 'Is this your bag?'

Karen shook her head.

'It was found near the body. Your photographs were in it. Have you any idea how they got into the dead woman's bag?' Rachel asked coolly. She had taken an almost instant dislike to the woman sitting opposite her. Karen looked back at her contemptuously.

'How the fuck should I know, love. That's for you to find out.'

Wesley tried again. 'When did you get these pictures taken?' He held out the strip of photographs.

Karen touched them and turned them over. 'I look a bleeding fright, don't I? Bride of Frankenstein. I didn't like these. I had more done.'

'For a passport?'

'I wouldn't have my photo taken like that for anything else, now, would I?' She studied her nails. 'I'm used to having my photo took by professionals, aren't I?'

'Of course.' Wesley remained calmly polite. 'What happened to these pictures, then? Did you throw them away or what? Please think hard. It's important.'

Karen lit another cigarette. 'I'm trying to bloody think.'

'When did you have them done?'

'Few weeks back.' She screwed up her face as if the process of thought were a huge physical effort. 'I had the new photos and I was filling in the passport forms. I must have left these ones there.'

'Where?'

'The office . . . the agency. I can't remember throwing them away or anything. I probably left them there.'

Wesley sat up. Now they were getting somewhere.

'Phil from the agency reminded me I had to have a pass-port to go abroad on this job. I went to the post office for the form and had the photos done in one of those booth things. I took the lot back to the office to fill it all in.' She sat back. 'I've always wanted to travel, me. Don't want to end up like my bloody mum – never been south of Stoke on Trent.'

'She has now,' said Rachel pointedly. 'She's staying just down the road.'

Karen snorted disdainfully.

Wesley tried again. 'Think back. What happened to the pictures you didn't use? Please, it's important.'

'I told you, I left them at the agency.'

'Whereabouts? Where did you fill the forms in?'

'The reception desk, I suppose.'

'Who was there?'

'Phil, the boss.'

Rachel nodded. She had met Phil briefly – a harassed, balding man who gave the impression that his long-legged charges existed solely to give him a hard time. 'Anyone else?'

'Another of the girls. I showed her the duff photos and we had a laugh about them.'

'Name?'

'Maureen. Don't know her surname.'

'Is this Maureen blonde?' Rachel looked at Wesley and caught the implications of his question.

'No, love.' She looked Wesley up and down appreciatively. 'She's dark. Like you. Why?'

'Was anyone else there?'

'Can't remember.'

The door opened. Heffernan crept into the room and sat unobtrusively on a chair behind Karen. He raised his hand to indicate that he would be an observer for the present. Karen turned and gave him a bored look then lit another cigarette.

Wesley repeated his question. 'Was there anyone else there when you left the photographs on the desk? Please think.'

'That girl, what's her name, Sharon. She was probably somewhere about.'

'Sharon?'

'The girl who works in the office.'

'What does she look like?'

'Fair hair. Never noticed her much.'

'About your height?'

Karen nodded. 'Suppose so.'

'How well do you know her?'

'I didn't really. She was quiet. Never chatted, like.'

'Did she have any kids?'

'Not that I know of. Why?'

At this point Heffernan stood up and introduced himself. Karen looked unimpressed.

'Your mother's waiting downstairs, Miss Giordino. If you'd like to come with me . . .'

Heffernan, like Wesley and Rachel, had weighed Karen up and didn't much like what he saw. But for the sake of the woman downstairs, the woman he had just taken to the local Catholic church on Higher Street to light a candle of thanks to the Virgin for the return of her only child, he was glad to see her. However, his hopes of a touching reunion were shattered when Karen Giordino turned to him and spoke.

'The old cow can wait. Get us another coffee, will you.'

The inspector tried in vain to recall that saying from Shakespeare about serpent's teeth and thankless children. Maybe Wesley would know.

Wesley reckoned he was becoming fitter. People paid good money for the use of those step machines in gyms. His fitness training came free – every evening when he trudged home up through those cobbled streets.

Pam was at a parents' evening so there would be nobody to notice what time he returned home. It was seven thirty: too early for the Tradmouth Arms. Neil might still be on the site.

Wesley found his friend in the wooden hut that was used as the site office and a temporary repository for finds. The hut was more impressive inside than Wesley had expected.

In one corner was a sink, edged with various items in the process of having the mud of centuries cleaned off them. There were labelled drawers for the smaller finds against one wall, and against the other a desk on which stood a flickering computer.

'Have a look at this.' Neil, eyes shining like those of a child with a new and fascinating toy, pressed a few buttons. Wesley watched as a simulated picture appeared on the computer screen of how the Banized house would have looked when it was still a thriving merchant's dwelling. With the aid of technology they walked through the rooms and the courtyard. Things had certainly come on since Wesley's student days when he would have had to have made do with the efforts of human artists.

'I'm impressed.'

'So you should be. We were lucky to get it. Good, isn't it? How's Pam, by the way? I've not seen her yet.'

'She's at a parents' evening. She won't be back till . . .'

'You're not, er. . . . You two are okay, aren't you?'

'Yes . . . er, yes. Why?'

'Just hoped there was nothing wrong. You hear of so many couples . . .'

'No. She's just had a bit of a medical problem, not been feeling too good.'

'Nothing catching?'

'Women's troubles.'

Those two words prevented Neil from enquiring further. He changed the subject. 'I've had some good news.' He looked pleased with himself. 'We're going to do an exhibition about this place in the County Museum. All the finds, reconstructed shop.'

'Great.' Neil's enthusiasm was infectious.

'I had a word with Dr Bowman about reconstructing that skeleton's face for the exhibition. Get Professor Jensen on to it when he gets back from the States. The Woman in the Cellar, that sort of thing. Always goes down well.'

Wesley nodded. 'Let me know when it's on. I'll be there.'

'Have you got any news on our break-in?'

'I've got one of our PCs contacting all the jewellers and

111

antique shops in the area. That's the best we can do unless we catch them having another go.'

'Let's hope they don't. Thanks, anyway. Let's hope something turns up. Have you looked at those parish records yet?'

'I haven't had a chance. We've been a bit busy. Especially when our murder victim turned up alive and kicking.'

Neil raised his eyebrows. 'So you've got no murder, then?'

'We've got a murder all right. It's just that the victim wasn't who we thought it was. I'll try and have a look at those records tonight.'

'They're all there, the Banizeds. Hatched, matched and dispatched. All except one – Elizabeth, wife of the son, John. She wasn't buried at St Margaret's.'

'She'll have died somewhere else and been buried at the local church.'

'She died before her husband because John married again when he was about forty-five. He's buried with his second wife.'

'There'll be an explanation.'

'Pity it's not all on computer. You could just call up the records of other churches and track her down.'

'One day, Neil. One day. It'll all be on the Internet. No more dusty archives in the brave new world of technology. I'd better be off.'

'Not coming for a drink?'

'I'd better be there when Pam gets back.'

Wesley walked home up the hilly streets to the modern enclave where his house stood at the top of the town. Pam wasn't home.

He put a ready meal in the microwave and sat down with his case notes, scanning Karen's statement for anything he'd missed. But his mind went blank as he stared at the pages. He put them to one side and picked up Neil's photocopies. A quiet retreat into the past always proved relaxing, put the troubles of the present into perspective.

Then he spotted the book open on the coffee table, the title *Women and Infertility* emblazoned on its lurid yellow cover. She had been reading again.

After making a mental note to remind the inspector about

his clinic appointment on Thursday, he began to read through the parish records. His mind happily returned to the age of the first Queen Elizabeth . . . until he heard Pam's key turning in the lock.

Chapter 16

Oh, Lord forgive my failing for today I did grievously sin.

I came upon Jennet in our chamber bringing in my wife's clean linen. She stood by the bed and looked me in the eye as if she knew all my thoughts. I was roused to desire and did shut the chamber door so that we two were alone.

I found myself next to her, kissing her. I could tell from her kisses that her desire was as great as my own. I went into her and had my pleasure of her then we parted without a word, she back to her duties and I praying vainly for God to forgive my weakness.

Oh, Jennet, why did you come into this house?

Extract from the journal of John Banized,
3 June 1623

The next morning Wesley and Rachel arrived at the office of Tradmouth Models which was housed in a Victorian row of shops near the market, above an expensive-looking shoe shop. Once inside, the office was pleasantly appointed with a newish pale wood reception desk and a row of filing cabinets to match; thick sage-green carpet tiles covered the floor. Wesley had been in worse places.

Framed photographs of the agency's protégées lined the walls. Rachel thought it was amazing what lighting, make-up and a professional photographer could do for a woman's looks. She noticed a small pile of business cards lying on the reception desk, picked one up and showed it to Wesley with a significant nod. 'Snippers and Curls.' Mr Carl had been right when he said his cards were everywhere.

As there was nobody on reception, Rachel walked past the desk and knocked on the door marked 'Phil Tebbit, Director'. Wesley followed her, thinking that Karen Giordino had come up in the world. The pictures on display in this establishment were considerably more tasteful than the ones taken of Karen by Mr Keffer of Manchester at the beginning of her career.

Phil Tebbit managed to make the words 'come in' sound pathetically harassed. He was a small, dark man, balding. He scurried around clearing files off chairs so that Rachel and Wesley could sit down. He reminded Rachel of a small, busy rodent.

'I'm so glad you've found Karen alive . . . and thank God she's been with Maurice. If she hadn't turned up for the job it wouldn't have done this agency's reputation any good. Our models have to be reliable . . .'

Wesley wasn't there to listen to Phil Tebbit's professional problems. 'If she'd been dead, sir, she wouldn't have been able to do very much about it.'

Tebbit blushed visibly.

'Now, sir, we know she left a set of passport photographs here; on the reception desk, we think. We're trying to trace who might have had them, if someone could have picked them up.'

Tebbit thought hard. 'I remember something about . . . let me think.'

Rachel tried to help. 'Did anyone mention them? Anyone show them to you?'

It did the trick. 'I remember now. Someone found them. Now who was it?' He shook his head. 'No, no, it's gone. I really didn't take much notice. It was just one of those things that was going on in the background when you're doing something else. Do you know what I mean?'

Rachel nodded. She knew. 'Is there anyone else who might remember? Your secretary? The receptionist?'

'Same job, I'm afraid. Actually, the girl I've got now is

new. She wasn't here when...' His eyes lit up. 'It was Sharon. I remember now. Sharon came in with the photos and said one of the girls had left them.'

'Can we speak to this Sharon?' Wesley asked, trying to create order out of potential chaos.

'She's left now. She was my old secretary, left in August.'

'Have you got her address, sir?'

'Oh, yes. I can give you her address.'

'And you don't know what became of the photos, what she did with them?' asked Rachel.

'No, no, I don't. I said to give them back to Karen next time she came in. I presume that's what she did. I never thought about it.'

'Why did she leave, Mr Tebbit?'

'She never said. Personal reasons, that's all. She was a quiet girl, never spoke much. Not one to tell you her troubles. Not like some – kept herself to herself.'

'And she gave you notice, did she? She didn't just disappear?'

'Oh, yes. She gave a week's notice, did things properly. And I told her she could use me as a reference any time. She was a good worker. I was sorry to lose her.'

'Can you describe her?'

Tebbit suddenly looked uncomfortable. 'Blonde, medium height. Why?'

'Have you any pictures of her?'

'I've got enough on my plate having pictures taken of my models without taking them of my secretary too. Sorry.'

Rachel and Wesley looked at each other.

'Thank you very much, Mr Tebbit,' said Wesley. 'You've been a great help. We might want to talk to you again. And perhaps some of the ladies who work for you...'

'Or gentlemen,' corrected Tebbit seriously. 'We have gentlemen on our books as well. There's a lot of call for male models nowadays.'

'I'll bear that in mind,' said Wesley, winking at Rachel. 'If you'd like to give us that address, we'll be off. Thank you for your time.'

Phil Tebbit watched them go, relieved that no potential clients had dropped by. Police were bad for business.

When they reached the street, Wesley suggested they go straight to the address Tebbit had given them, but Rachel had another suggestion.

'There's one person I think we should see before we go. It's only across the road.'

'Who's that?' asked Wesley, following automatically.

'I think it's the hairdresser who cut the victim's hair. Come on.'

Wesley didn't argue.

Chez Danielle didn't possess the intimidating atmosphere of Snippers and Curls. Rachel could quite imagine herself having a cut and blow-dry here. There was something homely about the Laura Ashley wallpaper and matching frilly blinds. The staff looked non-judgemental and a good proportion of the seats facing the mirrored wall were occupied by blue-rinsed pensioners. The prices displayed in the window seemed reasonable to Rachel. She looked upon the establishment and judged it to be good: clean, friendly and obviously popular.

She produced her warrant card at the reception desk and asked for Denise Wellthorne. The woman behind the desk, of maturer years than Mr Carl's Michelle, looked worried as she called through into the back room; the worry that anticipates bad news rather than the concern that comes from a guilty conscience.

Wesley had looked uncomfortable as they had been about to enter Chez Danielle, so Rachel had taken pity on him and told him she could manage alone. She'd meet him at the Butterwalk in half an hour. She felt perfectly confident dealing with members of the hairdressing profession: she'd had plenty of practice.

She knew where he'd go. He seemed to spend every lunch-time with that friend of his who was working on that excavation in St Margaret's Street. She'd heard him arranging to meet the archaeological friend for a drink in the evenings too. She wondered what Wesley's wife thought: from the vibrations Rachel had managed to pick up, it seemed as if their marriage was going through a bad time.

Denise Wellthorne seemed nervous when she appeared

from the back of the salon. She had thought she'd done her duty as a citizen; she hadn't expected to hear any more. Rachel smiled to put her at her ease and assured her it was just routine.

Denise led her through to the back. 'I'll get us a cup of tea,' she said nervously. 'There's just one thing. I've got a lady booked at twelve o'clock and . . .'

'That's all right, Mrs Wellthorne. This won't take long.'

Denise visibly relaxed and offered Rachel a seat. The little staff sitting room was clean and cosy, the kettle and cups having pride of place on the melamine table in the corner. Rachel sank into a well-worn chintz-covered arm-chair, somebody's cast-off pressed into use at their place of work. She accepted a mug of steaming tea gratefully and took a chocolate digestive; she was sick of dieting. They lived well at Chez Danielle.

'Sorry to bother you again, but new evidence has turned up and we think the lady who came to you on the seventeenth could have been the murder victim after all. What can you tell me about her?'

'She came in at lunch-time, when I was on my own. I told you that, didn't I? She had straight blonde hair – natural blonde, not dyed – down to her shoulders. She said she wanted a trim, wanted it tidying up 'cause it was getting a bit straggly. I gave her a wash and blow-dry. I asked her if it was a special occasion, if she was going out that night, like you do. I mean, it's one of the things you talk about in my job, isn't it? That and holidays, and the weather.'

Rachel smiled. 'Of course. What did she say?'

'She said she had an important meeting, wanted to look her best.'

'She didn't say anything about this meeting? What sort of meeting it was, who it was with . . .?'

'No, and I didn't like to pry. You've got to be tactful; can't be too nosy.'

'Did she say anything else? Anything at all? Where she lived? Her job? Her family?'

'Nothing. We talked about the weather mostly, and she said she hadn't had a holiday. She seemed a bit on edge – you know, like there was something she was nervous about.

She said she had something to sort out and that's why she hadn't managed to get away. I can't remember her exact words. Something like "We wanted to get away but we didn't manage it. We had something to sort out." Then we talked about Tenerife. She said someone at her work had gone last year. That's all, really.'

'She said "we", did she? "We wanted to get away?" Please think. It could be important.'

'I think so.' She hesitated. 'Oh, now you mention it, I can't really be sure. I'm sorry.'

'That's all right. Don't worry. Did she pay by cheque or credit card?'

'No, cash. Look, will I have to make a statement and all that?'

'Please. If you can come down to the station, I'll get the police artist there so we can get some idea of what she looked like.'

'You think it's her then? You think she's dead?'

'We can't be absolutely certain but it's a strong possibility.'

Denise Wellthorne opened the drawer under the sink and took out a sketch pad. 'There's no need to get a police artist, I can draw her myself. I do art at evening classes. I'm not bad on faces.'

Rachel nodded. Why not? It would save time and the budget. She watched as Denise's pencil moved over the clean white paper and a woman's face appeared.

Rachel ran across the street, narrowly missing being hit by a passing Range Rover. She ran up the stairs to the offices of Tradmouth Models and burst in on a startled Phil Tebbit. He confirmed it: the picture Denise Wellthorne had drawn was indeed a likeness of Sharon Carteret.

Rachel knew where to find Wesley. He was there at the dig, deep in conversation with a scruffy-looking man, almost unkempt enough to be one of the travellers she had encountered at Neston. She called across to him and he signalled her to come through the gate onto the site. The sergeant seemed to be preoccupied by two ragged bits of tile he was attempting to fit together.

He turned to Rachel, his eyes aglow with enthusiasm.

'These are the original Elizabethan roof tiles. Most of the stuff gets carted away when the place is demolished but you can always find a few fragments. See how they fit together. And there's a nail hole. Look.' He put the pieces in Rachel's hand. 'Just think. These were handled by people on this site before the Spanish Armada sailed.'

Rachel, who had hated history at school, was unimpressed. 'Very interesting, Sergeant. I've just confirmed that the dead woman's Sharon Carteret. I'll tell you about it on the way. We've got to go over the river, remember? Check that address.'

Wesley turned to his friend who, to Rachel's eyes, looked like he was covered by a layer of dust and needed a good bath. 'Tomorrow, then, Neil. Let me know how you get on at the museum.'

Farewells said, Rachel led Wesley down the narrow side streets towards the river.

'We'll have to go back for the car.'

Rachel shook her head. 'No need. It's quicker to take the passenger ferry. The address is only a short walk from the station at Queenswear.'

Wesley followed her down the steep gangway to the ferry, acknowledging reluctantly that his unplanned exercise programme was indeed making him feel fitter. The sun was out so they sat on deck for the short journey across the River Trad, the smell of the ferry's diesel fuel in their nostrils masking the salty smells of the river. The light glinted on the choppy water and flickered off the steel masts of the yachts moored on both sides of the river. So many yachts. Wesley wondered if the Drug Squad kept a regular eye on this place.

The ferry moored with a solid clunk and they disembarked. They found themselves beside the small railway station, painted in Great Western colours and now home once more to steam engines which chuffed their way between Morbay and Queenswear. In the summer the station would stream with tourists, but now it was quiet.

Rachel seemed to know where she was going. Did she have a remarkably good memory for street maps, Wesley

120

wondered, or did she just know the area from childhood? He suspected the latter.

The streets of Queenswear were as steep as those of the larger town of Tradmouth on the opposite bank. A long flight of stone steps led up to a narrow street of tall stuccoed houses painted, like their counterparts across the river, in pastel pinks, greens and creams. Number 38, a three-storey double-fronted dwelling, had two bells. The address Tebbit had given them indicated that it was Flat 1 they were looking for. Rachel pressed the brass bellpush.

The door was opened by a middle-aged man, wearing dark-rimmed glasses and a sour expression. 'Whatever you're selling I don't want any. I'm sick of you people. You can't get a minute's peace.' He was about to shut the door in their faces. Wesley fumbled for his warrant card. 'Now go away or I'll call the police.'

Wesley held out the card. 'We are the police, sir. If you could just spare us a few minutes ...'

The man stood back and held the door open. As his anger diminished, he seemed to deflate like a burst football and turn into a pathetic-looking man in a grey cardigan. 'You'd better come in. I'm sorry about ... but we get so many people knocking on the door: double glazing; burglar alarms; those lads with big bags who say they're unemployed and try and sell you things. I thought you were Jehovah's witnesses. Er, I hope ...'

'That's quite all right, sir,' said Wesley politely. After the embarrassing start, this one would be only too eager to oblige. 'We're making enquiries about a lady who lives at this address, a Sharon Carteret.'

The man shook his head. 'There's nobody of that name here. There's a Mrs Hughes lives on the other two floors. It's her house. She just rents out the bottom floor as a self-contained flat. She's a widow, lives on her own. But there's no one called Sharon.'

'How long have you lived here, Mr, er ...'

'Jackson, Dennis Jackson. I moved in at the end of August. Me and the wife, we, er, split up. She got the house, the lot. You know how it is.'

Wesley nodded sympathetically. 'Yes, sir. So you can't help us?'

'Sorry. No. Your best bet is to ask Mrs Hughes. I think it was a young woman lived here before me. I don't really know. Mrs Hughes'll be able to tell you.'

Wesley thanked Jackson, who looked relieved when they went back to the front door and rang the bell for the other flat.

Mrs Hughes was a tall woman: a woman possessed of a natural elegance. Her clothes were expensive; Jaeger probably, thought Rachel. Her steel-grey hair was cut in an immaculate bob. She looked at Wesley enquiringly, fingering the Hermès scarf at her throat. Wesley introduced himself and they were invited in.

The living room on the first floor matched its owner. It was simply decorated, the wall dotted with muted watercolours. They were asked to sit down on the soft leather chesterfield but they were not offered tea. Rachel produced Denise Wellthorne's sketch and watched Mrs Hughes's face as she studied it.

'Yes, this does look a little like Sharon – the girl who lived downstairs.' She handed the sketch back to Rachel. 'Since my husband died, this place has been too big for me and my son's married and lives up north, so I had the bottom floor made into a self-contained flat.'

Wesley spoke. 'Could you tell us about this Sharon, Mrs Hughes? Did she live alone? How long did she live here?'

'She moved in around three and a half years ago. She seemed a very nice girl, very respectable. She worked as a secretary in a bank or building society, not sure which – came with the best references from her employers. She seemed such a quiet girl. I like my tenants to be quiet, Sergeant. When they're living in such close proximity, that sort of thing's important.' Wesley nodded. 'As for living alone, well . . .' Mrs Hughes's lips tightened. 'She did at first, then this boyfriend of hers virtually moved in – a real ne'r-do-well. If he worked I don't know what he did, and I heard he was in debt – gambling, I believe.'

'Did he actually move in? Live here?'

'I shouldn't have allowed that. He lived somewhere in

Morbay, I believe. No doubt paid for by the state,' she added bitterly. 'But he spent a lot of time here. I felt most uncomfortable about it but the place wasn't let furnished so there wasn't much I could do.'

'Did Sharon have a baby, Mrs Hughes?' Rachel asked casually.

The woman looked indignant. 'No. No, of course not. It's a strict rule in the lease – no children.'

'And why did she move out?'

'She didn't confide her reasons to me and I didn't ask.'

'This boyfriend, was he on the scene all the time? Till she moved out?'

'As far as I know. I didn't enquire into her private life. He came and went.'

'Did they have any rows?' asked Wesley. 'Any shouting, threats?'

'I can't say I heard anything if they did.'

Wesley leaned forward. 'Do you know the boyfriend's name? Can you describe him?'

'I think his name was Chris. Don't know his surname, of course, as we were never formally introduced. Dark hair, average height . . . and he wore an earring,' she added with distaste.

'Did Sharon leave a forwarding address?'

'No. She left no address. I presume she's moved in some-where with her, er, boyfriend.'

Mrs Hughes's curiosity overcame her composure. 'Can you tell me what this is about?'

'We think Sharon may have been murdered, Mrs Hughes.'

Wesley watched her face. Her expression gave nothing away.

'We'd like to trace this boyfriend of hers urgently. Do you think you could help to build a picture of him?'

'Oh no, I'm sure I couldn't. I never actually saw him close to. I could only give the most general description. I'm afraid I'm not very observant . . .'

'You noticed the earring,' said Rachel sharply.

'Well, you couldn't really miss that sort of thing, could you? All I can say is that he had dark hair, medium length; average height. I really can't tell you any more. I'm sorry.'

It was clear that no more information was forthcoming so Wesley and Rachel took their leave politely, but with hints that they might want to talk to Mrs Hughes again.

As they walked off down the street, she stood at the living-room window, face impassive, watching them go. When they had disappeared from view she turned, heart pounding, and poured herself a whisky from the cut-glass decanter on the sideboard. She needed to steady her nerves.

Chapter 17

I did vow never more to have dealings with Jennet. I
did resolve to send her from the house but I cannot
now help myself. Last night I did go to her chamber
and as she watched me enter she did take off her
nightgown and she stood naked before me. Then in
her arms I did know such sweet pleasure and she
did give me all that I desired. It was past midnight
when I did take my leave of her and returned to
my wife's bed. Elizabeth was asleep and suspected
nothing.

> Extract from the journal of John Banized,
> 7 June 1623

The jeweller recognised Darren. He was one of that little
gang who hung around the Embankment with their metal
detectors when the tide was out.

As the boy left – without the ring; that was being kept
for 'valuation' – the jeweller looked through the pile of
cards and papers by the side of the till. Where was the
number that young policeman had given him?

But before he picked up the phone he studied the ring
again. It was a nice piece; very old, possibly even
Elizabethan or Jacobean. He looked at the stones, admiring
their undamaged settings. But it was the inscription that
intrigued him most: 'To Jennet with all my thanks. JB.' It
was quite clear; not worn.

He dialled the number of the police station while Darren,

hands in pockets, strolled down the street towards the Embankment, kicking an empty Coke can in front of him.

Gerry Heffernan sat back in his executive swivel chair. Things were moving. The identification was positive.

In common with practice in many offices, the employees of Tradmouth Models each had their own mug for use at tea breaks. Sharon hadn't bothered to take hers with her when she left and nobody else had used it. The fingerprints on the mug matched those of the dead girl. Her prints were on the photos of Karen too, and they had found her dentist, a man over at Queenswear: the dental records matched. Heffernan cursed himself for wasting so much time chasing after Karen Giordino. But, he thought philosophically, these things happen. They were on the right track now.

At least Mrs Giordino had gone back to Manchester happy. Karen had relented and grudgingly met her mother, whose tears of joy at their reunion had seemed pathetic in view of the daughter's attitude. John Fielding had also been treated with contempt. She mocked him for fussing; for going to pieces; for being so stupid when he knew perfectly well that she was in France with Maurice. He'd done it all on purpose; he was jealous. John had hung his head and said nothing. That was a relationship, Heffernan thought, that might not weather the twin storms of boredom and Maurice.

Heffernan had seen no point in detaining Karen and John further: he could charge them with nothing as wasting police time is an offence only if the culprit does it deliberately. They had returned to their flat in Morbay.

The inspector looked up as Wesley walked into the office.

'We've been in touch with Sharon Carteret's bank, sir. They're faxing her account details through. Her salary was paid directly into her bank account so the agency had the details.'

'Good. Modern technology has some uses, then. Go on. Anything else?'

'I've got Steve and Rachel trying to trace her new address and making enquiries about this Chris. If he's unemployed he must sign on. We've tried all the Carterets in the phone book – all two of them – and nobody's heard of a Sharon. And I'm arranging statements from the staff at the agency to see if we can get anything on her family and friends.'

'Good. Shouldn't take too long to turn something up.'

'No man is an island, sir.'

'Couldn't have put it better myself, Wes.' He looked up at his sergeant, serious. 'I've not forgotten your appointment tomorrow morning. Take as long as you like. Hope it goes well.'

'Thanks, sir. I'm hoping it won't take that long.' He gathered his thoughts. 'I was just thinking that Sharon moved out of her flat around the same time as she gave up her job. Why? What had happened? Did she intend to move out of the area?'

'Good point, Wesley.' Heffernan stood up. 'I'll think about it over my dinner.'

Wesley forsook the station canteen for a lonely sandwich. His desk was piled high with paperwork; reports to be gone through; statements to be looked at, filtered for tiny nuggets of information. There would be no lunch-time trip to the dig. He would have to wait to find out how Neil had fared at the museum.

In the corner of the room a discreet electronic bleep heralded the arrival of the fax from the bank, strangely enough the same branch as Karen Giordino had used. Copies of statements crept off the machine. Wesley gathered them up and took them to his desk. There was a new address; an address in Morbay. He wrote it down.

Wesley was no accountant but even to his untrained eye there was something odd about the statements; something that didn't fit with what he knew about Sharon Carteret. Her salary was there and a regular sum out each month – presumably her rent. But in addition to the salary another sum of two hundred pounds was paid in regularly every month, the words 'cash or cheque' written by the entry. Wesley wondered about the source of this extra income. A second job, perhaps? Some sort of investment? There were also statements for a deposit account – a very healthy deposit account. Wesley felt a stab of envy. The Peterson family fortune had been depleted by the move from London and Pam's enforced unemployment, not to mention the medical bills they would have to face from the Morbay Clinic. Yet here was a young woman, a poorly paid secretary, with a substantial five-figure sum in her bank account. It might well be an inheritance or a win on the pools, but it was worth investigating.

The bank had sent statements only for the past year. He would pay them a visit and delve further into their records. He rang the bank and made an appointment to see the manager at three; next he made a call to Rachel to give her the address on the statement. Then he looked at the pile of paperwork on his desk and despaired.

Stan Jenkins was still wrestling bravely with salads. Heffernan had to admire the man; he would have given up after the first day.

'How's the sailing, Gerry?' asked Stan as they sat down at a coveted corner table. 'Must say I can't understand you nautical types; prefer golf myself.'

'If you think I'm odd, Stan, you should see my sergeant: he goes around digging things up. A mate of his has just unearthed two skeletons. As if we didn't have enough on our plates . . .'

'Speak for yourself,' said Stan, staring at his lettuce. 'Maybe the murder rate's not high enough for him here. He'll be used to London. You don't want to go encouraging him, Gerry, or we'll be rushed off our feet.'

'How's it going? Any developments?'

'No sign of Jonathon, if that's what you mean.'

'So your lady friend didn't come up with the goods?'

'Oh, her. She's left me alone for a couple of days, thank God.'

'Did you follow up that sighting?'

'We had to. Turned out to be a flat rented by a young couple. They had a little boy about that age. My lady friend, as you call her, saw him with his dad. Mind you, that's exactly what I was expecting.'

'Did you see the kid?'

'No. They'd moved away. But the next-door neighbours filled us in. They said the kid was the image of his father.'

'Oh well, keep on trying.'

'Mrs Berrisford, the mother, is coming down here tomorrow. I can't see any point but what can I say?'

Heffernan looked at his colleague sympathetically. The man was clearly troubled. He again offered a silent word of thanks that it wasn't his case.

Wesley Peterson prided himself on being methodical; on keeping on top of his paperwork. But today the paperwork was keeping on top of him – and the appointment at the clinic tomorrow wouldn't help. He resolved to take some work home with him and get it finished that evening. Neil's research would have to wait.

The phone rang and Wesley cursed under his breath. He needed some time without interruptions. But what he heard when he grabbed the receiver made him sit up with renewed interest. It was a jeweller who had a shop on the Embankment, calling to say that a boy had brought in a very interesting ring and that he should come round and have a look at it.

Wesley didn't need asking twice. He pushed the papers on his desk to one side and put on his jacket. On the way he called for Neil, who left Matt and Jane to continue their painstaking excavations.

'Found anything exciting?' asked Wesley as they squeezed themselves against the walls of a half-timbered antique shop to avoid being hit by a passing car.

'Only what you'd expect. A few coins, nails, pottery. We think we've located the midden: found some animal bones. Thought for one terrible moment that we'd found another skeleton. What did this jeweller say?'

'Some kid brought him a ring, very old. It might not be connected but I thought you'd better come along just in case.'

The jeweller's shop looked as though it had wriggled itself into a narrow gap between a restaurant and an estate agent's. Inside, it was small and cosy; its dark wood counter glowed like a new conker. It was an old business, established over a century ago, with an impressive array of antique jewellery on show in its small plate-glass window: the kind of jewellery Pam liked, thought Wesley, but could seldom afford.

The jeweller, a Mr Seddon, was younger than Wesley had expected: a plump man in young middle age, who wore an alarming waistcoat and velvet bow tie. Mr Seddon got down to business as soon as Wesley and Neil had introduced themselves, Neil's unkempt appearance becoming instantly acceptable when the jeweller learned of his profession. Mr Seddon produced the ring from a brown envelope and Neil picked it up.

'What a beauty. I've rarely seen anything like this so well preserved. Look at this, Wes: there's an inscription inside.'

He handed it to Wesley and the jeweller provided a magnifying glass. Wesley read. ' "To Jennet with all my thanks. J.B." Might not be contemporary with the ring, of course. It might be hard to prove it's from the dig.'

He gave the ring back to Neil, who studied it carefully. 'It certainly looks sixteenth-, seventeenth-century. Nice. I'd like to show it to someone at the County Museum.'

'The boy who brought it in has a metal detector,' said Seddon. 'There's a little gang of them hang around the Embankment at low tide. It could have come from the river, I suppose.'

'It wouldn't be in such good nick,' said Neil, looking at the ring. 'It looks almost as if it was buried when it was new.'

'The lad's here most evenings with his friends. I see them messing about making a nuisance of themselves by the castle ferry steps when I lock up. If you come back about six you might be able to ask him about it.'

'Thank you, Mr Seddon. In the meantime, if you could keep it in your safe . . .'

Wesley thanked Mr Seddon for being so public-spirited and walked back part of the way with Neil, who was trying not to become too excited about such a desirable find. The truth would have to wait until the evening.

Wesley looked at his watch. It was nearly time to brave the bank manager.

* * *

Rachel looked out of the car window as they drove through Morbay and thought how the place had changed.

In her childhood the resort was the very pinnacle of respectability: retired colonels; tea dances among the potted palms; high-class shops; young families consuming ice cream while seated in municipal deckchairs on the beach below the ornamental gardens. She had been brought there as a treat. Parts of the town still retained the aura of bygone prosperity: the white villas perched above the town, one of them the home of Karen Giordino, were still leafy and desirable. But the town itself, Rachel noted, was showing signs of wear, like an elderly lady wearing too much make-up. The purveyors of luxury goods in the main street by the marina were slowly being replaced by amusement arcades. Hoteliers, hit by hard times, were accepting guests from the DSS rather than the rosy-cheeked young families of yesteryear. Gangs of youths roamed the streets in and out of season. The Drug Squad kept a careful eye on the place. It was not how Rachel remembered it.

She asked herself why she had allowed Steve to drive, knowing perfectly well it wasn't one of his talents. She told him as much. 'Your driving's bloody lethal. I'll make sure I come with Sergeant Peterson next time.'

'Fancy him, do you? Is it true what they say about black men?' Steve leered unpleasantly and put his hand on her knee.

Rachel hit the offending hand hard with her fist and turned on him, furious. 'I've had enough of you, Steve. You're getting as bad as Harry bloody Marchbank.'

'Good copper, Harry Marchbank,' said Steve with a smile.

'He was an ignorant pig, Steve. And you'd better not follow his example or Gerry Heffernan'll have you back on the streets handing out parking tickets. Understand?'

Steve was silenced for a few moments, but he knew he had touched a nerve. Maybe Rachel did fancy Wesley Peterson. It was a situation that would need watching.

The address they had been given was on a fairly respectable side of town. Rows of Victorian semis, only a few divided into flats, stood each side of Albert Road. Number

33 had two bells. Rachel rang the bottom one. There was no answer, so she worked her way up.

The door was answered by an elderly lady, still sprightly, with sharp blue eyes. Rachel thought that here was a good witness: nothing much would get past her. She asked if a Sharon Carteret lived there.

'There was a young lady on the bottom floor. She introduced herself as Sharon, but she didn't say her second name. They don't nowadays, do they? She seemed a nice girl – quiet.'

'Did she live alone?'

'Dear me, no. She had a husband . . . and a little boy. Very sweet he was. Such a shame they didn't stay long. I did offer to baby-sit, you know. Won't you come in? I'll pop the kettle on.'

Rachel was longing for a cup of tea, Steve for something stronger, but he'd make do. They followed the lady, who had introduced herself as Mrs Willis, up the stairs.

Her flat was cosy and filled with the memorabilia of a lifetime. She had obviously lived in this top-floor flat for many years. Rachel said as much.

'Oh yes, dear. I've seen a lot of comings and goings in that bottom flat, I can tell you.'

'Can you tell us about this family downstairs? Are they still living there?'

'Oh no, dear. It's empty at the moment. They moved out very suddenly while I was away.' She suddenly looked coy. 'My dancing partner thinks they did a moonlight flit, but I wouldn't like to say.'

'What were they like?'

'As I said, she was very nice. He never spoke. Wore an earring.' She whispered confidentially. 'I think she might have married beneath her.'

Rachel nodded and tried to look suitably disapproving. 'And the little boy?'

'Such a sweet child – the image of his father.'

'What was his name?'

'Daniel. They called him Danny.'

'And the father's name?'

'Chris.'

'Did Sharon talk about herself?'

'No. No, she didn't. I came down and introduced myself. I always believe in being a good neighbour. Sharon was very polite, told me their names, but that's all really. I don't think he worked. If he'd been out during the day I would have invited her up for a cup of tea. It's surprising what you can learn over a cup of tea. But then I suppose you know that in the police force. What have they done? Why are you after them? Have they robbed a bank?'

'No.' Rachel decided to spare Mrs Willis's feelings. 'It's something quite different. What happened when they went? Did they say anything?'

'I'm afraid I was away. I've just spent three weeks at my daughter's in Brighton. When I got back yesterday they'd gone, just disappeared. I asked the landlord but he didn't know any more than I did. The rent was paid till the end of the month so he didn't worry. You know what these landlords are like nowadays, only interested in money. More tea?'

'No, thank you, Mrs Willis. That was lovely.' Rachel, ever a favourite with her numerous great-aunts, was good with elderly ladies. 'Is the flat downstairs occupied now?'

'Oh no, dear. It's still empty.' She delved into an empty vase and pulled out a key. 'I've got this. The landlord's left me one in case anybody comes to view it.'

Rachel took the key. 'Thank you, Mrs Willis, you've been very helpful. I'll bring back the key when we've had a little look.' She smiled sweetly.

Rachel stood in the hallway looking at the key. She could tell Steve was growing impatient. She drew another key from her pocket.

'Sergeant Peterson gave me this,' she said. 'It's the one that was found in the handbag.'

She tried it in the lock. It opened the door. They hadn't needed Mrs Willis's spare key after all.

The flat had a chill air, an unoccupied feeling. The furniture stood plain and unadorned, waiting for the next tenant to add their touch of individuality. The place was cleanish, modern and unpretentious. Rachel had seen better ... and much worse. But there was something bothering her,

133

something at the back of her mind. And she couldn't think what it was.

Wesley had once considered accountancy as a career, but after several seconds' thought had dismissed the idea. His visit to the bank confirmed the wisdom of that decision. Rows of figures had never been his strong point.

The bank's records, now neatly consigned to computer, had revealed that the large sum had been paid into Sharon Carteret's newly opened deposit account roughly two years ago; the monthly payments had begun a year after that. All the transactions had been conducted in cash. Where, Wesley wondered, had the money come from? He sat at his desk back at the station and looked at the information the bank had given him. It didn't make sense ... yet.

The bank's records also showed that Sharon had changed jobs a few months before the money was paid in. She had once worked for a building society in Tradmouth. Another line of enquiry.

He worked till six, managing to reduce the size of his paperwork pile by more than two-thirds. After explaining to Heffernan where he was going and being offered the services of PC Johnson, he set off for the Embankment. Johnson's presence in uniform would add a useful element of officialdom when he tackled the boy with the metal detector.

Mr Seddon had been right about the boy's routine. A few youths, too old for school and at a loose end, were hanging about at the top of the castle ferry steps. They weren't doing anything illegal, or even very antisocial, just slouching aimlessly, consuming cans of drink and cigarettes. Two of them clutched metal detectors like wands of office. The ferryman tied up his small blue-painted craft below and eyed the boys with some suspicion. Wesley strolled over to them casually. Johnson followed behind. He recognised some of these lads as younger alumni of his old school, Tradmouth Comprehensive. He hoped they wouldn't recognise him.

Wesley showed his warrant card and asked who had taken a ring to the jeweller's. Darren, who had never been mixed up with the police, stared at Wesley with hostile interest, but stayed silent. The boys all shook their heads and tried to look as blameless as a gaggle of choirboys. But unfortunately for Darren, Mr Seddon chose that moment to come out of his shop to lock up. The jeweller saw the policemen and started to approach the group, but Darren spotted him first and took to his heels, clutching the metal detector, his prized possession, to his chest. Johnson gave chase; he had not been Tradmouth Comprehensive's 800 metres champion for nothing.

The rugby tackle grazed Darren's elbow and his pride but didn't damage his metal detector. The other boys scurried away as Johnson brought Darren back. The police were bad news. They didn't want to get involved.

Darren looked as if he'd rather be anywhere than being frogmarched along the Embankment by a six-foot spotty policeman.

'Is this the boy, Mr Seddon?' Wesley said quietly. The lad stood pathetically in front of him.

Seddon nodded. 'I'll unlock the shop, Sergeant. You can talk to him in there.'

Darren, in Wesley's judgement, told the truth – or the truth according to Darren. 'It was only a bit of waste ground. I only dug it up like I do on the river. What's wrong with that? It don't belong to no one.'

Wesley explained patiently and in the simplest of terms about private property and archaeological digs. Darren hung his head. 'I've not got to go to court, have I? Me mum'll kill me. I never knew it were against the law. I never . . .'

The boy looked so small, so pathetic, that Wesley found himself feeling sorry for him. Strictly speaking he should have charged him, but he decided on this occasion to use his discretion.

'Darren, I'm going to ask you to come to the site with me and show us exactly where you found the ring and anything else you took that night. Okay?'

Darren nodded. His eyes had begun to fill with tears.

Mr Seddon watched them go. The ring was a nice piece; he could have made a few bob on it, he thought, but it wouldn't do to get on the wrong side of the law in his business. He shrugged and locked the shop.

Neil was surprised to see Wesley in the company of a boy in a baseball cap and a young uniformed policeman. Darren hung back, looking guilty, as Wesley explained the situation and returned the jewel of the dig to its rightful keeper.

Neil spoke to the boy. 'Has the sergeant explained about the damage those metal detectors can do?' Darren, crestfallen, nodded and shuffled his feet. 'Tell you what. Come round here tomorrow morning and I'll let you do a bit of digging.' Darren nodded again, eagerly this time. 'You'll have to do exactly as you're told, mind. And bring that infernal machine of yours and you can go through the spoil heaps, see if there's any coins we've missed. Okay?' Darren's eyes shone. Just wait till he told his mates. 'Off you go now. See you tomorrow. It's hard work, mind.'

Darren grinned widely and ran off before Neil could change his mind.

'Thanks, Neil. Nice bit of community service you've arranged there.'

'Come off it, Wes. We could do with a few extra pairs of hands, you know that. Time's short. I got to the museum this afternoon after I'd seen you. Turned up quite a lot of information. They even had the original accounts from when the place was built – three shillings for timber and all that sort of thing. And the records of the shop accounts. It's fascinating if you've got time to go through it all, which you probably won't have. There's even more stuff at that museum so I'm going back there tomorrow. The Banizeds were what you'd call comfortably off. They sent ships out to Newfoundland in the spring, brought back cargoes of salted fish and traded it for wine and luxury goods in Europe – that's on top of the cloth trade, of course. They can't have been short of a bob or two. One interesting thing – in 1623 they replaced the staircase and used a ship's mast for the centre post. It's all down in the accounts. An early example of recycling. And the cellar was flagged in 1624 so our bodies probably predate that.'

'You're going to use all this in the exhibition?'

'You bet your life I am. Pity we don't know who the bodies belong to.'

'Keep digging and you might find out. Jennet's a possible. Looks as if the ring was buried with her.'

'Trouble is, Wes, we might never know.'

'I'd better be off. Got a lot to catch up on.'

Wesley walked off slowly, reluctantly, heading for home. Pam had put the card proclaiming tomorrow's clinic appointment in pride of place on the mantelpiece. He hoped, for her sake, that nothing would prevent him from keeping it. He walked up the hilly streets wondering what mood she would be in when he got home.

Chapter 18

I am drawn to Jennet's chamber every night. I tell
my wife I am at work in the warehouse. How easily
the lie doth come to my lips. My lust hath made me
a deceiver but I cannot give up what I must have. I
plunge into Jennet's fair body each night as a man
doth plunge a burning hand into cool water. To have
her is to cool for a time the burnings of my desire.
But my appetite doth increase with consumption.

Elizabeth is glad that I have ceased my importun-
ings as she feels most unwell. I am unable to help
myself. I cease even to pray for the Lord's for-
giveness.

Extract from the journal of John Banized,
10 June 1623

In Steve Carstairs's wildest sexual fantasies, he was surrounded by a bevy of nubile young models, only too pleased
to do his bidding. He could hardly believe his luck when he
sat in the office of Tradmouth Models on a rainy Thursday
morning waiting to interview the last of Karen Giordino's
colleagues. It hadn't been like this when he'd been on the
beat. CID got all the good jobs.

The model, a willowy blonde named Mimi, crossed and
uncrossed her remarkable legs as Steve tried not to stare.
He asked her the questions on the list, the same questions
as he had asked the others.

'Did you know Sharon Carteret well?'

'Well as anybody, I suppose. She wasn't the sort of girl who mixed, if you know what I mean. She was very quiet.'

Steve nodded. 'Can you tell me anything about her? Did she talk about a boyfriend, for instance?'

'She never mentioned one. She didn't talk much about her private life. There are some of the girls round here don't talk about anything else, but Sharon ... well, she was just the girl on the desk, part of the furniture. She was a bit, you know, mousey. It's Phil we come here to see, after all. Nobody took much notice of Sharon.'

'Were you there when Sharon found Karen Giordino's photographs?'

'The ones there was so much fuss about? Yeah. I'd just called in and Sharon was twittering on about not knowing what to do with these bloody photos. I said to keep them and give them back when Karen came in next. She put them in her bag and said she might drop them off at Karen's if she got the chance.'

'You don't know if she did call at Karen's?'

'No. Karen was off to France soon after. Never heard any more about it.'

Mimi recrossed her legs and a shiver went down Steve's spine.

'What about when Sharon first started here? Did she tell anyone about herself then? Was there anyone she did confide in?'

'No. I told you. She kept herself to herself. There was one girl who used to use this agency – she's moved now, gone to London – she used to tease Sharon when she first started.'

'Tease her? What about?'

'About her weight. She was a bit plump when she first started here.'

'How did Sharon react?'

'She took no notice – never said anything. She did lose weight, though, so perhaps it might have upset her. I don't know. You could never tell with her.'

Steve looked at his list. He could think of no more questions – except one. 'If you're not doing anything tonight, do you fancy a drink?'

Mimi smiled and surreptitiously pulled up her skirt to reveal even more of her alarmingly long legs.

'Nice carpet,' whispered Wesley, trying to take Pam's mind off things. She smiled weakly.

A nurse strolled towards them, smiling. She wore a crisp blue uniform of the type nowadays only seen in Carry On films and private hospitals, the design having been superseded in NHS establishments by something more practical.

She bent over and spoke confidentially in Wesley's ear. 'Have you provided a sample for us, Mr Peterson?'

Wesley, recalling how he had recently experienced one of the most embarrassing moments of his life, swallowed hard and nodded. The nurse went away.

The couple sat in silence, not knowing what to say. The blonde on the reception desk asked if they'd like another coffee. They both said yes. At least it would give them something to do with their hands while they were waiting to see Dr Downey. It was the waiting that was the worst part.

After what seemed to Wesley like an age, the nurse reappeared and led them through carpeted corridors to Dr Downey's office.

There was money in private medicine, thought Wesley, as his eyes took in his surroundings: Dr Downey's office was worthy of housing the chief constable himself. The desk was dark and vast, expensively inset with tooled leather. The leather chairs moulded themselves to the body as one sat looking at the tasteful watercolours on the soft green walls – all originals. Pam found herself wishing that school staffrooms were as luxuriously appointed.

Dr Downey shook hands, smiling in welcome. He could afford his affability.

'Mr Peterson.' He turned to Wesley, still smiling. 'I've had one of my colleagues look at your sample under the microscope and I'm pleased to tell you that everything appears to be normal. We do have to investigate the possibility of the male partner's infertility as well, you understand. If the sperm count is low, we have a problem.'

Wesley nodded and wished that the medical profession

wouldn't keep underestimating their patients' ability to read medical textbooks. Pam had probably read the lot and passed the salient information on to him. He just wanted to know the test results. 'So where do we go from here, Doctor? What's the next step?' He thought he'd better stop Dr Downey in his tracks before he went on to explain about the birds and the bees. 'Will you want to perform a laparoscopy?'

Dr Downey, who had been about to launch into an explanation of the fertilisation of the human egg, sat back in his deep leather swivel chair and looked at Wesley. Perhaps he had underestimated the man. 'Yes. That's the next step. I usually like my ladies to stay in overnight, Mrs Peterson. We'll do our best to make you comfortable so you shouldn't find it too traumatic.' He smiled reassuringly. 'Do you know about the procedure and what we'll be looking for?'

'She reads about nothing else.'

Pam, self-conscious, gave her husband a look that said shut up and don't embarrass me.

'Let me assure you, Pamela – may I call you Pamela? – that we'll do our very best here at the Morbay Clinic to sort out any problems you may have. Many common conditions are easy to treat and we do have a full range of services here. You're in the best hands.' He smiled charmingly.

Wesley didn't see the smile, or Pamela's eyes shining hopefully. He saw only a diminishing bank account.

As they left the clinic Pam linked her arm through Wesley's. 'I feel much better after talking to him,' she said. 'I might even come out for a drink tonight if I've not got too much preparation to do for school. Neil'll think I'm avoiding him.'

Wesley kissed her cheek absent-mindedly. He knew he should be grateful to Dr Downey, even though he didn't like the man.

The harassed young woman at the benefit office had pointed out to PC Johnson that Christopher was a popular name and it was impossible to trace anything if he didn't provide a surname; besides, there was no record of anyone at the address given claiming benefit. It would be on the computer,

141

and the computer never lied. Johnson nodded, thanked her and left. Who was he to argue with a computer?

Gerry Heffernan took the news philosophically. Chris could be anywhere. But the child? That added a new dimension to the investigation. Somewhere along the way either Sharon or Chris had acquired a child; not a baby but a young child. And according to the neighbour the child looked like Chris. The inspector sighed; in these days of unconventional families, the child could easily be Chris's from a past relationship. There was one advantage: a man with a child should be easier to track down than a man on his own. Heffernan comforted himself with this thought.

Sharon's family too seemed conspicuously absent from the scene. Nobody at work knew anything about the secretary's background, although Phil, the boss, thought she'd mentioned once that she was an only child, that her parents were dead and that she'd been brought up by her grandmother. Nobody knew about her friends either; perhaps she hadn't any. Heffernan felt a wave of sadness that someone so young should pass from this earthly existence so unmourned. It was almost as though the dead girl had no life or personality of her own.

His thoughts were disturbed by a knock on the door. Wesley had returned.

'Come in, Wes. How did it go?'

He saw that the sergeant was smiling.

Rachel felt sorry for the female staff of the Devonshire District Building Society. They had to wear a uniform, whereas she had earned the right to abandon hers when she joined the CID.

Most of the staff had changed since Sharon worked there, but she found two women who remembered her.

The first recalled her but had had little to do with her, but the second, a middle-aged lady named Dot who sported gigantic earrings and lethal stiletto heels, remembered her well. She had sat beside her in the back office.

'She was a nice girl. Quiet but always ready for a laugh, if you know what I mean.' Rachel sensed there'd be no shutting Dot up once she got going. 'She had this boyfriend, thought the world of him. I think he was a bit of a Svengali. She'd do whatever he wanted – poor girl. She never had a family. Maybe that's why she clung to him. Who's to say? I tried to tell her but they won't be told, will they? I mean, I know that men aren't worth it and I told her to think more of herself, but would she listen? Would she heck.'

Rachel nodded sympathetically. 'Can you tell me anything about the boyfriend? Or about any other friends or family she might have mentioned?' She sensed she would have to work hard to keep Dot on the right track.

'Well, his name was Chris, I remember that much. I never saw him but she talked about him a lot. It was obvious she was smitten. She said he had money worries but she never said what he did for a living.'

'So he was in debt, do you think?'

'That's what money worries usually means. You don't worry if you have too much of it, do you? I remember her saying she'd gone with him to the races at Newton Abbot. Maybe he gambled. But that's just a guess.'

'Did she have any particular friends that you know of?'

Dot pursed her lips, biting back her disapproval. 'Gave them all up, didn't she. Chris didn't like her having her own friends. She said as much. Poor girl.'

'What about when she left? What happened? Did she say why she was leaving?'

'No. She didn't give a reason – just handed in her notice.'

'She never confided in you?'

'No. But I had my suspicions.'

'Suspicions? What about?'

'When you see a girl throwing up in the loo in the mornings and putting on weight you don't have to be in the CID to put two and two together.' She looked at Rachel and winked.

'You mean she was pregnant?'

'I'd stake my pension on it. Such as it is in this place.'

'How long did Sharon work here?'

'About three years.'

'So she'd have been entitled to maternity pay and maternity leave if she'd stayed. So why did she leave? She wasn't signed off sick, was she?'

143

'No. She definitely handed in her notice. She showed me the letter, asked me if it was all right, but she never said anything about having a baby. I mean, in this day and age nobody'd worry that she wasn't married, and usually once girls here find out they're pregnant there's no stopping them talking about it.'

'And did you ever see her again after she left? Did she ever come in to visit . . . show off the baby?'

'Never saw her again. No, I tell a lie, I did see her in the street about a year later. But she didn't see me.'

'On her own?'

'Yes. Near the Butterwalk one lunch-time.'

Rachel nodded. 'Did she say where she was living?'

'She didn't say much about her domestic arrangements. But I reckon this boyfriend had her under his thumb all night.'

Rachel thanked Dot, who reluctantly returned to the routine of the day. A visit from the police had been a welcome respite from the tyranny of the computer screen.

When Rachel stepped out into the High Street, she began to walk towards the police station. Then, at the Butterwalk, she suddenly remembered what had been bothering her about Sharon's flat in Morbay.

Chapter 19

Last night my wife was awake and did ask me what business was so pressing that it kept me from my bed until this late hour. I lied to her and did claim to be counting the goods in my warehouse and making ready for our ships' return.

Jennet doth always keep a modest demeanour before her. She can suspect nothing. I am sunk deep in my sin and want nothing more than to lie in Jennet's fair arms. I know not what to do and I cannot call upon the Lord for guidance.

Extract from the journal of John Banized,
20 June 1623

Wesley put the phone down and walked into Heffernan's office.

'I've just been in touch with a mate of mine at the Met, sir. He's going to St Catherine's House to look up births, see if we can find out anything about this baby Sharon was supposed to have. He'll let me know if he comes up with anything. I've been in touch with all the local adoption agencies too – drawn a blank.'

The inspector breathed deeply and played with his ballpoint pen. After a long pause he spoke. 'Don't you find all this a bit strange, Wes? I could understand if we were living fifty years ago when having a baby out of wedlock was a big disgrace. Girls got sent away to aunts at the seaside so that nobody'd know – it'd all be swept under the rug. But today everyone's doing it – film stars, the lot. It's no great scandal any more. I don't know if I agree with how things have gone, Wes, maybe the pendulum's swung too far, but there we are, that's the way things stand.'

Wesley nodded. 'Maybe there was a reason for her hiding it. Maybe this Chris was married.'

'Maybe. But from what we've heard of him, he didn't act married. I suppose his wife might have held the purse-strings and he didn't want to go so far as leaving her. In which case I'm surprised he didn't persuade Sharon to have an abortion.'

'Perhaps it was against her beliefs . . . or maybe she did. We've not talked to anyone who actually saw her heavily pregnant, have we? I've got Rachel checking all the maternity hospitals in the area, see if she comes up with anything. The child he was seen with in Morbay could have been his by his wife or even another woman.'

'It's all ifs and buts, isn't it, Wes? What have we got? This Sharon, according to her landlady and her workmates, was a good little virgin until she falls into the clutches of the evil Chris; she gets pregnant and hides the fact; gives up her job and doesn't get another till after the baby's born . . . or maybe till after she gets over an abortion. She then disappears from her flat and her job and shacks up with Chris and some child he's picked up on the way; then she gets herself murdered on a cliff top by person or persons unknown. It must make sense, but let's face it, until we come up with this Chris character, we're a bit scuppered.'

'There's one interesting thing, sir. I've just been on to the bank. The amount that's usually paid into Sharon's account, the two hundred pounds . . . it's not been paid this month.'

'Meaning?'

'Meaning that whoever was paying it in knew she was dead on the twentieth of September. It was always paid in on or around the twentieth of the month. With the mix-up in identification, only the killer could have known she was dead then.'

Heffernan sat back and looked up at his sergeant in admiration. 'Good thinking, Wesley. I think you've got something there.'

'I'll do some checking, sir.'

'You do that.'

A few phone calls later, Wesley returned to Heffernan's office with the results of his investigations. Results that Wesley found puzzling to say the least.

They were interrupted by Rachel's return. She gave an obligatory knock on the inspector's door and burst in; she obviously had something to say. Wesley and Heffernan looked at her expectantly.

'I've checked the maternity hospitals. No record of Sharon having a baby at the time in question. She might have used a different name; there's no way of knowing.'

Heffernan sighed.

Rachel obviously had something else to report.

'And I've just remembered, sir. I knew there was something wrong when I went to Sharon's flat in Morbay. It was a furnished flat and the woman who owned her old flat said that it was unfurnished. What happened to her furniture? If she left it there it might mean she left in a hurry. Why?'

Her colleagues stared at her, trying to make sense of what she was saying.

Wesley spoke. 'She could have put the furniture in storage. Get someone to contact all the local firms.'

'I'd like to go over to Queenswear again. See if she left anything interesting behind.' Rachel looked determined.

'It's worth a try,' said the inspector. 'You two get over there.' He looked at Wesley. 'What were you going to tell me before Rachel came in?'

'It's interesting, sir. Those monthly payments into Sharon's bank account ... they were made in cash through various branches in the north-west, mainly the Manchester area.'

Heffernan sighed. 'This is all getting very odd, Wes; very odd indeed.'

Stan Jenkins's heart beat faster as he approached Hedgerow Cottage. Was it nerves? Blood pressure? He didn't know. All he knew was that he didn't want to be there.

The WPC who was driving the car looked at him, sensing how he felt. 'We're here, sir.'

There was no need to tell him; he knew. Hedgerow Cottage had become as familiar as his own house. But whereas his home conjured up thoughts of evenings by the television and dull domestic security, the thought of Hedgerow Cottage brought with it the mental demons of despair and hopelessness. He didn't want to see Elaine Berrisford; didn't want to look into her eyes.

He had expected her to be alone. But the door was opened by a man; her husband. Stan had met him only a few times before, although of course he'd spoken to him often on the phone; he had had to return to work, had a business to run. He shook hands with him solemnly.

'My wife's gone to bed, Inspector.' Alan Berrisford looked tired. 'Is there any news?'

Stan suddenly hated himself for not being able to supply balm to this couple's suffering. 'I'm very sorry. We've followed up a few sightings but they've all come to nothing, I'm afraid.'

Alan Berrisford poured himself a whisky. He offered one to Stan, who refused in the best traditions of the police force. Berrisford was a good-looking man in his mid-thirties; about five foot ten, he had dark hair, blue eyes, a charming smile and an easy manner. Elaine Berrisford must once have considered herself a lucky woman.

'My wife tried to go back to work, you know. She teaches in further education. But she found she could only stick it one day. Couldn't concentrate, couldn't keep her mind on it. I tried to tell her not to come back here but she insisted.'

Stan nodded. He understood. 'Is there anything you need? Would you like me to arrange for a WPC to stay?'

'No, thank you, Inspector. You've been very kind. I'm going to have to go back up north soon. I really can't stay too long. Business, you understand. I'll try and persuade my wife to come back with me. I think it's unhealthy for her being here, where it happened.'

'Quite, sir. We're doing our best, you know. God willing, we'll find him.' Stan tried to make himself sound convincing.

There was a noise behind him, the opening of a door. Stan turned and saw her. She stood in a long white nightgown, her hair uncombed, her eyes staring and sedated. He was

148

reminded of that poem he'd done at school; the one by Tennyson. 'The curse has come upon me, said the lady of Shalott.' Her face looked blank, exhausted, showing all the empty despair of the damned. Some curses were worse than Tennyson's.

As Wesley followed Rachel into the entrance hall of the police station, he nodded to Bob Naseby on the desk and noticed that Bob was looking him up and down speculatively.

'Sergeant Peterson, can I have a quick word?'

'Sure. What about?'

Bob leaned forward confidentially, as if it was important that Rachel didn't hear. 'Do you play cricket at all?'

Wesley, whose mind had been firmly fixed on murder, was unprepared for the sudden change of subject. 'Er, it has been known . . . but I'm no Brian Lara. Why?'

'We're a bit short of men for next season. Wondered if you fancied . . .'

'Can I give you an answer nearer the time, Bob? We've only just moved here and . . .'

'Oh, don't worry, I quite understand. You think about it. What are you, then? Batsman, bowler, all-rounder?'

'Er, bit of everything, but I wouldn't go so far as to say I'm an all-rounder. I'll have a think about it and let you know.'

When he'd made his escape, Rachel looked at him. 'Cricket, was it?'

Wesley nodded.

'Bob's what's known as a fanatic. Take my advice and don't get involved. Your wife won't thank you for it. It's not like football, ninety minutes then it's over. It goes on for hours, days on end. Your wife's got her career – she won't want to hang about a muddy field all weekend making sandwiches in her spare time. Just like I didn't. I speak from experience.'

Wesley detected bitterness in her voice. So that's what had happened to Rachel's last relationship. He had wondered.

'I told Bob I'd think about it. I didn't say I'd do it. Anyway, I doubt if I'll have the time.'

Rachel smiled. She was a pretty girl; she reminded him a bit of Pam when they had first met.

'How did you get on at that clinic?' she asked gently. 'Have they said anything?'

'Pam's got to go in for an investigative operation.'

'My sister-in-law had the same trouble, you know. She had all the tests going and they found nothing wrong. Then the doctor told her to relax and forget about it 'cause it's quite common, apparently, for people to adopt or give up hope then find they're pregnant once the pressure's off. She's got three kids now – little horrors, all of them.'

Wesley smiled at Rachel. If only Pam possessed her gift of common sense. They walked on.

Rachel still refused to go to Queenswear by car. Why pollute the place when you could take the ferry and get a bit of exercise into the bargain? she explained to Wesley, who had to accept the logic of her argument. They took the boat across the river.

Wesley was becoming used to travelling by water. He would have to, living in Tradmouth: the whole town centred on the river. The mouth of the Trad had been mentioned as a haven in the Anglo-Saxon Chronicle and the port had thrived in the Middle Ages and beyond, but, unlike the inspector's native Liverpool, it had been spared the curse of nineteenth-century expansion by its relative inaccessibility. If Wesley wanted to settle here, he would have to learn to live with water – and the noisy seagulls that screeched overhead.

When they got to Queenswear, Rachel and Wesley climbed the steps to number 38 and rung the bell to Flat 1. Of the two residents, Wesley reckoned that Mr Jackson would be the more amenable. Fortunately they found him in.

'Sorry to bother you again, Mr Jackson. If we could just ask you a few more questions?' Jackson let them in and mumbled something about putting the kettle on. He seemed resigned to their presence but not nervous.

They looked around the flat. The carpets were good-quality Axminster, but old and unfashionable. The furniture was an eclectic mixture; the type picked up over the years

150

in second-hand and junk shops: no better than the contents of the flat in Morbay, but no worse either.

When Jackson brought the tea in on a cheap tin tray decorated with stylised 1970s orange flowers, Wesley decided on the direct approach.

'This furniture, Mr Jackson . . . is it yours?'

'Good Lord, no. My wife kept all the furniture – everything. She got the lot,' he spat out bitterly.

'So where did it come from?'

'It was already here. It's a furnished flat.'

'We were told it was let unfurnished.'

'Oh, no. I don't know where you got that from.'

'So this furniture was here when Sharon Carteret lived here?'

Jackson shrugged. 'Must have been.'

Wesley leaned towards Jackson, taking him into his confidence. 'I must admit, Mr Jackson, we haven't got a search warrant at the moment. But we would like to have a look for anything that might have been left behind by the dead girl. Did you find anything yourself?' Jackson shook his head. 'Now you must realise that we're not interested in any of your possessions and . . .'

'Go ahead. Search wherever you like,' said Jackson, indifferent.

Wesley thanked him. He felt sorry for Jackson, a man defeated by life.

The search was concentrated on forgotten places: the backs of drawers where objects might have fallen unnoticed; the rear of the airing cupboard; behind chests of drawers. Wesley wished he hadn't worn a suit, and the dust made Rachel sneeze. They tried to ignore Jackson's sparse belongings. From what they had gathered, the man had been through enough without having the police nosing through his personal effects.

The harvest of finds was meagre: a cheese grater fallen behind the kitchen drawers; two pairs of washed-out Marks and Spencer's knickers behind the dressing table in the bedroom. It had been a good idea of Rachel's, but . . .

The living room was last. There was very little in it apart from a green Dralon three-piece suite and a television – and of course the bureau. The bureau was the only piece in the room Wesley would have described as a decent bit of furniture. It was dark wood, probably 1920s, with a sloping front that dropped down to form a desk. In contrast to the rest of the room's contents, its quality and solidity shone out. It was surprising that Sharon hadn't taken it with her. Perhaps she had left in such a hurry that she had had to travel light. Wesley began to take the drawers out. This was the last thing; they had searched everywhere else.

He found the address book wedged behind one of the small drawers in the top part of the bureau. Torn and bent, it had probably been discarded and forgotten when a new one was acquired. He picked up the small, tattered book and looked inside, making certain it didn't belong to Jackson. Then he called Rachel over and showed her his prize. Her face lit up with triumph. 'Has it got her name in?'

'Right here, in the front.' Wesley popped it into a plastic bag.

Jackson crept shyly into the room. He had been keeping out of their way. 'Did you find anything?'

'Yes, thank you, Mr Jackson. We found an address book behind one of the drawers in the bureau. You've not seen it before?' He held up the bag containing the book.

'No. I just put my things in the drawers. Didn't pull them out. You don't, do you?'

'No.' Wesley felt it was time they were going. 'Thank you again, Mr Jackson. You've been very helpful.'

Jackson smirked shyly and looked at his feet. 'I was glad of the company. Will you stay for a cup of tea?' The invitation was pathetically eager.

Rachel looked at Jackson, a man in a grey cardigan whose wife had robbed him of everything including his dignity. 'I'm sorry, Mr Jackson, but we are on a murder inquiry. Thanks for the offer anyway.' She gave him her sweetest smile and hoped it wouldn't be misinterpreted.

'Shall we pay Mrs Hughes a visit?' she asked significantly. 'I think she's in. I heard the floorboards creak above the bedroom.'

Wesley nodded.

They hadn't far to go to their next port of call. Once outside the front door, Wesley rang the doorbell for Flat 2. There was no answer.

Upstairs, behind the net curtain, Mrs Hughes stood very still, watching, hardly daring to breathe. She could see Rachel's face clearly – and the plastic bag containing something that looked like a diary in her hand. They had found something. Why, she asked herself, hadn't she searched the downstairs flat thoroughly when she had the chance? She watched the two police officers until they disappeared out of sight down the road.

Chapter 20

Last night as I lay with Jennet, after I had had my pleasure of her, she did tell me that she was with child. I know not what I should do. Elizabeth doth suspect nothing – of that I am sure.

Extract from the journal of John Banized,
1 July 1623

That evening Pam thought it was about time she made an effort. She put on her jeans and some make-up and walked arm in arm with her husband, as they had done when they first met, down the narrow streets to the Tradmouth Arms. She had felt better since her visit to Dr Downey; ready to face the world again.

And she was looking forward to seeing Neil again. She wondered if he'd changed at all after these many years.

Neil waved as they entered the pub. He still wore his hair long and straggly and his clothes looked like Oxfam's rejects. He hadn't changed . . . in appearance at least.

He greeted Pam with an apprehensive kiss. She smiled at him in a friendly way – but then her feelings had never matched his own. Once they had sat down he began telling her about the dig and the Banizeds' house. It was best, he thought, to keep to impersonal matters. When Wesley had tried once or twice to tell her, she had been in no state to take it in, but this time she listened with interest.

'So the skeleton might be this Jennet, whoever she is? She must have been murdered and buried in the cellar by . . .

well, I suppose the master of the house is the main suspect, don't you think, Wesley? Come on.' She nudged him. 'Wake up. We need your professional advice.'

Wesley, who had been contemplating the Sharon Carteret case over his beer, came back to the past with a jolt. 'What advice?'

'Pam wants to find out about our skeletons in the cellar,' Neil said. 'Your turn to get a round in, Wes.'

'Where are Matt and Jane tonight?'

'Gone to see a film in Neston. It's off and on with those two.' Neil finished his drink and returned to the subject that interested him much more than his colleagues' love lives. 'I've been back to the museum. They've turned up some wills. Got the copies here.'

Neil produced a few photocopied sheets and handed them to Wesley. Pam leaned over to see. Against her expectations, she was finding it quite interesting. 'This one's John Banized's will.'

'Yes.' An idea suddenly came to Wesley. Obvious – he should have thought of it before. 'JB, on the ring – John Banized.'

'Could be. Now there's a thought – about the right date too. In his will he left everything to his second wife and his son, Thomas, who eventually became mayor. He left small legacies to servants and relations as well but there's no mention of a Jennet.'

'Well, there wouldn't be if he'd bumped her off and hid her down in the cellar, would there?'

'It's the ring that bothers me – to Jennet with all my thanks. What was he thanking her for?'

Pam giggled. 'Services rendered, I should think.'

'I don't think he'd bother to say thanks. In those days the master of the house probably considered it well within his rights to tumble a few maidservants.'

'Maybe she wasn't a maidservant. Or perhaps he wasn't that type. Perhaps he had a conscience.' Wesley drained his glass.

'Someone killed her,' said Pam. 'Conscience or no conscience. We'll probably never know.'

'We might if we can find the journal.' Neil sat back, watching the effect of his words.

'What journal?' asked Wesley, suddenly interested.

'It's mentioned in all the wills since the middle of the seventeenth century. They all say more or less the same thing – to my eldest son the journal of John Banized, to be kept privy. It seemed it was passed from father to son. Probably contained some dreadful family secret.'

'Jennet's murder?' Wesley wasn't a detective for nothing.

'Could be. It's not mentioned again after the middle of the eighteenth century. I'd love to know what happened to it . . . if it still exists.'

'Mmm.' Wesley got up to go to the bar. 'Keep digging, Neil. You never know what might turn up.'

Pam sat back, relaxed. For the first time in months she felt able to take an interest in what was going on around her; she even found herself interested in the Banizeds and Jennet. The drink had gone to her head slightly and she felt a glow of wellbeing.

On the way home, she hardly noticed the steepness of the streets. She and Wesley walked arm in arm again. And when they went to bed that night they made love as if it was their first time.

'You look as if you're in a good mood, Wesley,' observed Rachel as he walked into the office the next morning. 'You can give us a hand ringing round some of the numbers in this address book.' She threw a typewritten list at him good-humouredly.

'Any progress?'

'I've tracked down one of her old friends. She told the same story as that woman, Dot, at the building society. As soon as Sharon took up with this Chris character, she dropped her old friends like hot bricks.'

'Did she have many friends?' He found himself feeling sorry for the girl.

'Those she did have she seemed to lose when this Chris came on the scene. She must have been very easily led.'

'Or infatuated. Love is blind, as they say.'

Love had so far never rendered Rachel even mildly

156

short-sighted. She shook her head. 'I've found her grand-mother's address in here too, by the way.'

'Did you contact her?'

'I'd need a medium. She's dead.' Rachel studied the sheets. 'The rest seem to be people like dentists, work colleagues, hospitals, that sort of thing.'

'Keep at it.' Wesley moved to his own desk and shifted round some paperwork. After a few minutes contemplating his workload, he spoke to Rachel again. 'That Mrs Hughes . . . hasn't it struck you as odd that she didn't mention Sharon being pregnant?'

'If she'd had an abortion she might never have known.'

'Mmmm. I'd still like to speak to her again. I didn't like her, did you?'

'No, not particularly. But we can't go round arresting people we don't like – cells'd be full.' Rachel smiled. 'All the same, I don't think she was telling us the whole truth. And why lie about the furniture?'

'Is the inspector in yet?'

'No sign. Bet he's slept in again. When it's Christmas we should all club together and buy him an alarm clock.'

'Don't suppose it's easy getting up on time when you're on your own. Pam always wakes up first.'

'I don't think it's been easy for him full stop since his wife died. He wanders round like a lost soul in that scruffy old anorak of his. He needs someone to take him in hand.'

The door opened and Heffernan trudged in. The subject of the conversation swiftly changed.

'Morning, everyone. No excuse. Can't blame seagulls on the line at Queenswear Junction. I overslept, all right? What's new? Anyone confessed?'

'I've been going through the address book, sir. Tracked down one of her friends. I was just telling Wesley, it seems she lost touch with everyone when she took up with this Chris. Her grandmother's dead so I don't know if there are any relatives. I've only done a few pages though, sir.'

'Keep at it, Rach. What about you, Wes? You look full of the joys of spring. Anything to report?'

Wesley explained his misgivings about Mrs Hughes.

'You reckon she was in when you searched the bottom flat but she didn't answer the door?'

'Rachel heard a noise upstairs, sir.'

'And then the lie about the furniture ... I think we ought to drop in on Mrs Hughes for a cup of tea, Wes.' Heffernan began to put his anorak back on. 'If we're lucky we might get chocolate biccies.'

They left Rachel dialling another number from the address book.

Stan Jenkins looked around for something to put his cup of tea down on. He didn't want to damage the polished surface of the coffee table. He pulled a glossy magazine towards him and used that. Nice coffee table; nice place for a holiday cottage. There must be plenty of money in wine.

Elaine Berrisford reappeared from the kitchen. She was dressed in dark trousers and a patterned shirt and looked calmer than he had seen her before, but still pale and drawn.

'Just called to see how you were, Elaine. Nice tea ... Earl Grey?'

She nodded.

'I had an aunt who always gave us Earl Grey. Never have it at home, though. Wife's not keen.' He was aware he was rambling on but he felt he had to fill the silence.

She spoke; well spoken but with a slight Northern intonation. 'I don't suppose you've ...'

'No, er, sorry, nothing to report. You'd be the first to know.'

'You said yesterday there'd been sightings. Where?'

'Well, we always get lots of calls in cases like these. From all over the place. They're all looked into, I can assure—'

'Have you had many round here?'

'None that have come to anything. If we thought we'd found him, you'd be the first ...'

'Tell me about them.'

'Well, I don't see that it'd do any good. They've all been ...' Stan was starting to feel flustered. The woman was leaning towards him, her eyes desperate. He didn't want to get her hopes up, nor did he want her to think he was keeping something from her.

'Please, Stan. Tell me about the sightings round here. I've got to know . . . please.'

Stan felt awkward. He knew he was about to do the inadvisable. 'It was just this old woman – bit of a nutter. She said she'd seen Jonathon in Morbay. She's been let out of somewhere, if you see what I mean. Totally unreliable, I'm afraid. You mustn't get your hopes up.'

'Jonathon . . . Did she say he was on his own?'

'Well, she saw him with a man. Turned out to be his dad.'

'Did you see him, talk to him?'

'No, we didn't, actually. They'd moved out by the time we tracked them down. But the neighbours said they were father and son – said the lad looked the image of his dad. And the hair was the wrong colour – darker than Jonathon's. I'm very sorry. I shouldn't have told you, should I. It's upset you . . .'

She sat back and took a sip of her tea. 'No, no, it's quite all right. I'll be okay now.'

Stan thought he saw hope return to her eyes.

Gerry Heffernan looked at Wesley. 'Doesn't look like she's in.'

'My guess is that she's not answering the door.' Wesley rang again; three loud, long rings. He wanted to show her that they weren't prepared to go away. His persistence was rewarded. The approaching footsteps were slow and reluctant.

Wesley smiled when Mrs Hughes opened the door, hoping it would put her at her ease. 'I wonder if we could have another word with you, Mrs Hughes. Do you remember me? Detective Sergeant Peterson. And this is my colleague, Detective Inspector Heffernan. May we come in?'

Mrs Hughes was dressed as immaculately as before. She held the front door open disdainfully and let them pass. Tea wasn't mentioned.

'Just a couple of things I want to clear up, Mrs Hughes. May we sit down?' She nodded, unwelcoming.

Heffernan spoke. 'Nice flat you've got here, Mrs Hughes. You own the one downstairs, I believe.' She nodded again. 'My daughter rents a flat in Manchester – she's a student at the music college. Furnished, it is. Pretty grotty, but then I don't suppose they notice their surroundings at that age, do they? Too busy having a good time. I told her to get one unfurnished – it'd be cheaper, and she could always cadge some sticks of furniture.'

Mrs Hughes was staring at the inspector, wondering where this was all leading. She hadn't got all day to listen to the housing problems of some scruffy middle-aged Liverpudlian's daughter. She looked away impatiently.

'I suppose the one downstairs is furnished?'

So this is where it had been leading. Mrs Hughes swallowed hard and hoped the policemen wouldn't notice her unease. 'Er, yes. It is.'

'The thing is, you told my colleagues that Sharon Carteret rented the flat unfurnished. Is there a reason for that?'

The woman shifted in her chair and thought quickly. 'Yes. It was let unfurnished then.'

'So where did the furniture come from? Did you decide to let it furnished, buy the stuff after she'd gone, or what?'

Mrs Hughes looked distinctly uncomfortable. 'Er, she left it. I presume she moved to somewhere furnished or . . .'

'She left everything?'

Mrs Hughes nodded, looking for the first time at a disadvantage. 'Yes. It wasn't very good furniture. She might have bought new or . . .'

'Can you tell us what happened when Sharon Carteret left, Mrs Hughes?' Wesley became formal.

'I . . . she just left, didn't give me any notice. I was rather annoyed.'

'Were you here when she moved out? Did her boyfriend help her to move her things?'

'I wasn't here. I went away to stay with friends for a few days. When I got back she'd gone. She'd posted the key through my letterbox.'

'She left no forwarding address, no hint of where she'd gone? Never mentioned a new flat?'

'No.'

Gerry Heffernan stood up to leave. Wesley watched the woman's face and saw relief. 'Thank you, Mrs Hughes, you've been very helpful.'

Wesley stood up to follow his boss. Surely he'd missed out the most important question of all. But Heffernan turned to Mrs Hughes as she was about to open the front door.

'How did you get on when Sharon was pregnant? You don't allow kids here, do you? What happened to her baby? Did she have it adopted or what?'

Neat, thought Wesley. The woman had been caught completely off guard.

'I . . . I . . .'

'She was pregnant, wasn't she, Mrs Hughes? What happened to the baby?'

'I don't know. I just told her she couldn't keep it here. I never asked what arrangements she made.'

'Were you here when she went into labour? What hospital did she go to?'

'She led her own life, Inspector. I didn't know and I didn't want to know. If these girls mess up their lives, I'm not responsible. Ours was purely a business relationship – landlord and tenant. I was the last person she'd confide in. Now, if you'll excuse me, I have an important appointment.'

Once outside, Heffernan spoke first. 'Hardly a product of the caring, sharing nineties, is she?'

'Hardly, sir. We didn't even get a cup of tea.'

Rachel picked up the heap of files and saw the yellow rectangle of paper she had fixed to her desk after she had returned from seeing Mrs Willis in Morbay. 'Get in touch with landlord.'

She had the address and number from Mrs Willis; she picked up the phone and dialled. A Liz answered. When Rachel introduced herself, Liz sounded vexed but grudgingly granted Rachel permission to call into the office, saying pointedly that she'd been bothered by the police before. Rachel thought she'd better take Steve, but she would do the driving.

When they drew up outside the office, with its flashy logo and vertical blinds, Steve announced he'd been there before – with Wesley, on the trail of Karen Giordino. The firm had been her landlord too; but that was hardly surprising as the company owned over half the private rented property in

Morbay. Steve got out of the car, squaring up for another encounter with the assertive Liz.

Liz kept them waiting; she was with a client. When she eventually emerged, she gave Steve her best scowl and looked Rachel up and down with suspicion. She led them into her office and reluctantly delved into her pale wood filing cabinets for the appropriate records.

The flat had been rented in the name of a Ms Sharon Carteret. She had paid by cheque, a deposit and a month's rent in advance. She didn't know the names of the other occupants, although she heard from the tenant upstairs that there was a child – not against the rules in this particular property. The tenant only stayed a month, moved out some time in late September.

Rachel felt disappointed. Liz had told her nothing they didn't know already. She thought of one more question. 'Does it say in your file when she rented the flat, what date?'

Liz pursed her lips and opened the folder again. 'Yes. August fifteenth. Let furnished.'

'Thank you very much for your help.' Rachel gave Liz her most ingratiating smile and left. August 15 – that must mean something. What had made Sharon Carteret leave her flat and her job at the end of August? The renting of the flat a couple of weeks earlier suggested a plan of action, hardly a spur-of-the-moment decision. What change had occurred in Sharon's routine life? Rachel pondered the question all the way back to Tradmouth.

Elaine Berrisford parked her VW Golf by the promenade. Morbay was a big place. It was a question of where to begin looking.

The day was sunny for late September – an Indian summer. Mothers with young children wandered up and down the promenade enjoying the bonus of sunshine. Some ventured onto the beach. Elaine's eyes watched them all, hoping to see one child. Jonathon had been here – she knew he had. A mother always knew.

Chapter 21

I have had little time to keep this journal as Oliver hath been ill again of the sweating fever and the shop hath been most busy. Yet I am glad of the occupation as I do not have much dealing with my wife whose sickness hath abated and who rules the household once more.

Jennet's condition doth not yet show. I continue to go to her each night and have the sweetest pleasure in her bed. Her breasts do grow larger. I find her more comely now than ever. What shall become of this?

Extract from the journal of John Banized,
15 July 1623

Sitting at her desk in a first-floor office of Tradmouth police station, Rachel, using a telephone, fax and computer, was gradually building up a picture of Sharon Carteret's life. When it comes down to it, she thought in a rare fit of philosophising, our lives these days can all be reduced to a series of electronic impulses.

She was on to the back page of the address book and had just spoken to an old friend of Sharon's with the surname Williams. The friend had been at school with her in Morbay but had lost touch about four years ago when Sharon had taken up with Chris – a story now familiar to Rachel. The friend thought Chris might be in the building trade, didn't know for certain. Rachel made a note. It was worth following up.

There was one other entry on the page. No name, just a number. She picked up the phone and dialled.

'Good morning. Morbay Clinic. How may I help you?' said a female voice on the other end of the phone. Rachel hadn't expected this. She introduced herself. The voice became wary. 'I'll put you through to our Clinical Director, Dr Downey.'

The line went dead for a while then a smooth male voice broke the silence. 'Good morning, Constable. Dr Downey, Clinical Director. What may I do for you?'

Rachel explained.

'I'm very sorry, Constable, but I can't help you. I've never heard of this young woman. I'm sorry not to be of more assistance. But she's not been a patient at this clinic, of that I'm sure.'

'Perhaps your records ...'

'I'm absolutely certain, Constable. I've never treated anybody of that name.'

Rachel felt it would be fruitless to argue with the man. 'Well, thank you for your help, Dr Downey. I'm sorry to have bothered you.' She put the phone down. Dr Downey seemed very sure of his facts. Too sure? And he had assumed Sharon to be a patient rather than an employee. Perhaps that was a natural assumption, but Rachel had phrased her questions to encompass both possibilities. Maybe she mistrusted smooth-talking men and her prejudice was affecting her judgement.

Gerry Heffernan, who certainly didn't fall into the smooth-talking category, came out of his office and asked her how she was getting on. He made a mental note to ask Wesley about the set-up at the Morbay Clinic.

It wasn't often that Stan Jenkins wandered into Heffernan's office. But wander in he did, resembling the proverbial lost soul. He was looking for someone to talk to, preferably someone of his own rank.

'How's it going, Stan? Take a seat. We're out of cyanide, you'll have to make do with tea. God, man, you look

164

depressed. What's happened?' Heffernan hesitated for a moment as the possibility occurred to him. 'You've not found Jonathon, have you?'

'No. I almost wish we would – get it over with one way or the other. It's the not knowing. It's the mother – she's come down here again. It's getting to me, Gerry, it really is.'

Heffernan nodded sympathetically.

'I can't take much more, Gerry. When this lot's over, I'm taking early retirement.'

'Your wife won't like it, you getting under her feet all day.' Stan gave a weak smile. 'We all have bad times, Stan. We all feel like jacking it in when it's not going as we want it. You've got too involved. It's easily done in a case like this – a missing kid gets to everyone.'

'The mother's taken to wandering round now, looking for him herself. I mentioned that woman, the nutter, and next thing I know Mrs Berrisford's taken herself off to Morbay. She's only going to make herself worse.'

'At least she thinks she's doing something. It's probably what she needs.'

'She rang me when she got back. She seemed so sure she'd find Jonathon, so sure he was alive.'

'Try and forget about it, Stan. I'll take you for a pie and chips this lunch-time if you're feeling naughty.'

Stan fingered his waistline and nodded.

Steve Carstairs was getting used to building sites. The trouble was that every time he thought he was getting close to finding out about the stolen building materials he came up against a metaphorical brick wall. The stuff he'd found at Mr Carl's sister's cottage was pinched, right enough, but the builder hadn't known the name of the man who sold them to him – just a bloke in a pub, a dark, youngish bloke with an earring – no names; always better to keep names out of it.

He picked his way over the foundations of some embryonic executive homes on the outskirts of Neston, looking for the site manager. PC Johnson was following behind, trying not to get mud all over his highly polished boots. Steve stopped and consulted his notebook. That batch of plastic guttering was nicked – he could tell by the reference number on the packaging. That would be the second thing he would ask about.

Steve thought it was a bit of a long shot – one of Sharon's friends thought Chris might, just might, be in the building trade. He had asked on five sites already that morning. He wasn't getting his hopes up.

The site manager was a middle-aged man with sparse oily hair and an oily manner. He was only too happy to help the police – always was.

Steve asked the routine question, trying to keep the boredom out of his voice, expecting the usual negative reply. It hardly registered when the manager answered in the affirmative.

'Yes, there's a bloke called Chris – brickie. I suppose he fits your description. He's casual, like. Hasn't been in for a couple of weeks. Domestic commitments, he said.'

Steve looked at Johnson and grinned in triumph. 'I don't suppose you've got his details, have you?'

The manager went over to a battered steel filing cabinet and pulled out a card. 'Here we are. Christopher Manners.' He gave the address too – it was the flat in Morbay.

'He's moved on since then. Have you got his new address?'

The manager looked surprised. 'No. He never said he was moving. He'll let me know when he comes back to work, I suppose.'

'What sort of man is he? What's he like?'

'Doesn't say much, doesn't cause trouble. Good worker – that's why I keep employing him. Keeps himself to himself. Strong silent type, I suppose. You can ask any of the blokes, they'd all say the same.'

'Is he married?'

'Don't think so, but he mentioned a girlfriend once. Needed some time off, said she hadn't been well.'

'Was her name Sharon?'

'Don't know. I told you, he didn't say much.'

'That guttering . . . where did you get it?'

'Chris got it for us. Knew somewhere giving a good deal.'

'Is that usual?'

166

The manager shifted uncomfortably in his chair. 'It happens. You save a bit on materials. It benefits everyone, doesn't it?'

'Not when they're nicked it doesn't.'

The manager sat there open-mouthed, pretending innocence very convincingly.

Wesley looked forward to getting out of the office. It was far more pleasant to wander round Tradmouth than to trudge the streets of London. Today he was torn between buying a sandwich from the cake shop near the police station or a pasty from the little dark shop on St Margaret's Street that sent out such inviting smells whenever he walked past. The pasty won. He sank his teeth into the soft flaky pastry and wondered why he'd never sampled this delight before.

As he was in St Margaret's Street already, he told himself, he might as well go and say hello to Neil. Jane was hard at work in a trench when he let himself into the site. Darren stood watching, obviously fascinated. Jane handed him a small trowel and he gave her a brush, like a theatre nurse assisting a surgeon. Darren's metal detector lay discarded in a far corner of the site. It seemed that Neil's experiment in community service was a success.

It turned out that Neil wasn't there. Matt was in the hut and he invited Wesley in to view the latest finds: a buckle; a small pile of leather shoes, preserved but so matted together that they were unrecognisable; some pottery. Neil had gone to Exeter to organise the reconstruction of the skeleton's face with Professor Jensen.

As Wesley wandered back to the station, his hands greasy with the remains of his pasty, he wondered about the conversation Rachel had had with Dr Downey. It was strange that the doctor had denied having met Sharon Carteret without checking through his records. Wesley's memory wasn't that good – he could hardly recall every person he'd ever had dealings with in the course of his career; and his career hadn't been as long as Dr Downey's and many of the characters he had met were far more memorable. Either Dr Downey possessed a remarkable memory or he was lying.

He would mention it to Heffernan, see if he shared his misgivings.

When Wesley returned to the station the inspector was pacing up and down his office floor. He shouted to the sergeant to come in.

'I've had a thought, Wes. I can't get an answer from Stan Jenkins at the moment but I'm going to check if that woman – the nutter, the one who keeps saying she's seen the missing kid – if the house where she saw the kid with his dad is the same one as this Chris character was living at with this mysterious child of unknown origin.'

'You think there's a connection? You think the kid might be . . .'

'Hang on, Wesley, I don't know what to think yet. It's just a thought. Probably nothing in it. Even if it was Chris it still doesn't mean . . . Oh, I wish someone'd find this kid and put Stan Jenkins out of his misery. The mother's back down here and apparently she's started looking for the kid herself. Stan's got himself in a right state about it. He's talking of early retirement.'

'I'll go up to Inspector Jenkins's office, sir, see if anyone knows if it's the same address.'

Heffernan nodded and Wesley changed the subject and told his boss about Dr Downey.

'When's your wife's op?'

'Tomorrow. Nine thirty.'

'We'll send someone round at eleven, then, to look through the records. Can't have the good doctor upset before he slices your nearest and dearest open, can we?' He grinned wickedly. 'Doesn't matter if he kills a few in the afternoon. Tell Rachel well done, will you.'

Wesley left Heffernan's office and went up to the second floor where the search for Jonathon Berrisford was being co-ordinated. After a few words with a detective sergeant assigned to the case, he had the information his inspector was looking for. He hurried down the stairs back to the office, wondering what Heffernan would make of it.

Elaine Berrisford went over to Queenswear on the car ferry. She was feeling more positive than she had for weeks. The car thudded over the ramp as she drove off the ferry, and she thrust the gear lever into second to negotiate the steep street to number 38. She parked up on the pavement outside the house; there was still room for cars to get past.

She hesitated by the front door then rang the top bell, still unsure whether she was doing the right thing. She had kept away since it happened. Should she be back there now?

The footsteps from inside the house drew closer. Elaine felt like running back to the car and driving away before the door opened. But she stood, waiting.

When Mrs Hughes opened the door, she stared at Elaine for a few seconds before standing aside to let her in. Once in the hall she put her arms around her and Elaine, exhausted and past tears, clung to the older woman.

'Elaine, I'm so sorry. Why didn't you come when it happened? You should have come.'

'I couldn't. I couldn't face anyone. Oh, Mary, you don't know what it's been like.'

Mrs Hughes led her through to her living room and sat her down on the sofa. She knelt on the floor beside her.

'If I'd known all this would happen . . .' She stood up and walked to the fireplace, her back to Elaine. After a while she spoke again. 'Oh, Elaine, I blame myself for all this, I really do.'

Chapter 22

In the shop today Mistress Webb did remark upon Jennet's figure and did look most knowingly at my wife. Elizabeth did speak to me of it and asked if Jennet was courting a young man. I did say I knew not.

Jennet hath never reproached me nor spoken of the child. It can not be long before Elizabeth doth discover the truth of it. I am afeared and I have begged Jennet to conceal her condition.

Extract from the journal of John Banized,
14 August 1623

'You were right.' Wesley looked triumphant as he strode into Heffernan's office. 'It is the same address. It was Chris that that woman saw with the kid.'

'I think it's worth another visit to Morbay. I could do with a trip to the seaside. I'll come over with you.'

They set out in the late afternoon sunshine. It was a pleasant drive across the river on the car ferry then through the field-lined country roads until they hit the outskirts of Morbay. The journey gave Gerry Heffernan a chance to gather his thoughts.

'So what have we got, Wes? A young woman has a baby two years back and nobody knows. Baby disappears and there's no record of its birth. She continues to see her boy-friend, who we can assume is the baby's father – there's been no suggestion otherwise. She carries on in her job till

170

the middle of August then she packs it in and gets a flat with her boyfriend and a child who's about the right age to be the one she had. Any ideas, Sergeant?'

'The child is hers. She either had it adopted or someone looked after it for her. She gave up her job and her flat in anticipation of getting the child back.'

'So why was she killed? And why did the boyfriend disappear as soon as he knew she was dead? And what about the money? Those payments into her bank account?'

'Could she have sold the child to someone, sir, then changed her mind?'

'I think you might have something there, Wes. You've been through it yourself, you can imagine how desperate some people get for a child of their own. Would you buy a child, Wes? How far would you go?'

'I don't know about me. But Pam; I reckon she'd go as far as it takes.' He thought for a moment. 'But the boyfriend's still got the child ... well, we can assume he has. If someone – the person who adopted or looked after the child – killed her to get him back, the plan went wrong.'

'Or maybe this is all speculation. The child Sharon might have died at birth. She might have had it in that flat in Queenswear and Mrs Hughes helped her cover the whole thing up. Maybe once Sharon and Chris were living together with this kid – maybe his by another girlfriend – things snapped. They had a row and he bashed her head in. Simple domestic, like most murders.'

'Why give up her job ... and change flats?'

'Presumably so they could have this kid living with them.'

'Would she give up her job to look after someone else's kid?'

Heffernan shrugged. Wesley had a point. They had arrived at 33 Albert Road. Wesley stopped the engine.

'There's an old lady lives upstairs; a Mrs Willis. Have you got the photograph, sir?'

The inspector nodded. 'Will we get tea, do you think?'

'According to Rachel as much as you can drink.'

Mrs Willis looked genuinely pleased to see them. 'Oh, come in, come in. Haven't you brought that nice policewoman with you? Come upstairs. I'll get the kettle on.'

Settled comfortably with tea and chocolate biscuits, Gerry Heffernan produced the photograph.

'The little boy who lived downstairs . . . is this him?'

She studied the picture and handed it back. 'It's like little Daniel but his hair was darker.'

'You've not had a visit from the police before about this child?'

'No. I've been away at my daughter's, but my neighbours mentioned the police had been round. Some poor woman who keeps claiming that every child she sees is this missing child, I believe.' She was sharper than Heffernan had given her credit for. 'That is a picture of that missing boy, isn't it – that Jonathon Berrisford? You think little Daniel may have been Jonathon.'

'Is it possible?'

'Anything's possible, Inspector. But I must admit it never occurred to me; Sharon seemed so . . . loving with him, just like any other young mother, and he seemed happy with her. Hardly how a kidnapped child would behave. I think you can forget that idea, Inspector, I really do.'

Heffernan was comfortable. He was reluctant to get up out of the ancient sofa that had moulded itself to his body like a living entity. But they had to leave. There was an important question he had to ask Stan Jenkins.

Rachel had an aversion to building sites and it was the third she had visited that afternoon. Messy, muddy places populated by leering male chauvinists. She let Steve lead the way.

The bricklayer glanced up from the neat section of wall he was creating. He looked warily at the warrant cards they showed.

'Chris Manners? Yeah, he works casual, like. I don't know him well, mind, but I know he sometimes goes in the Anchor on a Saturday night. You might find him there.'

At last, something solid. Rachel decided to push her luck. 'Do you know much about him?'

'Oh, he keeps 'imself to 'imself, like. He sometimes gets materials cut price, I know that. And he works off and on. Comes and goes.'

'Is that usual?'

'Not usual. Most of us work when we can – we've got mouths to feed. I reckon he only works on a site when he runs short. All right for some. But as I say he gets these materials – reckon that's where he gets his living.'

'Where does he get them?' Steve asked sharply.

The bricklayer became wary. Rachel cursed Steve. Just when things were going so well.

'Don't rightly know ... couldn't tell you. I don't ask no questions. Boss buys 'em, we build with 'em.'

'Are there any of his materials on the site now?'

'Couldn't tell you, mate. I just lay the bricks.'

Rachel tried to retrieve the situation. 'The Anchor? The one in Tradmouth?'

'That's right, my luvver. And don't tell him I told you.'

The bricklayer turned away from them and resumed his work, as if to make a point. The interview was over.

'Why the sudden interest, Gerry?' Stan Jenkins looked up from his computer screen.

'To tell you the truth, Stan, there are a few coincidences. The kid your favourite witness saw and swore was Jonathon Berrisford just happens to be the kid living with Sharon Carteret's boyfriend.'

'Did you show Jonathon's photo to anyone who knew this child?'

'The lady upstairs. She said it was very like him but the hair was the wrong colour.'

'Could always have dyed it.'

'That's what I thought. But the kid's name was Daniel and he treated Sharon like his mum.'

'Kids of that age are adaptable.'

'Is there any chance ... do you know if Jonathon was adopted by the Berrisfords? Is he their real son?'

'As far as I know he's the Berrisfords' child, all right. It's one of the first questions I asked.'

'That's that, then. Another theory bites the dust.'

Heffernan returned to his office. 'You know that mate of yours in London, Wes, the one who looks up birth certificates?' Wesley nodded. He knew what was coming. 'Can you get him to look up Jonathon Berrisford's? I've written down his birthday and parents' names.' He handed him a scrap of paper. 'See if you can track it down, will you. Probably born up north . . . Cheshire, I think.'

Two hours later the office fax bleeped into action and produced a copy of a birth certificate. The name, date and parents' names were as expected, but Wesley looked with interest at the place of birth. The Morbay Clinic.

The autumn sun streamed through the windows of the room in the university where Professor Jensen worked silently. His fingers moulded the modelling material and pressed it against the cast of the skull to recreate the muscles of the face. Some used computer simulation these days, but the professor preferred the real thing; the sense of creation.

Neil watched, fascinated. The professor was taking his time. Such painstaking work couldn't be hurried. He looked at his watch. He'd have to get back to the dig, see how things were progressing. There was a lot of paperwork to catch up on, and he had that appointment with the vicar tomorrow morning.

The vicar was keen. His eyes had shone when he talked of the Banized family tree he was creating. Family trees, he had said, could be the most revealing documents in existence, telling their story generation upon generation.

Neil wondered whether Wesley would like to come with him – he would certainly find it interesting. Then he remembered that Pam was going into hospital tomorrow. Wesley would have other things on his mind.

Pam had looked well when he'd seen her. It had been so long – must be seven years. She'd looked good, hadn't changed. If things had been different, if he hadn't taken her back to his flat and introduced her to Wesley. But he wasn't one to feel bitter about what might have been; he hoped things would go well for Pam tomorrow.

Neil stood up to leave and the professor, still kneading and pressing the modelling material, layer upon layer, nodded to him. The face was taking shape. Soon she'd be there . . . Jennet.

Gerry Heffernan found something liberating about singing his heart out after a day's work. After going through Sunday's anthem five times, he felt a good deal more relaxed – which was more than could be said for the choirmaster.

Dorothy Truscot warbled away in the front row of the sopranos, fully recovered from the ordeal of her gruesome discovery. Heffernan noticed that her fifteen minutes of fame, and having her name in the local papers, had given her a new confidence. She had been rather withdrawn after her husband had died but now she gossiped with the best of them over tea and biscuits after choir practice. He reflected sadly how fame changed people.

He found himself behind Dorothy in the queue for the tea urn. She was talking to a plump soprano somewhat younger than herself, another member of the League of Widows. He caught snatches of their conversation.

' . . . And she threw him out . . . kept everything. But he's got a flat now . . . Do you remember that woman who was on the jewellery stall at the WI . . . always dresses beautifully . . . lives over at Queenswear? Well, she had a flat vacant downstairs . . . so he's moved in there. You know her, don't you? . . . Mary Hughes . . . was Mary Berrisford before she married again. But that was before your time, Dorothy . . . a few years back now . . . people think she's a bit stand-offish but she's not so bad once you get to know her . . .'

'Excuse me, ladies, but I couldn't help overhearing. About Mary Hughes from Queenswear . . .' They turned and looked at him. How dare a member of the male gender intrude on their gossip. 'Do you know her?'

The plump soprano eyed him suspiciously. 'I don't know her well, only through the WI.'

'Did you say her maiden name was Berrisford?'

'Not her maiden name, her first husband's name. He was a solicitor in Queenswear. She married again. She's been widowed twice. Why?'

The plump soprano had been more than helpful. Dorothy Truscot was not to be forgotten. 'Is it something to do with the police?' She turned to her friend. 'Did you know Mr

175

Heffernan was a police inspector, Pearl? He was in charge when I found the body.'

The plump soprano looked worried. 'I hope I haven't said anything out of turn.'

'No, no, it's nothing, really, only a minor detail. Thanks anyway, ladies. Sorry to have interrupted.'

He walked away, his mind turning over this new information.

The fat soprano watched him appraisingly. 'Did I hear he was a widower, Dorothy?'

Heffernan's bedtime reading that night was a sheaf of interview notes. He scanned through them until he found what he was looking for. Mary Hughes had a son who lived up north. It was a long shot. Berrisford was a common name: the son might be in Scotland, Leeds, Newcastle ... anywhere. But if this was a connection between Sharon Carteret and the Berrisfords ... It was a long shot.

Chapter 23

I have left off writing this journal for many months. I have been much occupied with trade as my ships had a goodly season and I have not possessed the inclination to write of my affairs which have caused me much anxious worry.

Elizabeth is very near her time and she doth daily expect her pains to begin. She hath found it in her heart to keep Jennet in our employ. She doth consider it an act of Christian charity to help one so fallen by the wayside, as she says. She knows not the truth of it but I do sometime wonder if Jennet's looks toward me will betray our situation. But mostly Jennet is the most discreet of creatures and welcomes me to her bed despite her condition.

Jennet is also near her time and my wife doth think to employ her as a wet nurse if her own milk is not good. Jennet doth like this suggestion ill and I did promise I would put objections to my wife. Jennet did ask me last evening if I would marry her if my wife should die in childbed. I shall not succumb to such sinful thoughts.

Extract from the journal of John Banized,
1 February 1624

Pam had been taken down to the theatre at nine thirty that morning. It had only been a light anaesthetic but she felt groggy. She closed her eyes, only half listening to the woman who shared her room. The woman had had the same operation the previous day and was now fully recovered – and talkative. Pam was aware of the gist of the woman's conversation and was conscious enough to make affirmative noises when required. But she wished she'd shut up and let her get some rest.

The woman had somehow got on to the subject of America. 'It would be nice to get someone to do it all for you.' Do what? Pam wasn't concentrating. 'It would save all this messing about.' Pam managed a muffled yes, though she was in no condition to follow the woman's arguments, her talk of 'all those cases'. She just wanted to sink back into the pillows and sleep.

The woman droned on unheard for the next ten minutes until Wesley peeped cautiously round the door.

'Here's your husband,' the woman announced triumphantly. To Wesley she said, 'I think she's still a bit tired – it takes it out of you, you know.'

At last Pam felt inclined to sit up and take notice. Wesley nodded to his wife's room-mate and presented Pam with the flowers he'd bought. He hadn't liked to come empty-handed. He kissed her.

'How did it go?'

'Don't know yet. I think I've left my brain in the operating theatre. I just feel like sleeping.'

'Has the doctor been in?'

As if on cue, before Pam had a chance to answer, Dr Downey oozed into the room followed by a frilly-hatted sister, handmaiden to the high priest.

'Mr Peterson.' He shook Wesley's hand. 'So glad you're here. We've had a little look around inside Pamela and I'm pleased to be able to tell you everything appears quite normal. No sign of scarring or infection and all the other tests we've done so far have found nothing untoward.'

Pam hauled herself upright. She wasn't sure whether this was the news she wanted to hear or not.

'So what's been the problem? I mean, there must be something . . .'

'All I'm saying,' Downey continued with smooth patience, 'is that there doesn't appear to be anything physically wrong.

178

Of course, there are further tests we can do. We'll book you in for those if you wish. All right?'

He nodded to Wesley and turned to leave the room, having switched off his bedside manner.

Wesley, feeling superfluous, gave Pam a kiss on the forehead and left. Duty called. In the foyer he saw a familiar figure looming over the reception desk. It was time for work.

'Hi there, Wes. How is she?'

'Not too bad, thanks, sir. Still tired.'

'So our friend's finished with her, has he?' Heffernan asked quietly. He didn't want the receptionist to get any ideas.

'Oh yes, sir. All done, for now. Until he wants more cash out of us,' he added bitterly.

Heffernan spoke to the blonde in the unlikely-looking nurse's uniform who sat behind the desk typing at a computer terminal. 'Excuse me, love. Police. We'd like a word with Dr Downey.'

'He's doing his rounds at the moment. You'll have to wait.'

Heffernan showed his warrant card. 'Police, love. I think he'll see us. Isn't there some way of getting in touch with him?'

'Well, er, yes, but . . .'

'Then what are you waiting for, love?' He looked at her, challenging. She knew when she was beaten and picked up the phone.

Dr Downey didn't look pleased. He was a man used to deference. 'Really, Inspector, I am on my rounds and . . .'

'It won't take long, Doctor. You know my colleague, DS Peterson?'

'Yes. You should have told me you wished to see me in your professional capacity, Mr Peterson.' He looked at Wesley with distaste, a contrast to his previous charming manner.

'I didn't like to mention it, sir . . . in front of my wife.'

Downey led them through into his office. Heffernan looked around admiringly. 'So what can I do for you, gentlemen?'

179

'I wonder if you remember a patient of yours, an Elaine Berrisford?'

'I have to respect my patients' confidentiality.'

'I'm not asking you to give away any state secrets, I just want to know if she had a baby here.'

The doctor's expression remained impassive, but Wesley thought he detected a slightly guarded look in his eyes. He turned to his computer terminal and tapped the keyboard. The information came up on the screen.

'Yes, Mrs Berrisford had a son. Eight pounds two ounces, normal delivery. Named him Jonathon. Anything else?'

'How come she had her baby here when they lived up near Manchester?'

'I've really no idea, Inspector. Perhaps they liked the scenery. Now, if you've no more questions . . .'

'Just one. What did Sharon Carteret come in here for?'

'I beg your pardon? Who?'

'Sharon Carteret. Shall I spell it for you?'

The inspector sat back like a cat watching a mouse while the doctor fumbled with the keyboard. There was no mistaking it; the man was nervous.

'I'm sorry, Inspector. There's nobody of that name in patient records.'

'Perhaps she was a member of staff,' Wesley suggested helpfully.

'I can't recall anyone of that name.'

'Well, thank you for your help, Doctor.' Heffernan stood up. 'We'll be in touch.'

On that ominous note, they left the room. As soon as they were outside, the inspector spoke. 'That's given him something to think about, Wes. We'll just leave him to stew for a bit.'

Dr Downey looked up a number in his leather-bound executive address book and picked up the phone.

The vicar leaned over his handiwork, deep concentration on his face. The Reverend Richardson was not a young man, but then neither was he old. But a receding hairline and thickening waist concentrated the mind wonderfully on hobbies and personal interests. And local history was his particular obsession: he was the proud author of three volumes on the subject, prominently displayed in the local bookshop. He was fortunate in his calling: who better to have access to the records of the parish? The Almighty had placed the Reverend Richardson in the right location.

'This is great. Just what we need. Can we use this in the exhibition?' Neil was impressed with the painstakingly drawn-up family tree spread out on the table in front of them.

'Of course, Neil. I'd be honoured . . . very honoured.' The vicar's face glowed with satisfaction. He would have hesitated to call it pride. 'As you can see from the occupations, the Banizeds seem to have slipped down the social ladder in more recent times. These Victorian ones seem to have been fishermen, farmworkers – here's one who worked in the boat yard . . .'

Neil's eyes wandered to the bottom of the document; the most recent members of the family. There didn't seem to be many of them. 'What about these? Are any of them still alive?'

'Not in this parish. But the only daughter there, Rose, she married someone from the parish of Little Tradmouth. I suppose she might be dead by now. She was born in 1910. I don't know if they had children. You could check the parish records up there if you like. She's the only daughter of the eldest son. If this journal you mentioned has been handed down in the family, it could well have come to her.'

'I might try and track her down – or her descendants. If I've got time. We're getting a bit pushed at the dig. Time limits and all that.'

'If you ever need a hand,' the vicar grinned enthusiastically, 'I'd be only too pleased to help. Parish responsibilities permitting, of course.'

Neil thanked him. As the deadline drew nearer he might need all the help he could get. The discovery of a murder victim, even from the distant past, had slowed things up considerably.

Wesley was relieved to be back at the station. He didn't like hospitals, even those at the luxury end of the market.

Gerry Heffernan had suggested he spend some time with Pam, seeing he was on the premises, while he went back to Tradmouth and caught up with some paperwork. Thoughtful of the man, but Wesley would have preferred to get back to work . . . although he didn't care to admit it.

He had spent half an hour making polite conversation with his wife. It is impossible, Wesley thought, to talk normally to anybody, however intimately you know them, in a hospital. He had left as soon as he could respectably do so and drove back to Tradmouth. If possible he wanted to see Neil at lunch-time to find out how things were progressing.

The office was quiet; everyone intent on work. Heffernan came out when he saw Wesley had returned. 'I've not told you about my little discovery, have I, Wes?'

'What discovery's that, sir?'

'Our friend Mrs Hughes, Sharon Carteret's landlady. She was married before to someone called Berrisford, and they had a son who lives up north.'

'Er . . .'

'Stan Jenkins isn't in but when he gets back I'm going to ask him. I think she could be Jonathon Berrisford's grandmother.'

'And if she is?'

'I'm getting a feeling in my water that there's some connection. The kid Sharon was with looked like Jonathon. Her landlady was his grandmother . . .'

'That's just conjecture, sir. We don't . . .'

'I'm talking ifs here, Wes. When I first started in CID my old inspector told me to follow my instincts, so I'm following them. Okay? After lunch, when I've talked to Stan, I might pay Mrs Hughes another visit. You can come with me if you like. But make sure you have a cup of tea before you go. You'll not get one there.'

They were interrupted by Rachel. 'Excuse me, sir, but Steve and I have got a lead on Chris Manners. He sometimes goes to the Anchor on Saturday nights.'

'I think you've got yourself a date there, Rach. Get over there tonight and don't let Steve drink too much or pick up any fallen women.' She nodded, not relishing a night out with Steve Carstairs. Steve considered himself to be God's gift to women; and if this was the case, thought Rachel, the Lord was seriously short-changing the female sex.

The inspector had taken Stan Jenkins to the Tradmouth Arms for lunch. Wesley decided on a pasty and a visit to the dig.

Darren was standing proudly in a trench, holding a piece of pottery at arm's length. Wesley asked him what he'd found and Darren, overawed, responded enthusiastically. The boy was coming on: he clearly had a real interest. There was no sign of the metal detector.

Neil was in the hut, leaning over the sink, cleaning the mud off a few finds.

'I've just been to see the vicar. He's made us a great family tree. I told him we'll use it in the exhibition.'

'Any news on the journal?'

'I'm going to St Peter's church at Little Tradmouth to see if I can trace the surviving relatives. Fancy going over there now? It won't take long. How's Pam?'

'She'll be fine. They're keeping her in overnight.'

Neil nodded. He had thought about Pam last night – the kisses they'd exchanged at that long-ago party where they'd first met, how they'd gone out together for six months, how he'd introduced her to his family – then to his friend, Wesley. But Neil, wise enough to realise that the clock couldn't be turned back, liked Wesley and bore him no ill-will – except in the small hours of the morning when he thought of what might have been. But then Pam seemed happy with Wesley. She had shown no emotion when she had met Neil again other than pleasure at meeting an old friend after many years. Perhaps things had worked out for the best.

'Darren's shaping up well.'

'He's a natural.' Neil's mind returned to archaeology. 'He reckons he wants to go back to college and do his GCSEs then go on to university. I told him that if he helps out on digs as a volunteer he'll be getting involved – it'll all help. Have you got time to come over to Little Tradmouth?'

Welsey looked at his watch. 'If we're not too long. We can go in my car.'

St Peter's, Little Tradmouth, was built as a chapel of ease

in the eighteenth century, to relieve the overworked villagers of that small but expanding farming community from the pains of having to trail into Tradmouth itself for Sunday service. The church was plain, unlike the vicar's wife who greeted them. A tall woman in her thirties with a face and figure that would stop traffic even in London's busiest streets, she explained that her husband was responsible for five parishes and had had to go early to one of his churches to prepare for a wedding; such are the rigours of rural church life.

She unlocked the huge oak door and they stepped into the echoing silence of the nave. The vicar's wife walked in front of them to the vestry, her hips swaying provocatively under her tight jersey dress. Wesley, who had been brought up by strict churchgoing parents, felt a little uneasy at finding a clergyman's wife so alluringly attractive. Neil, from an atheistic family with no such hang-ups, watched her appreciatively and enjoyed the experience.

She pointed to a large oak cupboard. 'You'll find all the registers in there.' She unlocked it slowly to reveal a row of dusty leather-bound volumes. 'I'll leave you to it, then. Just drop the key in to the vicarage when you leave.' She smiled, a dazzling smile. 'And let me know how you've got on, won't you?'

When she'd gone they exchanged looks.

'Lucky old vicar,' said Neil appreciatively. 'We'd best get on. There's a lot to look through.'

Wesley, his eye on the time, thought he'd have to go back and leave Neil to it. Then they struck gold. At last, in a dusty baptism register, they found what they were looking for.

A boy, William, had been born in 1937 to a William Boscople and his wife Rose (née Banized). The deaths register revealed that the parents, William and Rose, had departed this life within a year of each other in 1982, their earthly existence reduced to ill-written entries in a country church register.

Their searches done, Neil and Wesley strolled back down the grave-lined church path towards the vicarage. Maybe the vicar's wife would know the whereabouts of William Boscople the younger.

But she didn't. They were new to the parish, she explained, only arrived six months ago and hadn't met everyone yet. She'd ask around for them. She uncrossed her beautiful legs and offered them coffee. Wesley happened to mention that his wife was in hospital and her expression changed to one of concern. She was not a vicar's wife for nothing.

Wesley started the car, leaving Neil enjoying a second cup of freshly ground ecclesiastical coffee. He had said he'd walk back to Tradmouth along the cliff path. The exercise would do him good.

Wesley drove along country lanes walled with hedgerow. When gates gave glimpses into the fields beyond, he noticed that the rich red earth was ploughed bare, the harvest gathered until next year when the cycle would begin again. There was something about this countryside, something that nagged away at his mind; some connection. If only he could remember where he had heard the name Boscople.

The midday meal that Gerry Heffernan had consumed at the Tradmouth Arms was considerably larger than Wesley's pasty. Wesley found him slumped in his swivel chair, sated and content. The inspector raised himself up.

'Come on, Wes. Let's get over and see this Hughes woman. I could do with a walk.'

'Good lunch, sir?'

'Very good. I think I've laid Stan Jenkins's diet well and truly to rest.' He smiled with satisfaction and stood up slowly. 'Nice walk and a little sail on the ferry – just what the doctor ordered. Come on.'

They reached Mary Hughes's house at around half past two. As Wesley rang the doorbell he was aware of a movement in an upstairs window, the flickering of a net curtain. She was in; he was certain of that. He tried again.

This time she answered, her expression cold. Her face looked strained and there were dark rings under her eyes which were visible in spite of her immaculate make-up. There was something bothering her.

'I don't know what you're wasting your time for,' she said grudgingly. 'I've told you everything I know. I really can't help you more than I have already. I'm sorry.'

She seemed to be about to shut the door on them when Heffernan pushed forward determinedly. 'If we could just have a word, Mrs Hughes. It won't take long.'

He was halfway through the front door. There was nothing she could do about it. 'Cup of tea'd be nice, love. I'm spitting feathers here.'

Wesley had to admire his boss's cheek. Mrs Hughes looked at the inspector as if he was something she'd found rotting in her dustbin. She complied in silence. The tea was served in bone-china cups.

'I think there's something you've not told us, Mrs Hughes,' the inspector said softly when they were settled.

The woman's eyes narrowed. 'I'm sure I don't know what you mean.' Wary.

'You've been married twice, I believe?'

'It's not illegal,' she snapped.

'Your first husband's name was Berrisford.'

Wesley sat watching her reaction, the bone-china cup halfway to his lips.

'Yes.'

Heffernan paused to increase the pressure. 'You have a son, I believe. What's his name?'

'Alan . . . his name's Alan.'

'And he lives where?'

'Up north.'

'Where up north?'

'Outside Manchester. Why?'

'Did his son go missing recently?'

She turned to face him, her face blank. 'Yes.' Whispered.

'Is his son Jonathon Berrisford? Is Jonathon your grandson?'

She nodded. 'I'm sorry, Inspector, I'll have to ask you to leave. This has been distressing for the whole family and . . .'

'Just one more question and then we'll go, Mrs Hughes. Have you any idea where your grandson is . . . any idea at all?'

She didn't answer. 'I'm feeling unwell, Inspector. I'd be grateful if you'd leave.'

They were halfway down the road to the ferry before Heffernan spoke. 'What do you think, Wes?'

'She knows something. Should we take her in for questioning, let Inspector Jenkins know?'

'One thing I learned when I went to cookery evening classes after Kathy died was that if you leave tough meat to simmer gently for a long time, it goes all tender and breaks up nicely. I find it works on suspects too.'

'So we leave her?'

'Oh, we keep going back to give her a stir from time to time.' He grinned wickedly. 'There's one thing, though . . .'

'What's that?'

'I think we can put Stan Jenkins out of his misery. I reckon that Jonathon Berrisford's most probably alive and well and living not a million miles from here.'

Chapter 24

Last night Elizabeth was delivered of a boy. He is small and scarce like to live. But he doth feed and clings to life.

Jennet's time is near and I do keep from her company. I must needs pray and repent me of my great sin.

Extract from the journal of John Banized,
20 February 1624

Rachel thought she'd better get changed for the evening. Jeans, her new black ribbed top: they'd do fine for the Anchor. Her mother had asked her if she was going anywhere nice, and why didn't she put that new dress on. Rachel had explained patiently that it was work, she didn't have a date. Her mother had looked disappointed.

Perhaps, Rachel thought to herself, she was outgrowing the farm. Perhaps it was time to start looking for a place of her own.

She met Steve outside the market and had to admit that he looked quite presentable, and there was a refreshing absence of suggestive banter. When they entered the Anchor Rachel felt relieved that she'd rejected her mother's advice and worn her jeans.

The Anchor wasn't the roughest pub she had been in, but it came close. The walls were shiny imitation wood, as was the bar. Fruit machines lined the walls like an alien guard from the pages of one of Steve's favourite science fiction novels. They sat at a round table in the corner, wood-effect laminate for easy cleaning, and sipped ice-cold, tasteless lager.

'Missing Sergeant Peterson?' Steve asked suggestively after a few minutes' silence.

Rachel had known that Steve's exemplary behaviour had been too good to last. She didn't answer.

'Like him, do you?'

She looked him in the eye, challenging. 'Yes, I do. He's a nice bloke. What's your problem?'

'He's a bloody graduate. They always come in over us, get the best jobs.'

'And he's black?'

'That and all.'

'I'm warning you, Steve, if Gerry Heffernan hears you say anything like that, you'll be out of CID so fast . . .'

'Okay, point taken.' He sat back resentfully and drained his glass.

'Just watch yourself, that's all. We've all got to work together as a team. We can't afford your stupid prejudices. If you don't change your attitude . . .'

'Okay, okay. Forget it, all right.'

For the first time Rachel thought she might just have got through to him. He sat for a few minutes, sulking in silence.

The place was filling up as Steve bought a second round. The predominantly male clientèle seemed to consist mainly of workmen and fishermen, some drinking silently, some having animated discussions about sport. At the bar, Steve, after glancing over at Rachel to see if she was watching, decided to try his luck.

'Is Chris Manners in tonight?' he asked the barman, trying to sound as casual as he could. 'A mate of mine said I might find him in here.'

The barman shook his head. 'Don't know him, mate. Sorry. Can't know everyone's name, can I?'

Steve returned to Rachel with the drinks. He felt eyes on him. He turned and saw a group of men at the bar watching him. As he looked they turned away.

'What did you say to the barman? That lot have been watching you like a load of hawks.' Steve looked sheepish and didn't answer. 'I don't feel very comfortable in here,' Rachel continued. 'It's not where I'd usually choose to spend a Saturday night.'

'So where would you choose, then?'

Rachel, sensing a chat-up line, didn't reply. She was watching the door. A man had walked in: mid-twenties, dark, with an earring . . . rather good-looking. He went up to the group at the bar and they said something to him, quietly. He looked over at Rachel and Steve warily and began to walk slowly out of the pub.

'That's him, Steve,' Rachel hissed at him. 'I'm sure it is. Come on.'

She stood up and walked towards the door, Steve following behind. Out in the street they saw the man disappearing towards the Butterwalk. Steve began to run and the man's pace quickened. Steve was catching up with him, Rachel trailing behind. The man looked back and began to run. The pavements at that time of the evening were fairly empty, but it was Chris Manners's bad fortune to collide with a middle-aged woman who had three Irish wolfhounds on long leads. His feet tangled with leads and excited dogs of huge proportions, Chris Manners lay on the pavement defeated as Steve Carstairs bore down on him.

The dogs seemed to be enjoying themselves. As their owner tried to calm them and release Chris from the tangle of leather, Steve stood over him, showing his warrant card and grinning.

'Mr Manners, I presume. Could we have a word down the station?'

Sludge and Donna didn't mind baby-sitting. When the bloke in the next caravan had asked them if they'd look after little Daniel while he met some people down the pub who could put a bit of business his way, they'd agreed. They'd seen little Daniel loads of times playing outside the caravans. He was a sweet kid, he'd be no trouble.

Daniel lay fast asleep in the spare bed. Donna found herself wondering what had happened to the bed's previous occupants, that Australian couple. Funny they should have disappeared like that. But people came and went on the travellers' site. She and Sludge were thinking of moving on soon themselves; Glastonbury maybe.

She wondered if Sludge should have given the kid that cider, but he'd seemed to like it and it made him fall asleep. She sat watching the child, the sweet-scented smoke from her oversized hand-rolled cigarette curling upwards towards the caravan roof. Sludge had retired to bed. He'd be waiting for her.

Chris was late.

Rachel and Steve had brought their suspect in and made him feel at home in the interview room with a cup of tea – probably preferable to the beer in the Anchor, thought Steve.

Gerry Heffernan, summoned from an evening in front of the television, lumbered into the interview room, announcing his presence to the tape recorder.

'I didn't know they were stolen.' Chris seemed to have his story thought out. 'This bloke I know supplies the stuff and I just sell it on.'

Heffernan looked at him. He was medium height, dark hair fairly long, even features. The man was good-looking, there was no doubt of that, but there was a hardness to his mouth, a calculation in his eyes. He could see why he had such a hold over Sharon. This one wouldn't be easy.

'I've not come to talk to you about the building materials, although we might want to question you about those at a later date. What I'm more interested in is what happened to your girlfriend. Sharon Carteret was your girlfriend, wasn't she?'

Chris swallowed and looked away.

'Was she or wasn't she? We've got enough witnesses who'll swear that you lived together . . .'

'Yes. She was my girlfriend. And I know she's dead but I had nothing to do with it.' He'd decided on the direct approach. Heffernan felt an alibi coming. 'We were living together in Morbay. I went to stay with a mate and when I came back she was gone . . . just disappeared. Then I heard that a body had been found but they said it was someone else. I thought she'd just done a runner till they said the body was hers.' There was emotion in his voice for the first time.

'So why didn't you contact the police?'

'I didn't want to get involved. I just moved out of that flat. I didn't want to be reminded of her.'

'You could have helped to catch her killer.'

'How? It was just some maniac, wasn't it?'

'We don't think so.'

'Well, you can't pull me in for it. Check my alibi. I wouldn't harm her, I loved her. We were making a new start . . .'

'With the child?'

'Yeah. How did you know about that?' He looked up, worried.

'When you stayed with this mate, when Sharon was killed, where was the kid?'

'With my mum. I took him to my mum's.'

'Where is he now?'

'With some mates. They're looking after him. But I've got to get back . . .'

'Tell me about your son, Mr Manners.' Heffernan sat back, prepared to listen to the proud father.

'He's two. Me and Sharon couldn't look after him till a few weeks back, then we got a place, the three of us. He's a great kid.'

'And he's yours?'

'Of course he's bloody mine. She wasn't no slag.'

'Why didn't you live together before this, Chris? Why leave it so long to play happy families?'

'I worked away a lot. And Sharon had her job. It just never played out that way.'

Heffernan leaned forward. 'So where has your son, Jonathon . . .'

'Daniel . . . it's Daniel.'

'Daniel. Where has Daniel been for the past two years?'

'With my mum.'

'Can we have your mother's name and address?' We'd like to confirm this.'

Chris meekly gave the required details – too meekly,

the inspector thought. It would be an unusual mother who wouldn't lie for her son.

'Is he with your mother now?'

'No. I thought I'd only be out for an hour or so. He's with the couple in the next caravan, on the travellers' site in Neston. That's where I've been living.'

'Why did you move there? Running away?'

'The flat got too dear. And there were too many things to remind me of . . . oh God, I hope you get whoever killed Sharon. If I got my hands on him I'd . . .' For the first time, Chris Manners seemed genuinely distressed. He was becoming aggressive. Heffernan knew the signs. 'Why the hell are you wasting time with me? Why don't you go out and find the maniac who killed her? My kid's without a mum and you waste your bloody time on asking me bloody stupid questions. You're useless, you lot.'

Heffernan leaned forward. 'This isn't helping, Mr Manners. Just calm down and we might get somewhere.'

Chris Manners breathed deeply and sat back.

'Have you any idea who'd want to kill Sharon? Anyone at all? Had she any enemies?' Chris snorted in derision and shook his head. 'Was she blackmailing someone?'

Chris looked up at him, shocked. This had touched a nerve.

'There was a sum regularly paid into her bank account, and a large sum in a deposit account.' Heffernan sat back, waiting for an explanation. Experience had taught him that expectant silences always provoke witnesses to talk.

Chris succumbed to the ploy. 'I don't know nothing about it.' Heffernan again said nothing. 'I knew she had this money, but I don't know where it came from. I thought she'd inherited it from her dad or something. I don't know, honest.'

Something told Heffernan that he was lying – or at least not telling the whole truth. But he'd had tougher cases. A night in the cells would do wonders.

'And Daniel is your son? Would you be prepared to take a DNA test, just to put our minds at rest?'

Chris nodded. Heffernan thought he looked a little relieved.

'By the way, Mr Manners,' he threw in casually, 'was Sharon upset when she found she couldn't have any more children?'

Chris Manners stared at him, uncomprehending. 'I don't know what you . . .'

Heffernan terminated the interview, returned to his office and rang Social Services. Someone had to think of the child.

Sludge had dropped off to sleep. Donna wished he didn't have to snore quite so loudly. He'd wake the kid if he wasn't careful. She sat on the end of the bed, watching the child sleeping. A sleep so deep, so innocent; so unlike Sludge's chemically induced slumbers. She reached out her hand and ran her fingers through his hair, surprised at herself; she had never been the maternal type. She turned the dark hair over in her hand; rich brown; a little gold underneath. She gently kissed his soft forehead. He was beautiful. She wondered if she and Sludge should . . . No. Sludge would make a lousy father.

Her thoughts, her uncharacteristic dreams of motherhood, were broken by a soft tap on the caravan door. Chris . . . it must be Chris back. She felt almost disappointed.

The long-haired, long-skirted woman who stood at the door wore earrings that outjangled even Donna's. She announced herself as Lynne Wychwood, Social Services. She had come about Daniel. Donna, resentful, stood aside to let her in.

Chris had eaten a good breakfast, or so the sergeant on duty had reported. Gerry Heffernan knew Wesley was picking his wife up from hospital first thing and wondered whether to wait for him to arrive or to proceed with the questioning without his sergeant's assistance. He decided on the latter course of action; he'd had a team of officers out checking the information the suspect had provided since seven o'clock that morning. Everything had been confirmed. Why waste time? He asked Rachel to sit in on the interview.

'You'll be glad to know that everyone confirms your state-ment, Mr Manners. We've contacted the friends you were staying with at the time of Sharon's death and your mother. They all back up your statements.'

'What about Daniel . . . is he okay? Is he still with . . .'

'Your son's being looked after, Mr Manners. I think Social Services might want a word with you, but I can assure you . . .'

Chris Manners stood up. 'You've not gone and taken him away. He was fine with Donna. He's not been . . .'

'Sit down and keep calm. Daniel has been seen by the duty social worker and she says he's all right where he is. He seemed to be well looked after. But they'd still like a word with you, see how you're going to cope.'

'Does that mean I can go?'

Heffernan saw hope in the man's eyes. 'You'll be charged with receiving stolen goods. Has the duty solicitor told you the procedure?' Chris nodded. 'Then I don't think we'll have any objection to bail. We'll get the formalities out of the way, then you're free to go.' He put his face close to Chris's. 'But don't forget we'll want to talk to you again, so stay put. If we're going to catch whoever killed Sharon, we'll need all the help we can get. Right?'

Chris nodded, all his cockiness gone. Heffernan gestured to Rachel, who rose to follow him out of the room. Halfway across the threshold, the inspector turned round. 'You're still willing to take that DNA test, are you?'

''Course I am. I told you.'

'I'll arrange it, then.'

Rachel looked at her boss and wondered what he was up to.

Chapter 25

I did baptise my son Thomas before he died. As I held him in my arms I did hear Jennet cry out in her pain from her chamber. I did not dare to go to her nor did I desire to in my grief. Elizabeth's tears do burn into my soul.

Jennet was delivered of a healthy boy. I did go privily to her chamber to see the child. As I looked at him I saw my Thomas. It was then I knew what I must do. But it must be done privily.

Extract from the journal of John Banized,
25 February 1624

Wesley wondered why Pam was so quiet as he drove the car down the sweeping gravel drive away from the Morbay Clinic and through the imposing gates. 'You okay?'

'Why?'

'You're quiet. I thought you'd be happy. They didn't find anything wrong with you.'

'That's worse in a way. At least if they found something wrong we'd know what we were up against.'

'I've got a confession to make,' said Wesley nervously.

'What?'

'I rang Maritia last night, told her. She's going to ring you today, have a chat.'

'You had no right to tell . . .'

'I had every right. This affects me too, you know.'

They drove home in silence. As soon as they got back to the house Pamela disappeared upstairs.

The telephone rang. He let Pam answer it. He could hear her talking and he resisted the temptation to listen in on the downstairs extension. After twenty minutes or so she came downstairs, looking a little better, more cheerful.

'That was your sister. She rang to see how I'd got on. I still don't know why you had to tell her.'

'Sorry.' Wesley didn't feel particularly apologetic. Maritia was working in the gynaecology department of the John Radcliffe Hospital in Oxford. She had been the obvious person for Wesley to confide in. 'What did she say?'

'She said it was good they hadn't found anything wrong. She said anxiety can sometimes stop women conceiving. That I should relax; try and forget about it; have a holiday.'

'Good advice.'

'You're only saying that 'cause you don't want to fork out for more medical bills.'

'It's not that,' he said unconvincingly. 'Maritia's a good doctor, and she's got no profit to make.'

Pam looked at him and attempted to smile. Then she put her arms round him. 'I'm sorry I've been such a neurotic bitch.'

Her husband kissed her. 'If I could get away, I'd suggest a few days of self-indulgence at a country hotel.'

'But you can't, and neither can I. I couldn't let the school down. I can't take any more time off.'

'Okay. But let's try and forget about all this business. That's what Maritia said – just try and put it out of your mind for a while.'

'It's difficult. I'm even covering for someone who's on maternity leave. It's all around me, reminding me that I'm some sort of freak.'

Wesley looked at her. She was near to tears. He had no words to say. He had said them all.

'You're not a freak. There are lots of people in the same boat. What about that woman you were sharing a room with?'

'That Jenny woman? She was awful, a real rich bitch. Husband owns his own computer company. She kept going on about her house and her Mercedes. She's been trying for a baby for five years; tried IVF, the lot.'

'But she's still not given up?'

'She heard about Dr Downey . . . heard he was good.'

'Expensive,' mumbled Wesley, who was still in shock at the bill for the doctor's services.

'And she said if all else failed, he could still come up with the goods. You could get anything as long as you were prepared to pay for it.' She looked at her husband, willing him to ask what she meant.

'Bound to be something that costs more than we could afford.' He shrugged, suddenly uneasy.

Pam stared at him, a look of determination on her face. If they had the money, he wondered, just how far would she be prepared to go to get what she wanted?

Chris kept the caravan quite tidy. He had to; there wasn't much room. He looked out of the window at Daniel who was playing outside with some dirty-faced children; he was following the bigger ones about happily, trying to join their game. A couple of girls, aged about ten, seemed to have taken him under their wing and were holding his hands. Daniel seemed content with their attentions.

Chris wondered if he should take the child to his mum's. It'd be for the best with all this business with the police going on. But Daniel was happy with the freedom of the travellers' site, happy to be with the children and the dogs. He saw a young woman approaching; he didn't recognise her as being one of the site's residents. Although her hair was long and she was dressed in a mildly hippie style, she looked as though she had access to a washing machine. She was coming up to the caravan, leaning to one side with the weight of her bulky briefcase. She was knocking on the open door.

'Hello, Mr Manners? Lynne Wychwood, Social Services. I wonder if I could have a word about Daniel.'

He invited her in and prepared to offer her a cup of tea. He didn't want to antagonise officialdom any more than necessary. 'He's out there . . . playing. He likes it here. Lots of kids to play with.'

'Would it be all right if I spoke to him, Mr Manners . . . or may I call you Chris?'

Chris went outside and led Daniel away from his minders, telling them he'd be back in a minute. Daniel toddled happily up the caravan steps and smiled charmingly at Lynne. She greeted him and got down on the floor with him to play with some bricks. After a while she looked up at Chris and spoke.

'I've been told the background to the case, Chris. I know all about Sharon. Daniel seems to be adjusting well.'

'Yeah, he is. He didn't live with Sharon, like, not from being a baby, so . . .'

'So the bond wasn't really there.' She completed his sentence. 'Do you mind if Daniel and I have a little chat?'

Chris nodded. There was nothing he could really do to stop her without setting off alarm bells.

'I thought I might take him to stay with my mum, while all this business with the police . . .'

Lynne looked up and smiled before returning her attentions to Daniel. 'That's a lovely tower you're making, Daniel. Can you make another one?' The child did so obligingly. There was certainly nothing wrong with his mental development, thought Lynne. 'Would you like to go to your grandma's for a little holiday, Daniel?'

The child looked at her, blank. He hadn't understood. 'You'd like to go and stay with your nan?'

'Want go home. Bike . . . want bike. Want go home . . . Mummy . . .' The child was beginning to cry. Lynne hated it when they cried. 'Want mummy . . .'

'I know, darling. Now you go to your daddy.' Chris picked up the crying child and looked at Lynne expectantly, praying she would leave.

'Well, it's obvious he's missing his mum. It's only natural. But I think, from what I've seen, you're coping well, Chris. It might be an idea to take him to his gran's for a few days. Familiar scenery and all that, and it'll give you a break. Remember, you've been through a bereavement too. If there's anything I can do, please ring me. I'll give you my number.'

Lynne scribbled down her office number. There was no

need to take any action on this one, no suggestion of abuse, and the man seemed to be coping and had the support of grandparents. And it was important not to be judgemental about the fact that he lived on the travellers' site and was in trouble with the police. Besides, she had eleven more cases to visit that day. She lugged her bag full of case files back to the car.

Chris held the sobbing child in his arms and mumbled comforting words, stroking the brown hair. Suddenly he looked down in alarm. There was something to be done . . . and he'd better do it quickly before anybody else saw what he had seen.

Pam felt lazy, guilty. It wasn't on to lie in bed all day reading the Sunday papers. Wesley had to go into work. It was always like that during a murder investigation. And she had work to do herself; lessons to prepare; reports to write. But half an hour more wouldn't hurt.

She turned the page of one of the glossy supplements. Another article about babies . . . She almost turned the page over in disgust. But a word caught her eye – America. This was what that Jenny in the clinic had been going on about. She began to read the article. It was about a woman who had paid another woman to have a child for her. One woman was childless, the other poor. Pam began to turn things over in her mind, things she'd heard at the clinic. She called down to Wesley.

'How's your wife?'

'She's fine, sir. On the mend. She's talking about going into work tomorrow. Anything new?'

'I sent someone round to take swabs from Chris Manners and the kid for the DNA tests and I told them to snip off a bit of the kid's hair while they were at it – but be discreet about it. I'm keeping Stan up to date. He's waiting with bated breath.'

'If you think this kid's Jonathon why don't you take the mother to identify him? That'd clear things up once and for all.'

'No, Wes. I think there's more to all this than meets the

eye. If it is him it'd muck up our murder investigation, and if it isn't it'd only get her hopes up. There's no way she's going anywhere near this kid till we know for sure. Social Services say he's okay where he is and I'll go along with that for the moment.'

'I've been thinking, sir. Pam was reading this article in the Sunday papers about places in America which arrange for poor women to have babies for rich childless women. The women are paid and their debts are cleared and it all goes through as an official adoption.'

'Surrogate mothers. It's illegal to pay here.'

'There was a woman sharing a room with Pam who was going on about Dr Downey being able to come up with the goods and that you could get anything as long as you were able to pay for it. What if Sharon Carteret . . . Chris Manners had debts from his gambling. If Sharon was so besotted with him, she might . . .'

'But how was it arranged?'

'Mary Hughes. She had a daughter-in-law who couldn't have a child and a girl who was desperate to pay off her boyfriend's debts living downstairs.'

'We don't know of any connection between Mary Hughes and this Dr Downey, and besides, there's no evidence that Jonathon wasn't born to Elaine Berrisford. The birth certificate says . . .'

'If it is done through Dr Downey it could all be fiddled. The real mother could go in at the same time as the adoptive mother. One woman comes out with a child and a valid birth certificate. Don't forget Sharon left work. Nobody saw her pregnant.'

'Except Mary Hughes, her landlady.'

'Exactly.'

'We haven't enough evidence. It's all supposition.' Heffernan sat back, deep in thought. 'I think we should give Mrs Hughes another stir, get her simmering gently, see what turns up.'

Wesley was getting used to the journey across the river. This time Mrs Hughes looked even less pleased to see them.

'I really can't tell you anything else, Inspector. You're wasting your time.'

'It's just a quick visit, Mrs Hughes. Nothing to worry about. May we come in?'

She could hardly say no. Soon they were upstairs in her immaculately tidy lounge.

'I wonder if you could do us a favour, Mrs Hughes. Have you got a photo of your grandson, Jonathon?' She nodded. 'Could I have a quick look, please, love?'

Slowly and resentfully, she left the room. As soon as she was out of the door Heffernan leaped to his feet and almost ran towards the telephone. With a swiftness that Wesley hadn't witnessed before, the inspector flicked through the address book lying by it. With a whispered 'Yes!' he turned to Wesley beaming triumphantly. 'His name's here. We've got her, Wes . . . we've got her.'

Mrs Hughes looked surprised to see the inspector standing by the phone, and she was even more surprised when he told her, with an air of official authority, to sit down. She obeyed, still resentful.

'How long have you known Dr Downey, Mrs Hughes?'

'I've known him for years. He was a friend of my late husband. They played golf together. Why?'

'When did you find out your daughter-in-law, Elaine Berrisford, couldn't have children?'

'She's got a child, Inspector. Jonathon.'

'How much was Sharon paid to have the child, Mrs Hughes? Did your son and daughter-in-law get in touch with her direct or through Dr Downey?'

Mrs Hughes squirmed uncomfortably. 'I really don't know what you're talking about, Inspector.'

'I'm talking about Sharon Carteret having a baby for your son and daughter-in-law for payment, Mrs Hughes. What went wrong? Did Sharon want her child back?'

'You've moved into the realms of fantasy, Inspector. Now if you don't leave I shall make a complaint to the relevant authorities.'

It was clear to Heffernan that she'd give nothing away. He looked at his sergeant. Mrs Hughes was calm, in control. This one would need more simmering until she was ready to break. There was nothing for it but to make a strategic withdrawal. But he had one more card to play before he left.

'We think we might have found Jonathon. But it's all very delicate. It might not be him, of course, and we couldn't just risk going in like a herd of elephants, not with a little kid of that age. We're doing DNA tests with the man who claims to be his dad and with samples taken from Sharon's body. That should clear it up once and for all. If, as you say, your son and his wife are Jonathon's real parents.' He smiled sweetly. 'Well, I'm sorry to have disturbed you, Mrs Hughes. We'll no doubt be seeing you again.'

As they left, Wesley noticed that Mrs Hughes's jaw had dropped and, even beneath her immaculate veneer of make-up, she seemed to have aged ten years in the past thirty seconds.

'She's not going to give anything away, is she, sir?' Wesley was perched on his boss's desk. They had made the journey back to the station in virtual silence, neither liking to intrude on the other's thoughts.

'I reckon I put the wind up her with that DNA stuff, though. We should get the results soon. And what's the betting they'll show I'm right. Did you see her face?'

'Yes. I reckon you touched a nerve there, sir. But we need proof. Anyway, surely if you're right the tests'll show Chris wasn't the father.'

'Not necessarily, Wes, not necessarily. Pity your wife's not in the force – she'd be perfect to do what I've got in mind, what with Downey knowing her already and . . .'

'What have you got in mind?' Heffernan was like a fox-hound in pursuit. Wesley just hoped that what he was contemplating didn't go against the regulations.

'Ever used an *agent provocateur*, Wes? Or don't they speak much French in the Met?'

Wesley felt uncomfortable. He hoped the inspector wouldn't go too far. The powers-that-be held a very dim view of officers who didn't stick to the guidelines. 'How do you mean, sir?'

'Is Rachel about? Tell her to come in, will you.'

Rachel was at her desk, wrestling with reports. She sensed

Wesley's unease and followed him into Heffernan's office with some apprehension.

The inspector was at his most jovial. 'Sit down, Rach, sit down. I remember a few years back you used to be in the divisional drama society.'

'That was when I first joined the force, sir. I haven't done much acting since.'

'How would you like to do some more ... in the line of duty, of course?'

Wesley listened with growing unease as the inspector explained to Rachel what he wanted her to do.

Rachel sat in Downey's office the next morning in her interview suit – very expensive; bought in last year's sales in Plymouth – and her mother's best pearl earrings. She hoped she was convincing.

She carried on with her tale of how she had had an abortion at eighteen which had left her infertile; how the adoption agencies had turned her down because her husband was so much older than her. Her performance, she thought, brought tears to the eyes. She really must try the drama society again.

She was enjoying herself. They were rich, she and her fictional husband, but no amount of money could make up for what they longed for – a family. She sat back, extracted a tissue from her handbag and dabbed her eyes. Dr Downey was watching her with speculation. Rachel looked up at him and for the first time felt uneasy. Had he seen through her act?

Downey leaned back in his deep leather chair, still watching her. 'Who recommended me to you?'

Rachel swallowed. This was the hard bit. 'A lady called Jenny. I don't know her well but I got talking to her last week. She was due to come in here for tests, I believe. Our husbands know each other. Please, Dr Downey, there must be something you can do for me. Please ... I'm desperate.'

'I could make the arrangements, you understand, but if you were to find someone willing yourself, a friend or relation perhaps, that's sometimes easier. Then I would arrange the medical side. The cost would be substantial but of course the result would be virtually guaranteed.'

'What do you mean ... someone willing?'

Dr Downey explained. Rachel listened intently.

Wesley sat in the hut waiting for Neil to finish talking to Matt and Jane. The office had been quiet; everyone was out and he needed some company. He wondered how Rachel was getting on. Heffernan shouldn't have put her in that situation, and he wasn't sure it was even permitted. If the super got to hear ... If anything went wrong ... He found himself worrying about Rachel more than he felt to be appropriate.

'You're quiet today, Wes. Pam okay?' Neil came in and carried on cleaning some finds, broken pottery mostly. They were down to the next layer – a house that had been on the site in the fourteenth century and burned down.

'Yeah. She's fine ... back at work.'

'Glad you called in. Got something to show you.' Neil wiped his hands and opened the drawer of his desk. He handed Wesley a Polaroid photograph. It was the head of a young woman; a small nose, high cheekbones, a wide, sensuous mouth, long blond hair. 'It's her. Our skeleton. Jennet. The prof's made a good job of it, hasn't he?'

Wesley stared at the face. 'She's beautiful.' He was suddenly filled with pity for this good-looking young woman who had ended up buried in a cellar. 'I wonder why she was killed ... what happened.'

'She's certainly a bit of all right, isn't she? Poor lass. Can't have been more than twenty, the pathologist reckoned. I'm still on the Boscople trail. Not found him yet. Might have moved out of the area.'

'I'm sure I've heard that name somewhere recently. I'll look through my case notes. I'm sure it was to do with work.'

'That'd be a help.'

Wesley heard a voice outside the hut, an unmistakable voice; the Scouse accent carried across the site. The door opened and Gerry Heffernan loomed in the frame, blocking the light.

'I thought I'd find you here. Get back to the station quick,

Wes. There's been a development. Rachel's Oscar-winning performance did the business. We've got enough evidence now for a search. Come on.'

Neil, a man who didn't like to be hurried, looked at his friend sympathetically and raised a hand in farewell.

They walked quickly back to the station.

'So what happened?'

'Our Rachel's missed her vocation . . . should be in the Royal Shakespeare Company by the sound of it. He told her the lot. How he arranged things, everything. What we need now is solid evidence. You're not telling me there aren't records of this lot somewhere in that place.'

It didn't take long to organise. The warrant was obtained and the clinic's records searched systematically. Wesley kept a low profile. All he could think about was what the staffs' attitude would be should Pam need more treatment. He would hardly be a welcome visitor after all this.

Administration staff stood about awkwardly as the search through the files and computer systems continued. Dr Downey was on the golf course, though no doubt he would have been notified on his mobile phone by now.

Everything seemed to be above board. Dr Downey seemed to have left no trace of his less-than-legal activities. But in a locked drawer in the doctor's office Wesley eventually made the discovery. A computer disk.

'Go on, then, Wes. I'm computer-illiterate . . . you have a go.' Heffernan stood back while the sergeant inserted the disk into the appropriate hole and pressed a few buttons.

The information came up on the screen. Names, dates, addresses, medical details. Among the names were those of Elaine Berrisford and Sharon Carteret. Sharon's pregnancy was detailed: her weight, blood pressure, urine tests – the lot. She'd certainly been well cared for. The doctor's fee appeared in the list of details. It had been a very lucrative business, exploiting people's innermost needs.

Wesley and the inspector left the team to get on with the search. Heffernan would see Dr Downey later and no doubt there'd be charges. But there were more pressing matters. Stan Jenkins had to know the truth.

'So you mean Jonathon isn't her child.' Stan had just about got the message but was still staring at Gerry Heffernan in disbelief. 'But I could have sworn she was the child's mum. She seemed so . . .'

'Well, I suppose adoptive parents feel just the same. And I suppose he is her husband's biological child. I believe that's the usual arrangement. It certainly said so in the records – child conceived by artificial insemination.'

Stan was starting to recover from the shock. 'So he's alive. Jonathon . . . he's alive, he's okay?' From the relief in his voice Heffernan would have supposed Stan to have known the child, even been a relative. Maybe Stan was right; he was getting past it, getting too involved.

'I think we should all go and break the good news to Mrs Berrisford, don't you, Stan?'

'But we haven't got the kid back yet.'

'She'll want to know he's alive. And I wouldn't mind a little word with the lady myself.'

'Shouldn't we go and get the kid first?'

'Oh no. It's a bit delicate, you see. It may take time before we know what's what.' Stan looked puzzled. Heffernan continued. 'I just want to nip back to my office on the way, if you don't mind, Stan. I'm expecting the results of some tests. They should be back by now. When we've got them, I'll be ready to go and see Mrs Berrisford with you.'

Stan Jenkins thought Heffernan looked smug. He wished he knew what was going on.

Chapter 26

I did take Jennet's child to Elizabeth who cried over it and did feed it. I did say to Jennet that she could have any sum she asked.

Jennet did help me bury my sweet Thomas in the cellar in the dead of night that none might have knowledge of the deed. I did give the child a Christian burial and read the words from the prayer book. I pray the Lord will understand. I did confess all to Elizabeth about my dealings with Jennet so that she will feel the child to be rightly hers as it is mine. We named the little one Thomas and he doth continue to thrive. Elizabeth is his mother now and Jennet doth seem well content with the arrangement. I did give her a goodly sum of money and a costly ring as a sign of my gratitude that after so many years without an heir she hath given me a son. The ring I had engraved on the inside. She took it and put it on her finger. I trust all will be well.

Extract from the journal of John Banized,
28 February 1624

Heffernan had not visited Hedgerow Cottage before. A nice property, he thought – beautifully renovated. The rambling rose round the stripped wood front door bore the last blooms of the season; a final desperate effort before its winter death. The small leaded windows sparkled in the

October sun. It was a cottage from a Sunday supplement, a desirable second home. It must have cost a packet.

The interior was plain and tasteful. White walls interspersed with oak beams gave an illusion of light and space to the low-ceilinged room. The furniture, antique and sparse, stood on a tasteful beige carpet on which were laid expensive rugs from the Middle East. It was clear that there was money about as well as good taste.

Elaine Berrisford sat forward on the antique sofa, looking nervous as Stan Jenkins introduced his colleague. Stan was being too soft, thought Heffernan. It was no use pussyfooting around now. He had to know the truth. If Stan wasn't going to speak plainly, someone had to.

'We think we might have found Jonathon, Mrs Berrisford. Did your mother-in-law tell you?'

Heffernan couldn't decide whether Elaine looked shocked or hopeful. 'No. Do you mean she knows . . .?'

'Well, I'm not really surprised she's not been in touch. You see, it's not as straightforward as it seems. Are you ready to answer some questions, Mrs Berrisford?'

'Of course. But where's Jonathan? Is he all right? When can we . . .?'

'He's come to no harm. But then he wouldn't, would he? Not if he's with his dad.'

The shock on her face was visible for a second, then she regained control. 'He's with Alan? What do you mean?' There was emotion in her voice. 'Why hasn't Alan let me know? Where is he? You've no right to keep me from seeing him if you know where he is.'

'He's not with your husband, Mrs Berrisford. He's with his real father. I had the results of some DNA tests today which prove Jonathon is the child of Christopher Manners. Do you know Mr Manners?'

She shook her head. 'You're wrong. Jonathon's my husband's child. How dare you suggest . . .'

'I'm not suggesting anything, Mrs Berrisford. Jonathon is the child of Christopher Manners and a young woman called Sharon Carteret. We've got proof.'

She shook her head in disbelief. 'It's impossible . . .'

209

'We know all about Dr Downey, and the clinic, and the arrangement you had with Sharon.'

For the first time Elaine Berrisford looked scared. Stan Jenkins was surprised at the change from bereaved, anxious parent to terrified suspect. He felt sorry for this woman whom he had comforted and supported over the past weeks, but somehow the professional in him took over. The child was safe, and this was now a murder inquiry. He let Gerry Heffernan get on with it – best not to interfere.

'Where's Jonathon?' she asked softly.

'I'm afraid I can't say at the moment, but he's safe and well. Tell me how you met Dr Downey. Was it through your mother-in-law?'

Elaine looked as though she knew when she was beaten. Her face bore the strain of the past weeks. She looked drawn and haggard and the dark shadows beneath her eyes betrayed lack of sleep. When she spoke it was almost a whisper.

'I had an operation when I was sixteen. It meant I couldn't have any children. Alan said he didn't mind at first – you know how it is, you're getting used to each other and getting your home together. He knew from the start. I was honest with him. He said he didn't care.' She took a tissue from her sleeve and blew her nose. 'Then our friends started having kids, one after the other. At first it didn't seem to matter, then I started to think about nothing else. I don't know if it's nature or what but ... Anyway, we tried to adopt but Alan had a criminal record. Something stupid he did when he was younger, before he met me.'

'What was it he did, Elaine?' Heffernan asked gently, not wanting to break the atmosphere of confidence.

'He got involved in an incident outside a pub. He was convicted of grievous bodily harm. The police said it was premeditated – a vicious attack, they said. I didn't even know about it until they looked into his background. I was devastated. It seemed completely out of character for him, honestly. He's never shown any sign of . . . It wasn't fair that we should be made to suffer for something he did when . . .'

'So what happened then?'

210

'Alan's mother – she lives in Queenswear, Alan was her only son – she wanted a grandchild almost as much as we wanted to be parents. She knew this doctor, at the Morbay Clinic. We saw him and he examined me and confirmed that I couldn't have any children, not even by IVF.'

She stopped talking for a minute, gathering her thoughts. Heffernan waited patiently. Then she continued, quietly and calmly. 'Mary, my mother-in-law, had this girl living downstairs. She'd got a boyfriend, a real no-hoper, always in debt. She kept asking Mary to let her off her rent for a month, that sort of thing. She was working but the boyfriend must have gone through her money, I don't know how: gambling or drugs, I don't know.' She breathed deeply before carrying on. 'Mary arranged it. I don't know how, I never asked. She told this girl that if she'd have a baby for us, we'd pay off all her debts and pay her a lump sum too. You're wrong about the boyfriend being the father. It was all in the agreement. The baby was Alan's, by artificial insemination. I wouldn't have liked . . .'

'Of course not,' Stan said puritanically. 'Go on.'

'I met the girl. She didn't seem too bright but I was so grateful to her. I thought it was all going to be perfect. She'd have our baby, we'd pay the money and then we'd never see her again. That'd be it.'

'So what went wrong?'

She looked up at Heffernan. It was as though he knew. 'She had the baby in the clinic. She had the best of care, no expense spared. I went in at the same time. I'd pretended to be pregnant at home. I'd even worn one of those corset things like they do on the stage. Nobody was going to know it wasn't my baby. Dr Downey saw to everything – the birth certificate, everything. I thought when we paid the money over and left the clinic with Jonathon that was it.' Tears began to well up in her eyes. 'I never thought we'd see the girl again. She'd done her job and got paid for it. That was going to be it.'

'But it wasn't, was it?'

'The boyfriend was greedy. He found out where we lived and said if we didn't pay them money every month, he'd say what had happened. We'd never legally adopted Jonathon –

Dr Downey said there was no need. That Chris, he said Jonathon would be taken away from us.' She began to sob.

'So you paid up?'

Elaine nodded. 'What we'd done wasn't legal. I knew that much. What else could we do?'

'So what happened when Jonathon went missing?' Heffernan looked across at Stan, who was listening intently.

'When he disappeared, I thought he'd wandered off or been abducted or something. It was like a nightmare.'

'What every mother dreads,' Stan said quietly.

She turned to him, pleading. 'I was his mother. She'd had nothing to do with him – she just had him, provided a service. I was his mother. I looked after him; nursed him when he was ill; he loved me. He called me Mummy.'

'When did you find out he was with Sharon and Chris?' Heffernan asked before things got too emotional.

'It was a couple of days later. Chris rang me to say he was with them and he was okay. I rang Mary but she said Sharon had moved out quickly and she didn't know where they'd gone. We drove round, we looked everywhere . . . and the police . . .'

Stan spoke gently. 'You really should have told us, Elaine.'

'I know but . . . I'm sorry. You were very kind. Everyone . . . I'm sorry.'

'So when did Sharon and Chris get in touch again?' Heffernan looked her in the eyes, challenging. Elaine shook her head and started to weep.

'So this is the place all the complaints have been about,' Gerry Heffernan commented as Rachel parked the car on the edge of the travellers' site. 'It's a while since I've been on the hippie trail to Neston.'

He got out of the car slowly and slammed the door. A barking dog followed them; not an auspicious start. Their progress was watched by a group of dirty-faced children and a young man in a multicoloured woolly hat who sat, whittling a piece of wood, on the steps of an ancient bus. The young man directed them wordlessly to Chris's caravan and returned to his task with studied concentration.

The caravan door was open. Chris was sitting with his

feet up reading a racing paper while Jonathon played with his bricks on the floor. When he saw his visitors, Chris sat up, apprehensive.

'Hello, Chris. You don't mind if we come in? You've already met DC Tracey, haven't you?'

Chris's expression gave nothing away. He gathered the child up protectively and sat him on his knee. The child buried his face in Chris's sweatshirt.

'I've just been talking to Inspector Jenkins. He's in charge of the search for that missing kid, Jonathon Berrisford.'

Chris looked wary.

'Jonathon.'

The child looked round.

'We've had some tests done, Mr Manners. DNA. It seems you're the kid's dad after all.'

'I told you.' Triumphantly.

'He does look like the missing kid, though. I was looking at a picture of him just before.' He paused. 'But the hair's wrong, isn't it? You can really change people's looks with hair, can't you? I mean, Jonathon Berrisford's hair was quite short. Daniel's is long. Jonathon was blond. Daniel's dark, isn't he, Mr Manners?'

Chris nodded warily. This was getting uncomfortable.

'I had another test done. The officer who took the samples also snipped off a little bit of Daniel's hair. You don't usually use hair dye on a kid of that age, do you, Mr Manners?'

Chris hugged the child to him.

'Hello, Jonathon. Do you like it here?'

The child nodded and grinned at the funny policeman who looked like a great big bear. Then he put his arms around Chris's neck and clung on.

'So what happened, Chris? Are you going to tell us here or at the station?'

'How much do you know?' he said quietly, stroking his son's hair.

'Quite a bit. We know about your debts and how you paid them. About Mrs Hughes . . .'

'That cow . . . she treated us like shit. Like bloody animals, breeding for her precious daughter-in-law. People who've got money treat people who haven't like bloody shit.'

'Leave the politics out of it, Chris. What happened?'

'Sharon was to have this baby, for this rich couple. She went to this posh clinic. They gave her this syringe thing with the man's sperm, told her what to do, but she didn't. She had some bloody pride. The kid was conceived in the usual way. I was the dad. Right?' Heffernan nodded. He suspected it had been Chris's pride rather than Sharon's that had dictated this arrangement. 'Anyway, she had the kid and everything was fine. She got paid and it saw off my debts, got the bookies off my back. I told her we could always have more kids when the time was right. She'd forget all about this one.'

'So what went wrong?'

'It was all fine while she was carrying this kid for that bloody doctor's rich friends. She was examined every week, had every test going. But once it had been born, Sharon had done her bit, she was no use any more. Just treated like a bloody farm animal. He never even examined her after the kid was born.' The child swung down off his father's knee and returned to his coloured bricks on the floor. 'She got an infection. She didn't know for ages, just had a few pains and that. They lasted so long she thought it was normal. We decided to try for a kid of our own but nothing happened. Turned out the infection had buggered up her insides, she couldn't have any more.'

Rachel, who had been in the background listening, squatted down and began to build a tower for the boy. He grinned at her and added some bricks.

'So you decided to get your child back?' Heffernan spoke softly, sympathetically.

'Yeah. I borrowed this mate's car and me and Sharon watched the cottage till we got the chance. He's a great kid, Inspector. We were dead happy. It was like he knew we were his real mum and dad. We had to dye his hair 'cause there were pictures of him everywhere. He was dead good when we did it. It was sort of a game to him.' He paused. 'I was always drifting, gambling, but when I had the kid to look after, and Sharon, it was different. We'd not lived together before: I'd had to work away a lot, stay in digs and all that. But we got on well, the three of us. Sharon's mum

214

and dad were killed and she'd not had a family before. It was all working out so well. And my mum knew. She helped out, looking after Danny and that. I don't think we did anything wrong.'

He looked at Heffernan. There were tears starting to appear in his eyes.

'Are you still in debt, Chris?'

'I've got my weaknesses. I'd always bet on anything, even when I was a kid. I tried to give it up when we got Danny back, but when Sharon went . . .'

'What happened to Sharon?'

'I don't know. That's the honest truth. I just thought she'd been attacked by some maniac. She was going on about making everything right, sorting things out with the Berrisfords. I'd rung them to say Danny was okay but she said she wanted to make everything right, legal. I told her not to be so daft. They might ask for the money back and there was no way . . .'

'So you killed her to stop her . . .'

'No. I didn't bloody kill her. You can get that right out of your heads. I didn't kill her. I was with those mates up in Tavistock. I did a job up there. You've checked already. Danny had gone to his gran's for a few days. She wanted to see him. Sharon was on her own in the flat. Why should I want to kill her? Danny needed a mum.'

'So you were away and you don't know whether she set up some sort of meeting with the Berrisfords?'

'I told her not to, to leave well alone. But I suppose she might have done it off her own bat. She did have this thing about letting them down and trying to make it okay.'

'Which one was she in touch with? Mr Berrisford? Mrs Berrisford? Mrs Hughes? Who would she contact?'

'I've no idea. As far as I know she didn't contact any of them. I just said she might have done. Danny can stay with me, can't he? I don't know what I'd do without him now.'

He reached down and stroked the child's hair.

Gerry Heffernan was going soft, just like Stan. There was nothing more he would have liked at that moment than to say yes to Chris's question. The man clearly loved his son, unconventional though the arrangement was.

215

'We'll have to ask you to come down to the station, make a statement.' Chris nodded, resigned. 'You can bring Daniel, or leave him with your friends if you'd prefer. It shouldn't take long. You'll get straight home afterwards.'

Chris went over to Donna and Sludge's caravan to ask if they could look after the child for an hour or so, then they went straight back to Tradmouth. When he got back to the station, Heffernan had an important question to ask Stan Jenkins. He practically ran up to Stan's office, probably not advisable for a man of his age and build. He didn't bother with any greeting. He just had one thing to ask.

'Was Alan Berrisford down here at the time of the murder?'

'Do you know, Gerry, now I think of it, I believe he was. He went back up north the day after. Why? Do you think . . .'

Wesley was going through statements when Chris Manners was brought in. Rachel came and told him about the latest developments.

'So you reckon he's in the clear?' he asked.

'All his alibis check out. He's a gambler and a bit of a villain on a minor scale but that doesn't mean he killed Sharon. The boss thinks it'd be worth checking the Berrisfords' alibis. They would have felt strongly enough about what had happened to do something about it.'

'What's happening now?'

'He's making a statement – about the clinic and how him and Sharon got the kid back. By the way, did you know Alan Berrisford's got a conviction for GBH? I've looked up the file. Vicious knife attack outside a pub in Morbay when he was about twenty. Lay in wait for this other bloke, apparently – quarrel over a girl. Got four months.'

Wesley raised his eyebrows. 'Is he down here at the moment?'

'No. Back up north.'

Wesley didn't fancy another trip to Manchester.

'Rachel, do you remember anyone called Boscople? I'm sure I've heard the name somewhere but . . .'

Rachel shook her head. 'Name seems familiar. Ask the

216

boss.' She turned to go but hesitated at the door. 'It does ring a bell. I think it's one of the people we interviewed when Sharon's body was found. But don't take my word for it.'

When she left, Wesley dug deeper into his files. Then he found it. PC Johnson had interviewed a Bill Boscople, one of the workers on Cissy Hutchins's farm, to see if he'd seen anything suspicious – which he hadn't, as he'd been working in another part of the farm at the time. The interview, confirming nothing, had been recorded and forgotten. There was a note on the file that said Boscople had also been interviewed because he was working in the fields near by at the time of Jonathon Berrisford's disappearance. There was an address, presumably a tied cottage at Hutchins Farm. Wesley wrote it down.

'Come on, Wes, we're off up north again. You drive.'

Wesley had hoped to see Neil with Bill Boscople's address, maybe even follow it up himself, but duty came first. This time they might even make an arrest, judging by what the inspector had said.

Gerry Heffernan sat in the passenger seat. There was a suppressed energy about him, an air of excitement.

'Will you get a chance to see your daughter while we're up there, sir?'

'Shouldn't think so. She'll be much too busy. Anyway, I reckon it'll be an interview, quick arrest and back down the M5. Won't have much time for socialising.'

'Do you think Berrisford did it?'

'He's a man capable of violence. This stupid girl, a girl who he'd paid well to provide a service, had just deprived him of his son and heir. He's got no alibi. He knows the area round the footpath well. I should say he's the prime suspect, wouldn't you?'

'Yes, I suppose he is. Nearly there, sir.'

With the help of the *A to Z*, they located the main road out of Wilmslow without too much difficulty. The Berrisfords' house was larger than anything Wesley would have aspired to. A substantial Edwardian detached with a sweeping drive, it smelled of wealth and good taste.

The front door, glossy with flawless red paint, was opened by a young woman with a ponytail who introduced herself as the cleaner. Mr Berrisford was at work as far as she knew. Wesley braced himself for a drive into Manchester.

It wasn't so bad out of rush hour. Gerry Heffernan looked out of the window as the scene outside changed from leafy suburbs to redbrick urban landscape to run-down districts to busy city centre. At last, after driving around for ten minutes, they found somewhere to park.

Berrisford and Brady, Wine Merchants was in the better part of town, near the business quarter, set amongst exclusive shops with exclusive prices. The two officers stepped through the etched glass door into a scene from a more elegant age. Discretion was the watchword here. The interior of dark polished wood had few bottles on display, and those there were looked alarmingly expensive. This wasn't the average high street off-licence. The customers here were connoisseurs and didn't mind paying for their indulgences.

'Not somewhere you'd buy a litre of Spanish plonk on a Saturday night,' Heffernan whispered to Wesley softly, in case the superior gentleman with distinguished grey hair and a bow tie, who stood expectantly behind the mahogany counter, heard and disapproved.

'May I help you, gentlemen? Perhaps I might interest you in a Côte du Rhone that we had delivered yesterday. I must say it's an excellent year. I really can recommend . . .'

Heffernan showed his warrant card and the sales talk stopped abruptly. 'We're looking for Alan Berrisford. Am I correct in thinking he works here?'

'Er, yes. He's my partner. I'm Geoffrey Brady. Alan's in the back. He deals mainly with the mail order side of the business. If you'd like to follow me, gentlemen.'

Brady led them through well-stocked storerooms. Rows of bottles gleamed on racks. Light wooden boxes, stamped with the names of vineyards even the inspector had heard of, were piled up against the walls.

'I hope it's not bad news, Inspector. It's terrible about Alan's little boy, it really is.'

Heffernan and Wesley were giving nothing away. Geoffrey Brady, denied information, knocked on a plain office door and announced them. Heffernan thanked him and waited for him to return to his post before stepping into Alan Berrisford's lair.

Berrisford was there at the desk, bent over a pile of invoices. He looked at his visitors apprehensively.

'Mr Berrisford, where were you on September the seventeenth?'

Alan Berrisford, with trembling hands, reached for his diary. 'I was down at the cottage, with my wife. Why?'

'Alan Berrisford, I'm arresting you for the murder of Sharon Carteret.'

Wesley looked at Berrisford's defiant face as the inspector gabbled the required words. It would be an interesting journey home. He hoped there would be no hold-ups on the motorway.

Chapter 27

All was well until my wife did discover Jennet holding Thomas in her arms. I had ordered that she have no dealings with the child and my wife was rightly angry.

No one suspects that the child is not my wife's. We did put it abroad that Jennet was delivered of a dead child as a consequence of her sin. I did offer Jennet more money but she did refuse it and did return that which I had already given her. I did order her from the house but she would not go without her child.

My wife is distraught. I must needs remedy the situation.

Extract from the journal of John Banized,
29 March 1624

Whatever Elaine Berrisford might have done, Stan Jenkins thought she had the right to know that little Jonathon was safe and happy. He had sat with her too many times and watched her suffer. He felt he couldn't just abandon the woman.

'So how do you feel, Elaine? You know if there's anything I can do . . .'

'Thank you. You've been so good, you really have.' She sipped her tea absent-mindedly. 'Can I see Alan?'

'Not at the moment, I'm afraid. They're still questioning him. I'm really sorry how things have turned out.'

'At least Jonathon's all right.'

'Yes. I've seen him and he's fine. You do realise that Sharon's boyfriend was his real father, don't you?' He spoke gently; he was on delicate ground. 'Sharon deceived you. She didn't stick to her side of the bargain.'

Elaine nodded. 'Does it mean he might be able to keep him?'

'I really don't know much about these things but I suppose there's a chance. I can't tell you about the legal position because I just don't know it. But Jonathon's happy and Social Services say he's all right where he is for the time being.'

Elaine twisted her handkerchief in her hands. 'I just want him back. That's all I ever wanted.'

'I know, Elaine, I know.'

'You say he's okay? Where's he living? What kind of place?'

Stan hesitated. There couldn't be any harm in putting the woman's mind at rest. After all, she'd been through enough.

'He's not exactly living in luxury but he's happy enough. He's got lots of other kids to play with on the site. I know it doesn't look very clean or conventional but then we mustn't judge . . .'

'Where is it? What site?'

He might as well tell her, he'd given enough away already. 'The travellers' site at Neston. It's not as bad as it sounds, honestly, and there are lots of children . . .'

Elaine stood up. 'I'm feeling rather tired, Stan. Thank you for coming. You'll let me know when I can see Alan?'

'Of course.' Stan rose and put his half-full cup of tea on the coffee table.

'Stan . . .'

'Yes?'

'If Alan killed this girl, he did it because he was provoked. She'd taken our child. They'll take all that into account, won't they? She wouldn't listen to reason.'

Stan didn't answer. He felt very uneasy as he left Hedgerow Cottage. He didn't know why.

Heffernan leaned forward. 'Why did you do it, Alan? Why did you do that to her face?'

The atmosphere in the interview room was tense. Wesley shifted a little in his chair. He needed a cup of tea ... or something stronger.

'Come on, Alan. Did she laugh at you? Is that it? After all you'd been through, after all the money you paid, did she tell you that you weren't the kid's real father? It must have really got to you. I mean, killing her's one thing, but doing that to her face. I saw her in the mortuary, you know, at the post-mortem. I saw what you did.'

Alan Berrisford seemed to have shrunk in stature since Wesley first encountered him. He sat hunched on his plastic chair. He looked pathetic, as murderers often do when their wrongdoings are discovered.

When he spoke, he was barely audible. Heffernan had to ask him to speak up for the tape machine.

'I was angry. She laughed. She turned round and I hit her. Then I kept on hitting her. That's it. That's what happened.'

'What did you hit her with?'

'A piece of wood ... a branch.'

'What did you do with it?'

'I threw it away.'

'Where?'

'I don't know ... just away.'

'Why were you meeting her?'

'She rang, asked to meet me, sort things out. She wanted to keep Jonathon, wanted us to agree ...'

'She was being a bit naïve, then ... a bit optimistic?'

Alan looked up as if he'd never thought of the situation in those terms before. 'Yes, she was. There was no way we'd give up our son, no way.'

Heffernan looked at the clock on the green-tiled wall, then at Wesley. He spoke to the tape machine. 'Interview terminated at fifteen hundred hours.' He nodded to the uniformed constable in the corner, who led the crumpled Alan back to the cells.

'He looked like he needed a break, Wes, and we've got to be there at four.'

222

The sergeant nodded. He had nearly forgotten about the funeral. It wasn't something he was looking forward to, but it was customary to attend. They left at half past three – plenty of time to get to Morbay crematorium.

The funerals of murder victims always seem to excite more interest than those of individuals who have died in more mundane circumstances. There was a good turnout. Chris Manners, his son in his arms, led the mourners; Sludge and Donna, out of place and awkward, provided a modicum of moral support. The model agency was well represented as their former receptionist went on her final journey. Phil was there, looking solemn. A few of the models stood about self-consciously, among them Karen Giordino. She wore a short black suit and Mr Carl had done her hair specially for the occasion. After all, there might be photographers.

Heffernan watched Karen. She looked pensive, as if contemplating her own mortality. At one time, everyone had thought it would be her in the coffin. What if . . . Karen shivered; it was too awful to contemplate. Life was unpredictable and you had to live each day to the full. That was why she had just ditched John. He was holding her back; cramping her. The previous evening she had also rung her mother. Life was too short to bear grudges. Karen felt tears prick her eyes as the vicar read the words of the funeral service. Her only thought as the coffin disappeared behind the chapel curtains to its fiery fate was 'They thought it was me . . . it could have been me'.

Chris's mum, who lived on the council estate on the edge of Morbay, invited people back for refreshments. Most declined. They had come for their own reasons – to pay their respects or out of curiosity – and now they just wanted to get home. Sharon had had no family so Chris's relations had to suffice. The mourners broke up into awkward groups, hung round for a while, then returned to their everyday lives.

Karen Giordino, as she was leaving, even managed to grace Heffernan and Wesley with a tentative half-smile. Life was too short.

It was after five when they got back to the station. Alan,

the inspector said, would keep till tomorrow. He had confessed. The charges had been made. It was all a matter of paperwork now – the blight of the modern policeman's life.

The statements lay on Heffernan's desk. Dr Downey had made a guarded statement in the presence of his solicitor. Even Mrs Hughes had come clean about her involvement in the case. She insisted she had done nothing criminal. No doubt Heffernan could think of something if he put his mind to it.

Chris Manners had named the men who were supplying him with the stolen building materials. The inspector had decided to ask for him to be treated leniently; he would recommend probation in view of the accused's co-operation and domestic circumstances. According to that long-haired woman from Social Services, it was looking increasingly likely that Chris might be able to keep his son. Heffernan hoped so. There was nothing like a bit of domestic responsibility to keep a young man on the straight and narrow: he had seen it before time after time.

Wesley knocked and walked in, interrupting the inspector's thoughts.

'All cleared up, sir?'

'Just about, Wes, just about. I had Stan in before saying he'd let slip where the kid was to Elaine Berrisford.'

'Hell.'

'It probably doesn't matter. She won't try and get him back now. Surely the woman's got more sense.'

Wesley nodded. 'Just have to keep an eye on the situation. Anyway, even if she did go down to Neston, the worst thing that could happen would be an embarrassing scene.'

'You're most likely right, Wes. Wish he hadn't done it, though.'

'Is it okay if I go now? I've got a call to make on the way home.'

'You go, Wes. See you tomorrow. We'll get some cans in, have a bit of a celebration tomorrow night – you tell everyone.'

There was always a celebratory atmosphere when a murder case was cleared up. And this one had the added bonus of the missing toddler being found alive and well. Wesley promised to spread the news.

Neil was preparing to pack up for the night when Wesley arrived at the site. Matt and Jane had left already. They were going to the theatre in Plymouth. Neil commented that it was all right for some. Wesley sensed a hint of envy and wondered why Neil hadn't a partner of his own: he had always been popular with the opposite sex at university; he had even gone out with Pam at one time, before Wesley had swept her off her feet, of course.

'How are you fixed for coming down to Little Tradmouth? I think I've tracked down William Boscople.'

'Great. Now?'

Wesley nodded. Now was as good a time as any, and Pam wasn't expecting him back for another couple of hours.

Wesley's car was at home. Neil's yellow Mini was squatting a quarter of a mile away in the municipal carpark near the waterfront. They drove out of Tradmouth up the steep incline of the main road. The Mini struggled valiantly. When it eventually reached its destination the poor thing looked out of breath.

Hutchins Farm Cottages were sited, as their name suggested, near Hutchins Farm. Number 3 looked less well cared for than its neighbours. The curtains hanging limply at the windows were in need of a good wash. Wesley used his knuckles to knock on the door; there was no bell or knocker visible.

Inside the cottage Bill Boscople put down his newspaper on the ancient settee which used to be green but was now an indeterminate shade of brown. He wished they wouldn't put those pictures on page three – it was no good for his blood pressure and the doctor had told him to take it easy and not to get too excited. Bad enough with all these murders and kids going missing. The place was getting like Chicago – he'd said as much to his mates in the Farmers' Arms the other night.

There was another knock on the door, louder this time.

''Ang on. . . . 'Ang on . . .' Bill Boscople stood up, stiff from shifting bales of hay. He was getting past it, he thought; the old joints weren't what they were. He was a wiry man,

225

average height with a mop of grey hair and the weather-beaten features of one who has spent most of his adult life working out of doors. He moved slowly towards the door, hoping it wasn't Cissy Hutchins wanting another job done just when he was settled for the evening. It was good on telly tonight.

He opened the door to find two young men standing there. He'd seen the black one before at the farm: he was one of the policemen who'd come up to interview that Mrs Truscot when she found the body. The other one didn't look like a policeman with all that hair, but you never knew nowadays. What did they want?

'I know you,' he said to Wesley in an accent that was pure West Country. 'You'm one of them policemen what come about the murder. Come along in. I don't mind helping the police with their enquiries.'

Wesley decided to do the talking, seeing he had a head start already. 'Mr Boscople?'

'That's me.'

'My name's Wesley Peterson. I'm a detective sergeant but I'm not here professionally.' He pointed to Neil. 'This is Neil Watson. We're doing some detective work of our own.'

'Private detectives?' Bill Boscople was impressed.

'I'll let Neil explain. He's with the County Archaeological Unit.'

Boscople looked confused, but as Neil gave an account of the dig and his discoveries, he began to nod with understanding.

'Aye, me mother were a Banized. I did hear tell that her family were not short of a bob or two at one time, but . . .'

'The wills in the museum at Tradmouth mention a journal, Mr Boscople. I know it's a long shot but we worked out from your family tree that if it still existed, it might have come to you.'

Boscople looked puzzled. 'What would it look like, this journal?'

'A book, I should think, handwritten . . . a diary.'

Boscople shook his head. 'I never seen it.' He paused, deep in thought. 'I don't know what's in them trunks, mind. Put 'em in the attic when me old mum died and never

226

looked in 'em. You're welcome to have a look if you like, if it's for the museum.'

Neil was longing to get his hands on the trunks but tried to contain his impatience. 'The vicar of Tradmouth's made up your family tree from the old church records, Mr Boscople. I'll take you along to see it one day if you want. And you must come to the exhibition at the County Museum – it's about your family, after all.'

'Aye, but they were a murdering lot by the sounds of it. What was it? Two skeletons you found. Don't know as I want to go.'

'If we find this journal . . .'

'Oh, aye, that's what you've come for.' He led them to the top of the steep, narrow, uncarpeted stairs and pointed up at a small trapdoor. 'They be up there.' He looked Wesley up and down. 'You'm not really dressed for it, me luvver. I'd send your mate up.'

Neil, clothes already grimy from the dig and game for anything, was provided with a ladder and a torch. Wesley stood at the bottom in his working suit, waiting self-consciously. Bill Boscople, he thought, probably didn't have a high opinion of people who wore suits.

It was a full fifteen minutes before Neil emerged, filthy but triumphant. 'You should have a look in those trunks, Mr Boscople. There's all sorts in there: war medals, old clothes, letters – fascinating stuff.'

'I'll take yer word vor't.' Boscople looked unimpressed.

Wesley could hardly contain his curiosity. 'Did you find it?'

Neil sat on the top rung of the ladder, grinning. He took a small brown leather-bound volume from his pocket and held it up.

'Would you mind very much if I kept this to have a good look at it? I'll return it as soon as we're finished with it, of course.'

'You'm do what you want wi'it. 'Tis no use to me. If it make you two gentlemen 'appy then you keep it. What'd I do wi'it?'

'Would you donate it to the museum, then, Mr Boscople? It'd be very much appreciated.'

'I told you, 'tis no use to me. What'd I want wi' old smelly books?'

'Thanks very much. We'll make sure there's a special notice up saying you kindly donated it.'

Boscople again looked unimpressed. He glanced at the cheap carriage clock on the tiled fireplace. It was nearly time for his programme. He suddenly had a thought. 'It's not worth ort, is it?'

'Not a lot in monetary terms, Mr Boscople,' said Neil earnestly. 'But in historical terms, for the museum, it's very valuable.'

'So it i'n't worth much money, then?'

'I'm sorry, probably not much. But as I said . . .'

'You 'ave it, then. More use to you than me.'

Neil and Wesley bade Bill Boscople a polite farewell before he changed his mind.

Wesley invited Neil back for an evening meal. Then they could have a look at the journal properly. If Pam hadn't cooked enough, he could always go down to Tradmouth for a takeaway. The journal lay on Wesley's lap. He opened it. The spidery handwriting was surprisingly easy to read. He read through the first pages, which were mainly accounts of how trade was going, interspersed with local gossip about the mayor, vicar and other solid citizens of the Banizeds' acquaintance. It seemed it would prove to be a fascinating account of life in a thriving port in the first quarter of the seventeenth century. He resisted opening the later pages. What, he wondered, would they reveal about John Banized, Merchant of Tradmouth?

When they arrived at Wesley's house, he carried the journal carefully inside and placed it in the centre of the coffee table.

Elaine Berrisford put on her coat; the nights were getting colder. She pushed the front door to make sure it was locked. The alarm was on, and the light in the living room. She shivered as she walked to the car, which was parked at the side of the cottage on the drive they had created by demolishing a section of hedgerow; it was amazing how

228

much life had been in that hedge – birds, small animals, insects.

She felt in her pocket. It was still there. She unlocked the car and got in.

Chapter 28

Jennet is beyond reason. Last night I did discover
her trying to lift the child from his cradle while my
wife was at her toilet. She says she will have him;
will take him from the house and back to her family.
She threatens to tell the truth abroad, that the child
is hers as a consequence of my lust for her.

I know not the remedy for this. The Lord doth
punish me for my misdeeds.

Extract from the journal of John Banized,
30 March 1624

Pam was nearly asleep when Wesley came to bed. He and
Neil had had a lot to discuss, and some cans of best bitter
to get through. Pam had gone to bed at half ten – she had
work the next day.

'You're a lucky man, Wes,' Neil had said wistfully when
Pam had said goodnight. Wesley found himself wondering
just how serious Pam's relationship with Neil had been
before he had met her. She had never mentioned him, but
now he had come back into their lives she seemed glad to
see him – even when he descended on her for an unplanned
dinner. But these were night thoughts, the kind rendered
insubstantial by morning light. Pam was just pleased to see
an old friend. Her spirits had certainly risen since her
conversation with Maritia. Maybe she was taking her sister-
in-law's advice to heart. He hoped so.

They had begun to read the journal, laughing at the

candid comments about the pompous citizens. The writing was lively and legible, but the pages were brittle and had to be treated with the utmost care. It had been decided that it should stay in Wesley's care for the time being, his house seeming safer than any alternative overnight accommodation.

Wesley couldn't resist it – just a quick read before he went to sleep. They had reached the part where Jennet had been taken on as a serving maid, but had decided to leave the next thrilling instalment for another night. But it was there, on the coffee table. Wesley gave in to temptation and carried the volume carefully upstairs. Pam turned over in bed; she was in that state between waking and sleeping.

'You're not bringing that dirty old book to bed with you, are you?' She turned away sleepily and closed her eyes.

Wesley undressed quietly and got into bed, turning his bedside light on. Pam hid her head under the duvet. He was tired, very tired, but the small brown book lying on the bedside table was more enticing than any amount of sleep. He picked it up, turning the pages delicately, carefully: he didn't want to damage such an ancient volume. He sat back against the padded headboard, making himself comfortable. This would take a long time. Pam shuffled further under the covers, as if to make a point.

Wesley began to read from where he and Neil had left off. He couldn't resist the temptation of discovering what had happened to Jennet, whether the master of the house had been considerate enough to commit his deeds to paper for future generations.

The master of the house had indeed been obliging; the journal had clearly been for his eyes alone. Wesley was growing accustomed to the handwriting and the style and he was able to read quickly as the account of John Banized's temptation unfolded. It was a familiar story, that of yielding to forbidden desire, well-known by policeman and clergyman in existence.

Adultery hadn't come easy to John Banized. His increasing helplessness as he faced the failings of his flesh, his seesawing emotions of pleasure and regret, were palpable. Wesley found himself wondering about Jennet's feelings on the matter. He turned the pages, unable to put the volume down as the story developed. He began to read about the substitution of the babies with unease. Had he not been dealing with a similar case, similar emotions, for the past few weeks?

He read on. Things were becoming more and more desperate, John Banized more and more helpless. He reached the part where Jennet wanted to take the child, her child. He could hardly leave the narrative at this point. He read on.

2 April 1624
May the Lord forgive the deeds I am to write of. I am cursed for my sins. I have paid for my wrongdoings a hundredfold.

Last night I did discover Jennet with the child. She wore her cloak and had with her her belongings. She did say to me that she would go from the house and take Thomas with her. He was hers and no man could deny her. She did vow to declare the truth across the district if I would not pay her a handsome sum for the upkeep of the infant. I did offer her a sovereign, hoping to persuade her but she did take it and say it would suffice for the journey.

I was pleading with her, kneeling to her, as my wife did enter the chamber. She saw me, my face buried in Jennet's lap as in our days of lust. She said she would speak to Jennet privily. I left them, praying that Elizabeth would move Jennet to reason.

When I returned to the chamber a good half hour later, a piteous sight did meet my eyes. I tremble now to recall. My wife stood, the babe in her arms. On the floor amid the rushes, Jennet lay, face downward. The leather belt which I had left upon the bed was fastened tight around her slender neck. I did lift Jennet in the hope that the spirit had not left her. But her face was blue and her tongue did protrude and her eyes did stare . . . oh, I tremble to recall it . . . her lovely face destroyed and showing all the corruption of our sin. My wife did not cry. I said to her 'What have you done?' She did say nought but sang softly to the child and rocked him in her arms.

I waited till the household was abed then I did bury Jennet in the cellar. I did throw the ring I gave her into the grave and some sweet herbs in memory of the pleasure we had shared. I read the prayers over her and begged the Lord to take her soul to Him. I could not have paid a higher price for my sin.

Wesley put the book down. The policeman in him realised he had just read an account of a murder, a statement of the despair and pain of a man and woman who lived four hundred years ago. No wonder the Banizeds kept the journal secret for so many years. Bill Boscople couldn't possibly have known its contents – and would he have been so willing to give it away if he had?

But something else struck Wesley. Something about this account reminded him so much of the Sharon Carteret case. Four hundred years might divide them but human feelings didn't change.

He looked across at Pam. She was sleeping and he didn't want to wake her. He crept downstairs and picked up the phone. It was late, but in view of what he'd learned he had to get in touch with Gerry Heffernan. It would be worth dragging the inspector from his bed to prevent another tragedy.

Elaine Berrisford had never been in such a place before. She hugged her expensive camel coat closer to her. It was cold. She could hear dogs barking. Lights shone in the windows of the old buses and caravans; worn sheets and dirty torn material sufficed as curtains to give the occupants of the vehicles a modicum of privacy. Voices carried in the dark: an argument in one old bus, a guitar being strummed in a caravan.

A baby cried. Elaine froze. But no, it was a young baby; it couldn't be him. She had left her car at the entrance to the muddy track that led to the site. She stood, watching, listening. He was somewhere here. Where was he?

233

Wesley drove down the steep main road into Tradmouth, in second gear all the way. When he reached the waterfront he turned and drove along the Embankment, getting as near as he could to the inspector's house. Tradmouth was quiet – just a few fishermen on the quayside preparing to set sail in the moonlit night. He walked the last few yards to Heffernan's house. The lapping of the river and the bobbing of the boats in the moonlight created an atmosphere of serenity; not a night to be considering death and its consequences.

Heffernan was ready. Wesley turned the car round and they headed down the empty country roads to Neston. They reached the lane leading to the site. Her car was there, the Golf GTi: Wesley recognised it from his visit to Hedgerow Cottage. He had admired it then, wondered if he could afford one. This time his mind was on less material matters.

He parked behind the Golf, blocking it in. He hoped they were in time.

Pressed up against the side of a caravan, Elaine had watched and listened, certain that the darkness would conceal her presence. She watched as a young man in a threadbare jumper and woolly hat knocked on the door of the caravan opposite. The door opened and in the rectangle of light she saw him, the man she was looking for. Her heart began to pound. The woolly-hatted youth didn't go in. Manners was handing him something; the youth was going away; the caravan door was closing. She would wait a few minutes; wait till there was nobody about.

She stood stiffly against the metal wall. Jonathon, she thought, Jonathon was only a few yards away. He would be so pleased to see her, to see his mummy. They would go back to the cottage. He would sleep in her bed. She would watch him tomorrow as he played with all the new toys she had bought him.

She had eliminated one of the obstacles that stood between her and her son. When Sharon had met her on the cliff path, she thought she'd be able to reason with her. But Sharon had rejected her pathetic pleas; had even asked for more money for Jonathon's upkeep. Then they had argued. Sharon had said, 'He's mine, he can never be yours. He's not even your husband's. I did it with Chris, he's Chris's kid, you've no right to him.' Then she'd turned away, smiling, smug.

The branch had just been lying there on the ground, thick, solid. Elaine had eliminated that smile, that gloating face, for good – kept eliminating it, blotting it out. Sharon hadn't been expecting it, had turned her back. It had been so easy.

She had got rid of the branch, thrown it over the cliff, and run back to the cottage. Alan had been there, had seen her clothes splashed with blood. She had had to tell him the truth. He had been so calm. He had burned the clothes in the garden incinerator, moved Sharon's body to a place where it might not be found for a few days, then held Elaine while she wept.

At one time she had thought she might lose Jonathon for good; that Manners would take him somewhere so she couldn't trace him. But now she was near him, would soon touch him, hold him in her arms. He would probably be asleep. She would carry him to the car and he would wake up the next morning, with his mother's loving eyes watching him. She imagined the expression of joy on his little face.

She felt in her pocket. It was still there. The site was quiet. It was time. She emerged from the shadows and walked slowly to Chris Manners' caravan. She knocked softly on the door, not wanting to wake Jonathon.

A shuffling from inside, then the door was opened; opened wide. He expected his visitor to be friend rather than foe. When he saw Elaine his expression changed to one of panic. He tried to close the door but he had opened it too wide. She was inside. He tried to push her out but she stood firm.

'I've come for Jonathon.'

'The kid's mine. Now get out.'

'Where is he?' She tried to push past Chris to get to the bedroom beyond.

He blocked her way. 'You heard me, you stupid bitch. Get out. I can keep him – they said.'

He gave her a push that sent her sprawling to the floor.

Jonathon was beyond that flimsy door. 'I'm not going without Jonathon.'

'I told you, I'm his real dad. I'm keeping him. And his name's Daniel. Now piss off before I get the police.'

He stood, blocking the door to Jonathon. She could tell by the expression on his face that he had no intention of giving way. But a father's love could never be as great as a mother's – never. She felt in her pocket; it was still there, comforting. If all else failed . . .

'Didn't you hear me? Piss off. Do you think I'd let you have him when your husband killed his mum?'

She was on her knees, all artifice gone. She uttered a primal sob. 'I'm his mum.' Tears streamed down her face.

Chris couldn't stand this. He turned his back.

He hadn't expected the sudden lunge, knocking him off balance. Then the sharp pain in his shoulder. He lay stunned and saw the knife flash as it began its downward journey again.

What occurred next seemed to happen in slow motion. His body tensed, expecting the blow. But instead of finding its target, the knife seemed to fly out of Elaine Berrisford's hand. Chris curled up, shielding his head with his arms. He expected pain but none came. Daniel, he thought, what was going to happen to Daniel? The woman was mad. There was no way he'd let her touch his son.

He looked up, prepared to fight back. But there was no need. Elaine Berrisford was standing, sobbing, held between two men. He recognised them, the inspector and the sergeant, but what the hell were they doing here? He didn't care too much. He'd never been glad to see the police but now he was.

Another face appeared at the door. Donna had come over to see what all the commotion had been about. Heffernan was pleased to see her. She could stay with the kid while they got Chris to hospital. Chris put his hand to his sore shoulder and felt something warm and sticky. He was bleeding. Someone was saying the ambulance wouldn't be long.

Chris heard the inspector's words. 'Elaine Berrisford, I'm arresting you for the murder of Sharon Carteret. You don't have to say anything but . . .' At this point Chris lost consciousness. He was unaware of the paramedics lifting him onto the stretcher.

Pam took a bite of toast. She had woken early and, puzzled by her husband's absence, had decided to make herself some breakfast. She wondered where Wesley was; he usually left a note.

There were things to do, a box of books and record sheets to sort and put in the car. Paperwork, paperwork: like a relentless tide, it never stopped flowing. She had just finished preparing for the day and was about to put the kettle on when she heard Wesley's key in the door. He came into the kitchen. He looked tired.

'Where have you been? Were you called out? I didn't hear the phone.'

'No. I rang the boss. That diary, the old one; I read it and it was just like history repeating itself, just like the case we've been working on. I had an idea so I got in touch with the boss. It turned out I was right. We made an arrest last night and we've been questioning her all night.'

'Her?'

'The mother of that missing kid. Don't ask me now. It's a long story.'

'Go on, tell me. I've got half an hour before I have to set off.' Pam's curiosity was aroused.

'No. Another time.' Normally he would have recounted the facts in glorious detail if she asked. She looked at her husband enquiringly.

Wesley turned away and put the boiling water in the teapot. Maybe later he'd feel like telling her. But something told him the time wasn't right; the case was too close to home. Heffernan had asked him how far Pam would go to get a child of her own and he had answered 'As far as it takes'. Elaine Berrisford had gone as far as it took, and further; the same with Elizabeth Banized four hundred years before. It was best to say nothing for the moment. Pam was noticeably more relaxed. He didn't want to spoil things now by raising the subject again.

Pam watched him as he got himself some cornflakes. It

was nearly time to set off for school. The kids would be waiting.

Bob Naseby wondered where he had seen the young couple before. Then he remembered. They were the Australians who had found that handbag. The pair of them looked sheepish as they came through the swing doors into the station foyer.

It was the girl who spoke first. 'Can we see Inspector Heffernan?' The accent was certainly antipodean. Naseby wondered if they had seen the Test match, England versus Australia, earlier in the year. But then not everyone shared Bob's passions. He rang the inspector's office.

A few minutes later, Rachel appeared. She would scarcely have admitted it to herself, but she had often found herself thinking about the male half of the Australian pair. She felt and quickly suppressed a twinge of disappointment that he was still accompanied by that hard-faced Julie.

'Do you remember us?' He grinned disarmingly. He really was rather attractive, thought Rachel unprofessionally. She nodded.

'We're here to pay that money back.' He drew some ten-pound notes from the pocket of his jeans. 'Thirty pounds. We've been working in a café in Morbay and we want to be off up north later this week, if that's okay with your lot.'

Rachel summoned the inspector. She knew he always liked to have the last word. He was in a remarkably good mood.

'We've got someone for the murder,' he told the pair chattily. 'And the money'll come in useful 'cause the murdered girl's got a little kid. I'll make sure his dad gets it.' He completed the sentence in his head: and hope he doesn't blow it all on the favourite in the 4.30 at Newton Abbot.

He shook hands with Dave and Julie and told them they were free to go and stood with Rachel, smiling benevolently, as they disappeared through the swing doors out into the street.

Rachel yawned. She was tired, having sat in on the interview with Elaine Berrisford the previous night. After the doctor had given her a sedative, Elaine had fallen asleep in her cell; Rachel had to carry on.

'Get over to Neston, will you, Rach. See how Chris Manners is. They let him out of hospital this morning; seems he wasn't badly hurt. Give Chris the money, will you, and see if Stan Jenkins wants to go with you. He might like to see the kid's okay.'

He returned to his office and sat back in his imitation leather executive swivel chair, contemplating life. He decided he would treat himself to a sail that afternoon, weather and tides permitting.

He summoned Wesley into his presence and studied his sergeant as he sat down. 'Credit where credit's due, Wes. You did a bloody good job last night. What's all this about a journal?'

Wesley explained patiently. 'It just seemed to fit in. Elizabeth Banized murdered the real mother of her child when she threatened to take him back. It got me thinking – there's nothing that the mother of any species won't do to keep its young.'

'Kipling – the female of the species is deadlier than the male.' Heffernan looked pleased with himself for remembering a literary quote. They usually went out of his head at the appropriate moment. 'Good thinking. You'll be after my job next. I'll have to watch meself,' he added mischievously.

'What'll happen to the kid, sir? Are they going to let him stay with Manners?'

'It's all up to Social Services. There'll be reports and what have you. I reckon there's a good chance, if our friend Manners can get his act together. It might be just what he needs, a bit of responsibility. Do you fancy coming sailing this afternoon, Wes? Thought I might give the *Rosie May* a quick run . . .'

Wesley, feeling queasy already, made his excuses and left.

Rachel made a cup of tea. The caravan kitchen was cramped and none too clean, but she thought she'd better show willing. She looked across at Chris Manners, who was sitting mournfully with his arm in a sling. Then found a cloth and started wiping surfaces. She was a good person to have around in a crisis.

Stan Jenkins sat opposite Chris, watching the child, who sat beside his dad reading a book that produced alarming electronic noises when a set of buttons was pressed. He had bought it for the boy, thinking he'd better not come empty-handed. Chris had been quite welcoming once Stan had explained his involvement in the case. The atmosphere when Rachel handed round the chipped mugs full of steaming tea was positively cosy.

'I'm just so glad to see him alive,' Stan said, shaking his head in disbelief. 'I had a case once when a child went missing and he was found dead in a river. I'll never forget his parents' faces. I've got to admit I feared the worst for Jonathon . . . sorry, Daniel.' There was emotion in his voice. 'I've got three kids of my own. They're nearly grown up now but you can't help thinking . . .'

He fell silent and reached across and stroked the boy's hair. The fair roots were just visible. In a few weeks his piebald hair would look strange, but it would grow out. Everything would be normal again; all crises pass. Daniel looked up at Stan earnestly, took hold of his finger firmly and placed it on one of the electronic buttons. A sound like a police car siren sprung from the brightly coloured page. Daniel, delighted, took Stan's finger again and repeated the action.

Rachel watched as Stan put his arms around the child and gave him a hug. The boy responded with a giggle and crawled along the seat on all fours back to his father's knee.

As they left, she saw Stan's eyes fill with tears. 'I'm getting too involved,' he said, avoiding her gaze. 'I'm thinking of taking early retirement. It doesn't do to get involved, Constable. Remember that.'

'But it means you're human, sir,' said Rachel quietly. 'We're all human.'

Chris, watching from the window of the caravan, took his son's hand and waved it at the departing police car.

Rachel had driven only a few yards when she saw a familiar figure approaching one of the caravans. She stopped the car.

'Excuse me, sir. I've just seen someone I want a word with. I won't be a minute.' She fumbled frantically to undo her seat belt. She had to get to him before he disappeared. She stumbled out of the car and walked quickly – she didn't want to run – towards the young man knocking on the door of a dilapidated caravan. He heard her and swung round, surprised. He looked a little guilty; she put that down to her profession.

'Hello, er, Constable. Er, I was just calling on some old friends. They put us up for a few days when we first came down here. I haven't seen them for a while.' Dave's Australian accent, Rachel thought, was very attractive; it put her in mind of sun-drenched beaches and wide open spaces.

'Where's your girlfriend?'

He looked sheepish. Sheepish, Rachel thought, but very good-looking. 'Er, we've decided to split. She's off up north and I fancied staying down here for a bit, getting more casual work. I was hoping these friends could maybe put me up for a while. The hostel's a bit, er ...'

She thought quickly. 'If you're wanting somewhere to stay, there's a flat in the old barn at my parents' place. They've got a farm just outside Tradmouth. We rent it out to holidaymakers in the summer but in winter it's mostly lying empty. If you want me to ask ...'

Dave's face lit up with an open smile, showing an array of well-maintained teeth. 'That's great. Thanks.'

She wrote down the address and handed it to him. 'Call round this evening. I'm off duty. I'll probably be there.'

She smiled shyly. As Rachel returned to the police car Donna opened the caravan door. She looked at Dave, not seeming in the least surprised to see him. 'Come in,' she said. 'Sludge is still in bed – you know what he's like. Was that that policewoman you were talking to?'

'Yeah. She said she might know of somewhere to stay. She's quite nice.'

'Pigs are pigs,' Donna announced dismissively. 'Where's Jules?'

He explained.

'We're off up north ourselves some time. Thought we'd try Glastonbury maybe.'

'When are you going?'

Donna shrugged. 'Dunno. Soon maybe. You got to keep moving on, haven't you?'

Dave nodded. Donna was right. You've got to move on. And that policewoman really did seem quite nice . . .

Epilogue

It is full six months since I wrote in this journal. It hath been a goodly season and my fortune in trade doth increase, yet I feel my life accursed. I am a man most wretched.

I watch my son, Thomas, grow. He is a strong, lusty little fellow who smiles and cries heartily for his food. He is my only blessing.

Elizabeth did depart this life full three months past. I know not whether it was by accident that she did drown in the river, but on the word of some common sailors the coroner did judge that she did take her own life. I know she never did sleep easy after what she did to Jennet, but that she did take her life . . . I truly know not. But maybe 'tis justice.

She was buried in unconsecrated ground with myself and Thomas the only mourners. I pray for her soul daily.

I had a new stone floor laid in the cellar. I do pray that they rest in peace . . . Jennet and the babe.

Extract from the journal of John Banized,
2 October 1624

25 March

Neil thought that having wine at an exhibition opening was a bit extravagant, considering the cuts in the museum's budget threatened for the next financial year. Still, if it was there he might as well help himself. He took a glass from the buffet table and drank it down thirstily.

He had been watching the entrance. They were late, he thought, as he fidgeted with his watch. He picked up a vol au vent and munched it absent-mindedly.

The exhibition was impressive, even Neil had to admit that. The museum had done him proud. After viewing a video about the history of the site and the dig itself, one walked through an avenue of brightly lit glass cases displaying the important finds, and eventually reached a reconstructed Elizabethan street. Even the sounds and smells were there, lovingly recreated. Neil wondered about the wisdom of recreating the latter.

The frontage of the Banizeds' house, copied from Victorian photographs, was the centrepiece of the exhibition. One could pass through the doorway into the shop itself. The Banizeds had lacked the display skills of their modern counterparts: the shop was filled with barrels and chests; leather goods, wool and bolts of cloth lined the lath-and-plaster walls.

An area beyond the shop was dedicated to its more gruesome history. The journal of John Banized was displayed in a glass case on the far wall, and as one circled the room, the story unfolded through photographs and extracts from the journal with transcriptions underneath. The ring was on prominent display, along with the buckle of the belt that had killed the unfortunate Jennet. In the centre of the room stood Jennet herself, reconstructed, looking so lifelike that Neil felt if he'd spoken to her she would have replied. It was a pity, he thought, that no one knew what John Banized looked like. His spirit – and that of Elizabeth, his wife – hung in the air, insubstantial. Only Jennet seemed real.

At last Neil heard Wesley's boss's voice; it was unmistakable, that Liverpool accent. He went through to meet them.

Heffernan spotted him first. 'Here's your mate, Wes.' To

Neil he said, 'Good spread here. Don't get this down at the station, do we, Wes? All right for some.' He was rewarded by scathing looks from a couple of lady councillors standing near by.

'It's not always like this,' said Neil, embarrassed. The hospitality was a touchy subject. Neil had heard that it was all to impress some potential commercial sponsors of the museum: a couple of men in sharp suits stood near the entrance watching the proceedings with jaded speculation.

'It's very impressive.' Wesley attempted to rescue the situation. 'Pam sends her apologies. She's not feeling too good.'

Heffernan came up and put a large arm around Wesley's shoulder. 'Did you know my sergeant here's going to be a dad? I reckon it was that posh hotel you went to at New Year did the trick. *En suite* jacuzzi indeed.'

Neil smiled weakly, trying to look happy, trying to hide the fact that his heart had sunk in a quicksand of disappointment at the news. 'Congratulations. Why didn't you tell us?'

'I've not seen you much since the dig finished, and we didn't want to say too much yet. It's early days. You know how it is.'

Heffernan mumbled something about sleepless nights, winked at his sergeant and went off to forage for chicken legs and a glass of Chardonnay. Wesley watched him go.

'Where is she, then?'

'Just through the shop. I'll show you.'

Wesley followed Neil through the exhibition. Things had certainly picked up in museums since the days when his parents had marched him round the V and A as a child for the good of his soul and his education. 'What's that awful smell?'

'Authentic smells of the period,' replied Neil matter-of-factly.

'I'll take your word for it, but I reckon someone should check the drains.'

They reached the room where Jennet stood. Wesley stopped dead as he felt a hand on his shoulder.

'Now then, Inspector, what you think?' Wesley turned, amused by his sudden promotion. Bill Boscople continued, 'Good, i'n'it? I got me name up there, by yon old book I gave you.' He quoted proudly. ' "Kindly donated by William Boscople Esq." ' He stood in his Sunday suit, well scrubbed and beaming with pride.

'And you can put your mind at rest, Mr Boscople,' Neil said comfortingly. 'The murderer was no blood relation of yours.'

Boscople looked confused. Wesley decided that an explanation was needed. 'You're a descendant of Thomas Banized, Mayor of Tradmouth.' Boscople nodded. 'And he was the son of that lady there, Jennet. It was her who was murdered by John Banized's wife.'

'Aye.' There was a glint of mischief in the old man's eyes. Wesley realised he had underestimated him. 'I'd worked that much out, Inspector.'

They approached the figure of Jennet, which stood in the centre of the room. She wore a plain russet gown and apron; a white cap covered her fair hair. She looked young, trusting, vulnerable. Wesley felt pity for her. But wasn't Elizabeth just as deserving of his compassion? Perhaps poor tortured Elizabeth needed his sympathy more. Who was to say?

'She's a right beauty, i'n't she?' Bill Boscople said softly, almost reverently.

'Yes,' replied Neil, considering Jennet the woman for the first time. 'She was lovely ... really lovely.'

The Armada Boy
Kate Ellis

Norman Openheim is an American veteran of the D Day Landings, on a sentimental journey with his old unit to their West Country base. His is the last body archaeologist Neil Watson expects to find in the ruins of an old chantry chapel...

Neil naturally turns to his old friend from student days, Detective Sergeant Wesley Peterson, for help. Ironically, both men are looking at an invading force – Wes the WWII Yanks and Neil a group of shipwrecked Spaniards reputed to have met a sticky end at the hands of outraged locals as they limped from the wreckage of the great Armada. Local memories are retentive, and Wes is soon caught up in old accusations, resentments and romances from fifty years before. But the coolness of Openheim's wife Dorinda, and her reliance on a fellow veteran in the party, offers an all-too-familiar motive for murder.

A belligerent group of homeless youths are also under suspicion: then another veteran's wife disappears. Wes's case grows more perplexing, while Neil uncovers a tragic story from the distant past. Over four hundred years apart two strangers in a strange land have died violently – could the same motives of hatred, jealousy and revenge be at work? Wes is running out of time to find out...

The Marriage Hearse
Kate Ellis

When Kirsten Harbourn is found strangled and naked on her wedding day, DI Wesley Peterson makes some alarming discoveries. Kirsten was being pursued by an obsessed stalker and she had dark secrets her doting fiancé, Peter, knew nothing about.

But Kirsten's wasn't the only wedding planned to take place that July day in South Devon. At Morbay register office a terrified young girl makes her wedding vows. And a few days later her bridegroom is found dead in a seedy seaside hotel. As Wesley investigates he suspects that this death and the bride's subsequent disappearance might be linked to Kirsten's murder.

Meanwhile the skeleton of a young female is found buried in a field that once belonged to the family of Ralph Strong, an Elizabethan playwright, whose play, 'The Fair Wife of Padua' is to be performed for the first time in four hundred years. Is this bloodthirsty play a confession to a murder committed in the reign of Queen Elizabeth 1? Or does it tell another story, one that might cast light on recent mysteries?

A SELECTION OF NOVELS AVAILABLE FROM
PIATKUS BOOKS

THE PRICES BELOW WERE CORRECT AT THE TIME OF GOING TO PRESS. HOWEVER PIATKUS BOOKS RESERVE THE RIGHT TO SHOW NEW RETAIL PRICES ON COVERS WHICH MAY DIFFER FROM THOSE PREVIOUSLY ADVERTISED IN THE TEXT OR ELSEWHERE.

0 7499 3698 3	The Armada Boy	Kate Ellis	£6.99
0 7499 3700 9	An Unhallowed Grave	Kate Ellis	£6.99
0 7499 3701 7	The Funeral Boat	Kate Ellis	£6.99
0 7499 3750 X	The Bone Garden	Kate Ellis	£6.99
0 7499 3606 1	A Cursed Inheritance	Kate Ellis	£6.99
0 7499 3702 5	The Marriage Hearse	Kate Ellis	£6.99

ALL PIATKUS TITLES ARE AVAILABLE FROM:

PIATKUS BOOKS C/O BOOKPOST
PO Box 29, Douglas, Isle Of Man, IM99 1BQ
Telephone (+44) 01624 677237
Fax (+44) 01624 670923
Email; bookshop@enterprise.net

Free Postage and Packing in the United Kingdom.
Credit Cards accepted. All Cheques payable to Bookpost.
(Prices and availability subject to change without prior notice. Allow 14 days for delivery. When placing orders please state if you do not wish to receive any additional information.)

OR ORDER ONLINE FROM:

www.piatkus.co.uk

Free postage and packing in the UK (on orders of two books or more)